PHILLY BARKER

AND THE MURDER AT DEVERELL GRANGE

ALSO BY JOANNE TRACEY

The Philly Barker series (cosy crime)

Philly Barker Investigates

Philly Barker Is On The Case

Philly Barker and The Murder at Deverell Grange

Clementine Carter series (cosy crime)

One For Sorrow

The Melbourne series (contemporary romance)

Baby, It's You

Big Girls Don't Cry

I Want You Back

Careful What You Wish For

It's In The Stars

Christmas At Mannus Ridge

The Queenstown series

Wish You Were Here

Happy Ever After

The Little Café By The Lake

The Brookford series

Escape To Curlew Cottage

Christmas at Fountains Hall

PHILLY BARKER

AND THE MURDER AT DEVERELL GRANGE

A PHILLY BARKER MYSTERY

JOANNE TRACEY

First published in Australia in 2025

by Joanne Tracey

https://joannetracey.com

Copyright © Joanne Tracey 2025

Print ISBN 978-1-7637768-2-1

Ebook ISBN 978-1-7637768-1-4

Cover design by Louisa West

Formatting by coeurdelion.com.au

A catalogue record for this book is available from the National Library of Australia

For Kali

Adventure Spaniel and Best
Dog In The World

2008-2024

CHAPTER ONE

'And you call yourself a guard dog,' I muttered to Balthazar as I watched a well-dressed middle-aged woman at the rear of my shop slip a small wooden box she didn't intend to pay for into the pocket of her cashmere overcoat. The cocker spaniel's snores didn't miss a beat.

'Hiya, Philly. Where do you want me to put these?'

With my attention still on the shoplifter, I glanced briefly sideways at the bear-like man standing in the doorway with a box of vegetables. 'Robbie, this is a pleasant surprise. What do you have there?'

'I've got leeks and purple-sprouting broccoli from the allotment. I've left some leeks, parsnips and onions in the café with Ginny.' He placed the box on the corner of my desk and hung his anorak from the coat stand behind it. Another sideways glance told me he'd picked up on the source of my preoccupation and was now also closely watching the would-be thief.

'She'll be grateful for that,' I said absently. The woman was now examining a pokerwork photo frame. 'Parsnip soup coming up.' Ginny Wilding ran the café here at Chipwell Barn Antiques, a conglomerate of antique dealers – of which I was one – in Chipwell, a small village in North Yorkshire.

'She said she'll do parsnip fritters as the lunch special tomorrow. Something about serving them with chutney and yoghurt dressing.'

'Why is your nose wrinkling in scepticism, Detective Inspector Dawkins?' The woman's head jerked up, and her hand reached into her pocket. She pulled out the box and replaced it on the shelf. 'You should know and trust everything from Ginny's café – even parsnip fritters.'

'Aye, you're right there.' Robbie had a habit of timing his visits to coincide with mealtimes.

Suppressing a grin, I strolled across to the woman. 'Is there anything I can help you with? I noticed you admiring this Mauchline Ware trinket box.' Pronouncing it as 'Moch'lin', I picked up the pale wooden box she'd replaced. 'This is quite a lovely example of a trinket box – mid to late nineteenth-century sycamore.' My finger traced the pattern of the heavily varnished black transfer scene of Alloway Kirk. 'I have some other pieces in the cabinet if you're interested – a small pinwheel and a goblet.'

'No, it's fine.' The woman lifted her chin. 'I was looking for something bigger and of better quality.'

With a little huff, she adjusted the handbag over her shoulder and stalked out. As she appeared to be heading next door to Ambrose and Eugene Ashton's militaria shop – the only other shop in the barn with goods small enough or transportable enough to be concealed in a jacket pocket – Robbie raised his eyebrows meaningfully and followed her. Within minutes, she was heading in the opposite direction and out of the barn.

'Nicely done,' When Robbie reappeared ten minutes later I patted him on the shoulder.

'I did nowt,' he said with his trademark half grin. 'I walked in, and she scarpered. I explained what was going on to Ambrose, and he made a note in his little book and said, seeing as I was there, could I help Eugene move some furniture.'

Knowing that a request to move furniture tended to expand into pictures that needed rehanging or ladders that needed climbing, Robbie was probably fortunate to have escaped the clutches of the tweed-wearing septuagenarian brothers within such a short time.

Correctly reading my thoughts, he grinned, 'I got lucky – they're closing up early so they can take Rochester home and head over to The White Horse at Dunthrop for quiz night.' He rubbed at a scratch on his hand at the mention of the Ashton's cantankerous cat.

I suppressed a grin and placed the Mauchline Ware box into the lockable cabinet it probably should've always been in. 'You did get lucky. What brings you out here today?'

He shoved his hands into the pockets of his jeans and wrinkled his nose. 'Nothing to be doing in this rain.' Robbie had recently retired from the police force and was struggling with the change, spending his days in his allotment – or hanging about here helping in my shop or assisting anyone who needed any heavy lifting done.

'What was that bit of wood she was trying to nick?' Robbie peered into the cabinet.

'Mauchline Ware.' I unlocked the cabinet and retrieved the box. 'Essentially, it's the Victorian equivalent of what we'd now call tourist tatt. If you were a tourist in Victorian times, you might've brought one of these back from your travels.'

'Oh, aye? A bit more practical than a snow globe.' His tone was dry.

'Exactly.' I returned his smile. 'It was all made from wood – boxes like these, egg cups, eyeglass cases, even book covers … pretty much anything that could be decorated with a scene of a popular tourist destination.'

'Is it valuable?'

'Not particularly.' I replaced the box and locked the cabinet. 'Certainly not worth stealing. I've got sixty pounds on this one – and that's only because it's in good condition. Some of the rarer pieces do better at auction. If memory serves me correctly—'

'And you have a photographic memory when it

comes to antiques,' he quipped.

My lips curled into a wry smile. 'I saw an unusual box come through for auction when I was working at Young and Johnsons several years ago. It was made from a patchwork of different timbers: a hawthorn said to have been planted by Queen Mary, a yew tree connected to William Wallace, and an oak from Alloway Kirk. To make it even more Scottish, they printed it with the lyrics to "Auld Lang Syne". And last month, a tourist guide to Doune Castle with Mauchline Ware binding came up for auction. On the front cover, it said the wood had come from the Old Gallows Tree at Doune Castle. I bid on it, but it went to a collector over Skipton way.' I wrinkled my nose at the missed opportunity. 'Every so often, a page-turner made from the same wood turns up in auctions – they're quite collectable.'

As I was talking, Ginny sauntered in. Robbie's eyes lit up when he noticed the tray she was carrying.

'You're a sight for sore eyes, you are,' he said, taking the tray with three cups of tea and a plate of Ginny's famous parkin from her and setting it on my desk.

Ginny beamed, her dimples forming deep holes in her cheeks. 'What's she lecturing you on now?' Her smile removed any implied rebuke. Slumping into the cane-backed Regency chair beside my desk, she lazily reached down to pat Balthazar, who deigned to open his eyes, his tail thumping rhythmically against his cushion.

'Tourist tatt made from trees that had been used as gallows and trees planted by dead queens,' said Robbie. 'What was it with these people and their fascination with things associated with death?'

I shrugged. 'It was a Victorian thing – there's a huge market for that sort of item.'

'I thought I heard your voice, Robbie.' Dressed as always in well-worn jeans, the ubiquitous band T-shirt (today's was the Dead Kennedys) worn under an open red flannel shirt, and the glasses he'd later be searching for hanging from a chain around his neck, Simon Bridges strolled in. Perennially untidy, Simon reminded me of a dog who occasionally forgot how tall he was. '

Simon's furniture shop filled one corner of the barn's rear – with stock overflowing into the café, my shop, and Isabel (Bell) Mayfield's vintage fashion and accessories shop. We knew better than to get attached to any chair he lent us, as it wouldn't be long before he'd swap it for something else. 'If you've got a few minutes, could I get you to help me move a couple of chairs? I've sold this one' —he gestured towards the Regency chair Ginny was sitting in— 'but have a late Victorian armchair I can swap it out for.' Seeing the longing glance Robbie directed towards the tea tray, Simon added, 'Don't worry, I'll have you back before the brew goes cold.'

With a resigned sigh, Ginny stood aside as the men carried the chair away.

'How's Robbie doing?' Ginny asked, perching on the desk and choosing a teacup from the tray.

'It's still early days, but…' I reached for a piece of parkin and bit into it, my hand catching the gingery crumbs. Ginny handed me a plate from the tray and waited as I finished chewing. 'After forty years in the police force it was always going to be an adjustment, I suppose. Although Stewart has promised to bring him back on a consultancy basis for the occasional cold case,' I said, referring to Robbie's chief superintendent and my ex-husband. 'Nothing stressful or dangerous, but enough to keep his mind active.'

'What about you and Robbie?' Ginny asked.

'What about me and Robbie?' I'd first met Robbie just before Christmas last year when he'd been investigating some fake Clarice Cliff pottery. One thing led to another, and I ended up assisting him with that investigation. I recently helped with another case involving a string of antique-related burglaries targeting elderly farmers. We'd become close friends and enjoy each other's company; Robbie was interested in learning more about antiques, and I was pleased to have him around – especially when his presence also meant gifts of the excess vegetable kind. 'We're just friends – nothing more.'

'Are you interested in making it more?' Ginny placed her cup on the desk and took a slice of parkin.

Shaking my head, I picked up a cup and sat in the

Georgian Captain's chair behind my desk. 'No. And nor, I think, is he.' Even though Robbie, a widower, had lost his wife several years ago, and I'd been divorced for even longer, we were both enjoying the perks of friendship without the pressures or complications of anything more.

'How long has Stewart been with Alison? What does Bell call her? The "child bride"?'

I chuckled. 'Ten years – and I don't refer to Alison as the child bride anymore.' While we'd never be best friends, I'd learnt to tolerate and respect Alison. Besides, she and Stewart and their children, Reuben and Misty, were always at any family gathering held by my son Ryan for his twins – Ada and Alfie. If I wanted to see my grandchildren for birthdays and Christmases, I'd had to learn to accept Alison's presence.

'Don't you think it's time?' Ginny asked gently. 'You're an attractive woman, Philly – especially when you haven't been climbing around in dusty barns or attics' —I brushed at a mark on my jeans, a bashful grin on my face— 'and you're still young.'

'I'm almost sixty!'

Ginny laughed one of her belly laughs. 'That's still young. I'm not that far behind you.' She took a sip of tea. 'Has Robbie spoken about how his wife died yet?'

I shook my head. 'Stewart knows, but I won't ask him – it's up to Robbie to talk about it when he's ready. And until he's ready to do that, he's not ready for anything else.'

The sounds of conversation outside grew louder and Robbie and Simon re-entered the shop carrying a walnut button-back grandfather-style armchair.

'Nice,' I said when they set it down. 'I like this tapestry upholstery.'

'And enough is going on in the fabric, so if you do happen to bleed on it again, it won't show.' Simon wore a teasing grin, referring to an incident before Christmas when I'd been involved in an altercation with an armed robber and his accomplice. 'Right,' he said, swiping a slice of parkin. 'I'll be off.' With a wave he was gone.

Robbie motioned Ginny towards the new chair. 'You take that' —he removed a pile of books from a Georgian oak spindle-back chair and set them on the floor— 'I can use this.' Settling himself down with tea, parkin and a contented sigh, he said, 'You could sell this parkin, Ginny.'

'She does,' I said drolly. 'In the café.'

Ginny chuckled, but there was an awkwardness to her chuckle. 'Actually,' she said, 'I wanted to talk to you two about something.' She ran her finger along the upholstered arms of the chair. 'Richard and I have been invited to stay in a sixteenth-century manor house this weekend.'

'Sounds fun,' I said warily, wondering where this was going.

'I was hoping you'd think that, as I'd like – we'd like

– you to come with us … you and Robbie.'

'Oh aye?' Robbie prompted for more information. Although he appeared to be casually sipping his tea, a slight frown told me his antennas were up.

'They're friends of Richard's – well, Serena is a family friend. She grew up next door to him; Richard said she's always treated him like a big brother.' Her eyes softened. 'The poor thing had a rough start in life – her parents died in a car accident when she was very young, and her aunt brought her up. She met Rupert when she was working in the city – he was into hedge funds or some such thing. It's the second time around for them.' She paused as if realising she'd been rambling. 'Richard Googled the house; it's in the middle of nowhere but looks to be quite the place. The attic is full of antiques, and Serena told him she doesn't know where to start working out what's good and what isn't.' Ginny sent me a diffident smile. 'And that's where you come into it. Serena saw the article in the paper about how you found that painting last year that ended up selling for a lot at auction. Then she remembered Richard saying how I had the café at Chipwell Barn so would know you, so rang him to see whether you'd be keen to have a rummage. She said to say they'd pay you, and you'd get first refusal for any items they chose to sell.' She paused and drew breath.

'Right…' I began to understand the direction Ginny was heading in.

'She thought you might like to come up for a night or two and take a look before accepting the job – and we thought it would be a good idea for you to come this weekend while we're there. There will be some other friends of theirs as well, and they're bound to be posh.' Her face fell, and this time, her expression held a tinge of anxiety. 'I was okay about going when I thought it was just us, but now I feel …'

Her voice trailed away, but she didn't need to say more. She'd probably already decided that Serena and her husband's posh friends would be rake-thin and stylish and look down their patrician noses at her comfortable size, colourful knits and exuberant prints. Ginny didn't see herself as we saw her. She didn't know that when she smiled – which was often – her brown eyes twinkled, and when she laughed, her mouth wide open, her hands clasped beneath her generous chest, no one in her vicinity could help but laugh with her. Ginny brought joy into a room just by being in it, yet was oblivious.

I squeezed her arm gently. 'They won't be able to help loving you as much as I do.'

Her smile was grateful. 'Thank you, Philly. I'd feel better if there was someone else there I knew …' I squirmed under her gaze. 'You could drive up on Saturday after work, and Richard said there's plenty of room for you both – he told Serena you'd need two bedrooms.'

'Right.' My voice trailed off as I considered the options. While the idea of a house party ranked about as high on my list of things to avoid as an outlet centre on the first day of the Boxing Day sales, I couldn't deny the excitement that rippled through me at the possibility of rummaging in an attic that probably hadn't been looked at in decades.

'You know you like nothing better than a good rummage.' Ginny must sense she's a smidgeon away from victory. 'I'm sure Bell won't mind taking Bally for a night or two, and if you want to make a full day of it, you can get Ellie in to watch the shop for a few hours.'

We'd recently employed Ellie, a local girl, to help in the barn a few days a week. This allowed us to get out and about to the auctions and house clearances we needed to without relying on each other to cover our respective shops in our absence. Ginny, it seemed, had all bases covered. 'Hmmm … what about the café? Are you closing for the day?'

'No need,' she said. 'As you know, we only open for morning tea on Saturday, and Josie Marsh has said she'll do that for me, so we'll drive up after work on Friday and head home on Sunday.' She paused, leant forwards and locked eyes. 'I'd really like you to come – and if you are interested in taking the job, why not go when we're going to be there too?'

'I don't know …'

'Did I mention they own a Stubbs?' Ginny grinned

cheekily as she saw my eyes light with excitement. George Stubbs was one of the most important British artists of all time. His paintings – mostly of horses – were sublime.

'No,' I said dryly. 'You probably should've led with that little gem.'

I glanced across at Robbie who lifted his shoulders in silent acceptance. 'Why not? Where is this place?'

'It's a great pile about ten miles northwest of Reeth at the top of the Dales National Park – near that pub where people get snowed in every so often at Christmas,' said Ginny.

'Tan Hill?' I guessed. 'I've never been out that way but have always meant to. And they definitely have enough rooms for us?' Robbie raised his eyebrows as I asked the question.

Ginny nodded. 'Richard told Serena you'd probably bring Robbie with you – especially now that he's retired.'

Robbie's thoughtful frown worried me. Had Richard's presumption that we were a twosome upset him? He flicked at his chin with his forefinger. 'Are you talking about Deverell Grange by chance?'

Ginny's eyes widened. 'Do you know it?'

'Aye.' He nodded slowly, his lips pursed. 'A long time back – one of my first cases as a detective constable. A disappearance – a young mother, Jenny Black. I'll always remember it …' His voice trailed off, his mind on a long ago regret. 'It's a strange house, but full of pictures and the like – none of it to my taste, but …' He tilted his head to the side. 'I reckon as how we should go.'

'Okay.' I searched his face, finding nothing concerning. 'I'll ask Bell if she can have Bally.'

Impulsively, Ginny reached for my hand. 'Thank you, Philly, that means a lot. Besides,' she said with a cheeky grin, 'you'll be in your element.'

'I will – and it's been a while since Libby had a decent run.'

Robbie sighed and shook his head. 'We'll take my car. As functional as your Land Rover is, Libby's suspension is not what it used to be.'

CHAPTER TWO

For over three centuries, the Chipwell Arms had been at the heart of Chipwell – a village that otherwise consisted of a few dozen cottages of varying sizes, mainly constructed from the local Yorkstone, a church, Chipwell Barn Antiques and not much else. Although Roger Marsh and his wife, Lynn, had been the landlords here for twenty years, some of the locals still regarded them as 'off-comers'. Even I'd been accepted more readily – thanks to Stewart having been born in the north and me having come from Australia. 'Aye, lass,' long-term residents would say whenever I said anything wrong, 'you weren't to know.'

After ensuring Bally was settled in his usual spot just far enough away from the fire – although it was early March and officially the beginning of spring, no one had, as yet, informed the weather gods of that fact and winter was still maintaining her grip on the temperature – I made my way to the bar where Robbie was placing our drinks orders and chatting with Roger.

'Ow do, Philly?' Roger greeted me with a warm smile.

'All good, Roger, thanks. You're busy tonight.'

'Aye, a few groups in tonight. If you're wanting your tea, you'd better order it soon.' Lynn placed our drinks on the counter – a pint of Black Sheep, a local ale, for Robbie, and Rioja for me. 'Usual for you, Robbie, pet? Ham, egg and chips? With some bread and butter on the side.'

'You know it, Lynn.' Robbie rubbed his stomach, grinning wryly.

Tilting my head, I squinted to read the specials on the blackboards on either side of the fire. 'I'll have the cheese and onion tart. Thanks, Lynn.'

'Done. I'll get that started for you.'

'So,' Robbie said when we settled at a table, his lips twisted into the beginnings of a smile. 'I assume you've bought me dinner so I can tell you more about the Deverell Grange case?'

My fingers traced the stem of my wine glass. 'Am I that obvious? Actually, don't answer that. But' —I grinned cheekily— 'Seeing as how you've brought it up… Tell me about the woman who went missing … Who was Jenny Black?'

Robbie's large hand cradled his pint glass. 'A local lass. She worked up at the Grange – housework and the like. Her husband, John, was the estate manager. He was a good bit older than her, but devoted, he was.' A brief frown furrowed his brow. Was he thinking about the loss of his wife? 'Folk said she left with the eldest Deverell boy – he left town at the same time.'

'Rupert?' My brows flew up.

Robbie shook his head. 'Edward Deverell, Rupert's older brother. I didn't meet Rupert – he was away at university. Oxford, I think.'

'When you say he left town, do you mean he went missing as well? Did they find him?' An involuntary shiver ran up my spine. 'Or is that how Rupert came to inherit?'

Again, he shook his head. 'No one knew he'd gone missing until a few days into the investigation. Then it came out that he'd bought two one-way tickets to Spain from a travel agent in Harrogate.'

'Did he use them?' I leant forward, my elbow on the table, my cheek resting against the back of my hand.

'We confirmed that Edward Deverell boarded a flight to Barcelona and drove down to Valencia, but the trail ran cold after that. The other ticket wasn't used.'

'Is that why you don't believe Jenny left with him?'

'Aye and nay.' Robbie waggled his hand. 'A suitcase and some of her clothes were gone, so the conclusion was she'd left too, but maybe not on the same flight. There was no obvious motive we could find for anyone to have harmed her – so the assumption was she'd left of her own free will.'

'But you don't think so.'

He shook his head. 'Even though it was a convenient explanation, something about it never rang true for me. Jenny wasn't long married, and she left behind a baby. There'd been no gossip about her and Edward Deverell, and in a community that size, if they'd been involved, someone would've known about it. Everyone we spoke to talked about how she seemed happy with Black. If it weren't for the fact they disappeared simultaneously, I don't think anyone would've linked her name with Deverell's. If I were a betting man, I'd say she never left Deverell Grange.'

'You think someone murdered her?'

'Aye.' With a solemn expression, he nodded. 'My guvnor disagreed though. In the first few days, we questioned her husband, John, and' —he twisted his mouth— 'and a few other people who knew her, but there was no evidence to hold anyone.' He stared into the milky depths of his tea as if he'd find the answers there. 'In the end, it was agreed she'd run off with Edward of her own free will.'

'Did you think the husband did it? Do you think he murdered his wife?'

Robbie shrugged but didn't look up. 'No,' he finally said. 'Not now. At the time, I had my suspicions, but I was young and new on the force – we're talking nearly forty years ago.'

'What about John Black and the baby? What happened to them?'

Again, he shrugged. 'I heard Black moved away. He was devastated. I've heard nothing about him since.'

The conversation paused as Josie March delivered our food.

After thanking Josie, I said, 'What about Edward Deverell? Was he ever questioned in relation to Jenny's disappearance?'

Lips tight, Robbie shook his head. 'That's the thing – we never found him. As I said, we tracked him to Valencia, but that was a dead end, and as far as I know, nobody's heard from him again. At some stage, the family must've applied to have him declared dead for Rupert to have inherited.'

'You seem to remember it well.' I tried to imagine Robbie as a young, green detective constable. He'd be as earnest as he was today, probably more so because experience wouldn't have smoothed his perception. His face would be unlined with none of the crags and furrows that age and long hours had brought, and his eyes wouldn't be shadowed and bagged by the pain he'd seen – and felt.

'Aye, it was my first case.' He drained his beer and grinned back at me. 'You might have a photographic memory for antiques, but I remember most of my cases – especially those with no result.'

Although I'd been out of the police force for twenty years, I knew exactly what he meant. The unsolved cases never left you. 'Is that why you want to go back?' I asked quietly.

'Maybe. Not that I think there's anything still there to solve, but …' He ran a quarter slice of buttered bread through egg and brown sauce, a slight frown on his face.

'It's always been unfinished business.' I finished his sentence.

'Aye.' He stood and held up his pint glass. 'Same again?'

'Thanks.'

The heavy wooden door closed behind us, and I wrapped my scarf tightly around my neck, pulling my jacket closed for the walk home.

After covering the short distance in silence, we paused at my iron gate, the movement causing the sensor light above the door to come on. 'Are you coming in for a brew?' My fingers traced the wrought iron white rose on my gate, the emblem of Yorkshire, Bally tugging at his lead, eager to be in and out of the cold.

Robbie stifled a yawn. 'Not tonight. I'll see you in safely and be off.'

He waited as I opened the front door before lifting his hand in farewell and retracing his steps down the path to his car.

Although we hadn't spoken again of the case at Deverell Grange, and his craggy face had given nothing away, there was something about Robbie's profile and the set of his mouth in the light as he opened the car door that told me his mind was still back there at Deverell Grange.

Chapter Three

Robbie eased his Vauxhall sedan into what was – given its location – a surprisingly full car park.

The weathered seventeenth-century stone building stood isolated, the icy wind whipping across the moors, reminding us that although the calendar said it was March, up here, that didn't mean cherry blossoms and sunshine.

Zipping my parka and pulling the hood up against the cold, I wandered away from the pub to the edge of the car park where horned, black-faced sheep were grazing. The landscape was bleak, windswept and uninviting but starkly beautiful in that way raw nature often is. There was, however, not a tree to be seen.

'It's quite something. I'd forgotten it looks like this.' Robbie joined me, his hands jammed into the pockets of his anorak, his shoulders hunched against the biting wind.

'When was the last time you were up here?'

'Twenty years, maybe more. Audrey and I used to come out here on a Sunday before we were married, but the last time I was here was a camping trip with our Jim. He was only thirteen or so and is almost forty now.' He squinted into the distance as if he could see back to those days. So rarely did he mention his wife and son; I didn't like to interrupt. 'I remember it were right parky even in the middle of summer.'

A little pulse beat in his jaw, his silence telling me he wasn't keen to say more. 'Tell me about the pub.'

'Well,' he said with a chuckle. 'That's a turn-up, me teaching you about a place.'

I snorted a laugh. 'How about you start with the sheep, then? They're a mean-looking bunch.'

'Aye, they're Swaledales. They're a hardy breed and suit the fells.'

'Does anyone own them?' As far as I could see, there were no fences.

'Aye, see their lug marks?' He pointed towards a yellow tag in the ear of the closest one. 'They're gathered down at tupping time.'

'Tupping time?' I wasn't sure I wanted to know.

'When the tups are put in with the yows.' A broad grin crossed his face.

'Is that what I think it is?'

'Aye. I reckon it is.' He inclined his head back towards the pub. 'Let's head inside – I'm so famished my stomach's begun to think my throat has been cut.'

If I thought the car park was busy, the bar was heaving with people, most of whom were dressed for rambling in multi-pocketed hiker's trousers and mud-spattered hiking boots and accompanied by equally muddy dogs.

We pushed through the crowd across the stone-flagged floor to the bar. I looked around the space as we waited for our turn to order. Even though there was ample headroom, Robbie had ducked instinctively for the low exposed beams, upon which were pinned beer mats, the welcoming bar fringed with horse brasses next to a roaring fire.

Robbie placed our lunch orders, and the barman deftly poured two pints of dark ale from gleaming gold-handled taps.

I sighed my relief when we'd fought our way through the crush around the bar to the restaurant and secured a seat. 'There's not enough cars out there for all these people in here.'

'Most of these would be ramblers,' Robbie said after lightly clinking his glass against mine. 'We're right on the Pennine Way here, and there are other paths you can walk from Keld, or you can do a quick out and back to the old mines.'

'Mines?'

'Aye, there were coal pits around here – the hotel was originally built to service the pit workers – the King's Pit, they used to call it. My nan told me there used to be miner's cottages all about here. The last mine was closed when she was a girl, and the huts have disappeared over the years. The pub stayed open for the farmers, but these days' —he waved his arm around the room— 'it's mostly day trippers like us and ramblers.'

He took a long drink of his beer. Robbie was a born-and-bred Yorkshireman, but his childhood was yet another subject he rarely discussed. 'You're from around here?'

'Aye,' he said. 'On a farm down the road a bit— near Hawes. My brother took over the farm …'

My eyes grew wider and I struggled to form a coherent sentence. 'You're … you're telling me your family is just down the road?'

His laugh was wry. 'It's not like you to be lost for words Philly, but aye.' He dropped his gaze to the table. 'My parents have long passed, but my brother and his family … It's been a while.'

'How long? After all, you only live ninety miles away.'

He exhaled, placed his beer back on its mat and cast his eyes around the room before answering, lingering on the piano in the corner. 'Since Audrey passed,' he finally said. 'But there were—' —he scratched the back of his head and grimaced— 'problems before that.'

The server chose that moment to bring our lunch, dumping our plates of pie, chips, peas and gravy on the table with enough force to make the chips in their little wire basket jump about. She whipped away the table number before we could thank her.

For the next few minutes, we ate in silence, giving the steak and ale pie the reverence it deserved. Robbie had disclosed more about himself in the last hour than he had in the few months we'd known each other, but while I was conscious of allowing him to proceed at his own pace, when it became clear Robbie wouldn't bring the conversation back to where it had been interrupted, I did.

'Is there something you're not telling me, Robbie? Something you need to tell me?'

His head subtly dipped. I waited as he loaded his fork with pie and peas and waited some more as he chewed thoughtfully, perhaps deciding what or how much to tell me.

'They interviewed my brother in connection with Jenny Black's disappearance.' Robbie looked up from his plate at my gasp. 'Ken was working on the estate at the time.' His shrug seemed casual, but the tightening of his grip on his fork told a different story. 'And it came out that he and Jenny had been involved. It was over well before she met John Black and it didn't last. Ken always had the impression she was keen on someone else and that he was either a rebound or used to make the other man – whoever he was – jealous. It had been casual between Jenny and Ken and over for a long time, but' —he shrugged— 'we talked to everyone she'd been associated with.'

He said it matter-of-factly, yet I heard the weariness of the decades behind his words and imagined how he must have felt when his brother's name came up. 'Had you known he'd dated Jenny?'

Robbie shook his head, the movement so slight I almost missed it. 'We … we weren't close.' His mouth twisted ruefully. 'He's a few years older than me and had been up at the Grange for a bit, and I'd been posted to Richmond.' He paused and dabbed the corner of his mouth with the paper napkin. 'Let's say me being a copper wasn't a popular choice, and when Ken was dragged in' —he shrugged lightly— 'I'm sure you can imagine.'

It was no wonder this case had stayed with him. Leaving aside the fact that it was one of his first as a detective constable and one of the first that had been unsolved, his brother's involvement would've ensured it was memorable.

'Surely he knew you were just doing your job?' I attempted to keep my words light, as though we had conversations like this every day.

Another half shrug. 'A job he disagreed with.' He took a mouthful of his beer. 'It was Audrey who got us back talking. I met her just before this case and' —he swallowed— 'she could be stubborn when she wanted to be and didn't give in until we were all on speaking terms again.'

'And since she passed?' I pressed gently.

He shook his head, his face clouding with sadness. 'Time's got away.' I understood without him telling me – he'd not wanted the sympathy.

'You're going to do some scouting around of your own this weekend, aren't you?'

'Aye,' he said after a brief silence. 'If I get the chance. I looked out my notebook from the case last night.' He pulled a black flip notebook from his pocket and passed it over. I'd seen plenty of these over the years – and had a box of my own somewhere at home from my time as a detective. The random observations captured in these notebooks often led to breakthroughs.

'Did you check out the case file too?'

He nodded. 'I dropped in at the station yesterday and got Lewis to look it up on the system for me. The original case file will be there, but I won't bother with that unless I need to.' Lewis Stanley had been Robbie's sergeant or, as he called him, his 'bag man' for the last few years. Now, he worked with Robbie's replacement, Detective Inspector Chris Whiteley, a youngish up-and-comer from down south. Robbie knew that any request for the file would find its way to DI Whiteley's attention, and Robbie would not have wanted that. 'I know the trail is long cold, but I wondered …'

'… if you would see something else with the benefit of experience that was missed back then?' He nodded. After a short silence, while we both finished our lunches, I said, 'Maybe you can call in on your brother on the way home.'

'Maybe.' His expression gave nothing away.

Chapter Four

The sky had taken on an ominous, darkened hue as we made our way down Deverell Grange's sweeping drive. Robbie peered through the windscreen, frowning. 'Those clouds look like snow.'

'This late in the season?' I asked sceptically.

'It happens – especially up here.'

'They were talking in the pub about a storm being on the way, but the weather forecast doesn't mention snow.'

'Those buggers sometimes get it wrong.' Robbie lifted a shoulder. 'Hopefully, there won't be much in it.'

I glanced sideways at him and wished I hadn't. His frown gave me no confidence that he believed his words. Before I could say anything, though, we got our first look at Deverell Grange. Robbie stopped the car so we could take it all in. The gabled house rose proudly on a plateau above Deverell Sike – more of a gully than a stream – its Yorkstone exterior darkened over the years to an almost-black deep grey that today matched the sky. The design was a hotchpotch of several styles and several eras, with the exterior of the main wing of the house marked by a two-storey porch with mullioned windows flanked by classical columns and a statement rose window beneath battlements and pinnacles.

'That's their grand hall.' Robbie pointed at the single-storey wing with high windows set into the ashlar to the left of the main house. 'I didn't see inside it last time, but the old viscount said they used it for balls and the like, but not so much now, or, rather, they rarely used it back then,' he corrected himself. 'It's the oldest part of the house. They've added to the rest over the years.'

'And the ruins?' Adjacent to the hall was the gabled facade of what I assumed was once a mirror image of the main house.

'Apparently the folly of the third or fourth viscount – who knows with that lot. He died before he could finish the renovations – in mysterious circumstances too, mind – and whoever came after had to clean up his debts, so all that's left is what you see.'

It was impressive, but something about it also sent a chilling sensation running down my back.

'It feels …' I was unable to finish.

Robbie shuddered. 'I know what you mean. I can't stand the place. When we were here investigating Jenny's disappearance, the old housekeeper told us that someone had cursed the house hundreds of years ago.

I don't believe in curses and the like, but I remember thinking this house could convince me they were true.'

'Well' —I squared my shoulders as if heading into battle— 'the sooner we get started, the sooner we can leave.'

We parked on the drive and, leaving our overnight bags in the car for now, approached the wrought-iron-trimmed double oak door and pulled on the bell chain. As if she'd been waiting for us, the door was flung open by a woman so slight it was difficult to believe she had the energy to fling anything, let alone a centuries-old oak door.

'You must be Philomena Barker,' she gushed. 'And Detective Inspector Dawkins. I've heard so much about you from Richard that I feel we're friends already. I can call you Philly and Robbie, can't I?' I'd no sooner nodded, without getting a word in, before she said, 'And you must call me Serena. I can't abide any of that Lady Deverell business. Besides,' she added in an undertone, 'I'm Rupert's second wife, so that means – including Rupert's mother, who I hope you never have to meet – there are another two Lady Deverells still gadding about.'

Suppressing a smile, I noticed Robbie's lips also held a suspicious twist.

'I probably shouldn't have said that about my dear mama-in-law, should I? Especially with us just having met.' Her English rose complexion pinkened prettily.

If Serena treated Richard as a big brother, she must be in her early forties, but her smooth skin, clear blue eyes and softly waving short light-brown hair made her look at least ten years younger. 'I'm so glad Richard and Ginny persuaded you to come. Ginny really is a dear, isn't she? I haven't seen Richard happier than he's been since he met her.' Again, I opened my mouth to answer, but Serena was still talking. 'If they hadn't managed to convince you to come, I had another secret weapon on my side.' Her smile was conspiratorial. 'I bet you can't guess who it is?'

Still smiling, she was silent, and I realised I was supposed to answer this time. 'No, I couldn't possibly guess.'

'My husband's cousin is Hilary Cunningham,' she announced. When I struggled to connect, she added, 'Lady Cunningham from Chipwell Hall. Tony and Hilary speak so highly of you.'

'Oh, really?' My eyebrows flew up in surprise — mainly at the idea that Lady Cunningham had spoken well of me. While I'd hit it off with Sir Antony, who, as a militaria collector, was one of the Ashton's regular customers, it had taken longer for Lady C (as Bell referred to her) to warm to me — and me to her.

'Yes. Tony said you have a real talent for divining antiques from fakes, and between you and me' — she shook her head, her turned-up nose wrinkled in disgust— 'I think they were both relieved that cousin

George hadn't hurt you in that awful business before Christmas.'

A few months ago, after breaking into my store and then robbing and assaulting another local man, George Cunningham had held me and the Ashton brothers at gunpoint over documents that brought his birthright into question.

'Then there was that business last month.' She turned to Robbie. 'Tony said it's no wonder you've retired; there's rarely a dull moment when Philly's around.' Her laugh was bright and reminded me of water tinkling down a beck. 'Anyway, what am I about leaving you on the doorstep in the cold? Come in, and I'll show you around before the others get home.'

'Where are the others?' I asked, peering over Serena's shoulder down the long hall, trying to catch the sound of voices.

'Rupe and Wenty had to go somewhere or other to see a business associate. Who knows what that's about?' She shook her head and lifted a shoulder. 'Everyone else has gone to lunch at The Blue Lion over in East Witton. Fabulous food, and normally I'd go too, but I needed to ensure everything was arranged for this evening. They should be home soon – we usually do tea in the drawing room from four. Anyway, come inside.'

As Robbie turned back to the car, his keys in his hand, she waved her hand dismissively. 'You can get your bags later. Now, follow me.' Robbie and I exchanged grins and did as we were bidden, his smile turning to a concerned frown when he noticed snow had begun to fall.

Stepping back into the flag-stoned entrance hall, Serena wrapped her pale blue cashmere wrap closer against the chill. 'This place is a nightmare to heat.' Her fingers waggled towards the stone walls and the imposing timber staircase that wound up from the hall's centre. 'Any heat that is generated goes straight up the staircase.'

A faded tapestry depicting a knight making an offering to a demure maiden, his horse pawing the ground behind him, two dogs, lurchers probably, at his feet, covered almost the entirety of one wall. Below it was a long oak bench with a high-panelled backsplash, and on either side were a pair of early Georgian waiting chairs. 'The tapestry would help keep some of the warmth in,' I mused, moving closer to examine the worn fabric. 'This is quite remarkable – possibly sixteenth century?'

Serena shrugged dismissively. 'I have no idea, Rupe may know – or there'll be records somewhere. I'd love to get rid of all this heavy furniture and the dreary paintings of dead relatives.' She sighed dramatically. 'Just wait until you see them; you'll know what I mean then. Unfortunately, most of it's entailed in the estate.' Another little shrug. 'Rupe has given me free rein with the attic, though, so I hope you find some treasures there. So yes, that poor old carpet on the wall does its best to keep a little warmth in here. We have central heating, of course, and light the fire in the drawing and dining rooms, but keep the ballroom closed unless we're using it. I'm sure you'll want to look closer tomorrow, but while we're here …' Another set of double oak doors to the left opened into a cavernous space that took my breath away. 'This is the Great Hall – we call it the ballroom.'

'Flippin' 'eck,' whispered Robbie, lapsing into Yorkshire vernacular.

Timber panels lined the walls as far as a dado rail, and above that, the walls were painted in a deep rose below an intricately decorated and corniced ceiling. As Serena had said, the room was full of oil paintings of long-dead relatives and the occasional hunting trophy. Timber bench seating adorned the long walls. At the opposite end from where we stood was a massive timber-surrounded fireplace constructed from the same local sandstone as the rest of the house and framed by two carved wooden panels.

If I closed my eyes, I could imagine the room filled with dancing couples in Regency finery, their steps softly gliding along the polished but worn floorboards, perhaps a band in one corner, tables with refreshments in another. 'Do you hold many events in here?'

Serena began walking, her steps soft on the floor, her hand trailing absently along the panelling. 'Just once in the five years I've been here — to celebrate our wedding. It's quite something dressed for a special occasion, with a fire blazing in the hearth.' Turning back to us, her eyes took on a dreamy expression. 'Maybe we should do it more often.'

Robbie's head tilted to the side as he took in the stag's head adorning the wall. As I passed him, I lifted my eyebrows slightly, just enough to let him know I wasn't keen on sporting trophies either.

Above the fireplace was a painting of a white horse tossing its head against the groom's attempt to restrain it. This must be the famous Stubbs. I leant closer.

Robbie stood beside me. 'That's not a dead relative,' he said, his expression deadpan.

'No, it's much more important than that.' Even though Serena was some feet away, gazing up at an image of one of the earlier viscounts, her wrap tightened against the cold, I lowered my voice. 'This place gives me the creeps.'

Robbie frowned and nodded, lightly gripping my elbow to lead me away from the fireplace towards where Serena waited. 'I felt it last time too.'

'Do you mind if we move on?' Serena said when we rejoined her. 'It's rather chilly in here.' With a little smile, she led the way back into the entrance hall.

'I'd love a closer look at the Stubbs,' I said, with a yearning glance back at the painting.

'Perhaps later. You are staying until Monday,

aren't you? Richard said you might because the shop is closed that day. The others will be leaving tomorrow afternoon, so besides Rupe and me, you'll have the place to yourself.'

'We'll see how we go tomorrow,' I said. While I was itching to have a look through the attic, a closer acquaintance with the house hadn't lessened the feeling of foreboding I'd had when I first saw it from the drive, but I would like another look at that Stubbs.

Chapter Five

Chatter from one of the other rooms greeted us as we emerged into the entrance hall. 'Oh good,' said Serena. 'The others must be back. If you want to get your bags from the car, I'll show you to your rooms and introduce you over tea.'

After quickly pointing out where we'd find the drawing room, dining room, library, kitchen, and access points to the attic, Serena showed Robbie and me to our rooms at the end of a long hallway, a shared bathroom between them. 'I must get back downstairs,' she said. 'But I hope you'll be comfortable.' She glanced at her watch. 'Tea is being served in the drawing room now, drinks at six thirty and dinner at eight. We don't stand on ceremony, so there's no need to dress for dinner.'

Once she left us, Robbie said wryly in an exaggerated Yorkshire accent, 'Somehow, I don't think tea means ham and chips, and dinner isn't in the middle of the day.'

I chuckled lightly. 'And when she says not to dress for dinner, I think she means there's no need for a dinner suit or ballgown.' Shivering slightly, I wrapped my arms around my body. 'She wasn't wrong about the heating, though; I think I'll put a jumper on before going downstairs.'

He nodded. 'Aye, I'll do the same. Ten minutes do you?'

My bedroom was small but tastefully furnished. The walls were papered with lilacs on a cream background, and the same design was on the curtains framing the window through which my view was of an expansive gravelled courtyard the width of the house and the Grand Hall. Bordering the courtyard on the left, almost directly behind the hall, was a detached stone building I assumed was once a barn but now appeared to have been converted – or was in the process of being converted – for a different purpose. Opposite it stood a collection of semi-detached cottages that probably housed the housekeeper, the estate manager and the estate offices. In the centre sat a three-tiered concrete fountain topped with the figure of a woman pouring water from a jug. It struck me as being incongruous, an attempt, perhaps, by a previous viscount to give the house a Georgian elegance.

The bed – Georgian mahogany – was topped with a fluffy duvet in a plaid cover in the same purple and cream of the wallpaper and curtains but with contrasting touches of red, while woollen tartan blankets in a similar colourway were piled on the end of the bed. Beside the timber-framed fireplace sat an armchair upholstered in the same plaid as the duvet cover, the cushion bearing a picture of a cocker spaniel that immediately had me wondering what Bally was up to right now – probably sleeping, I supposed. The overall effect was one of luxe cosiness and pure country-house style. While I longed to take my boots off and sink into that chair with a book, my allocated ten minutes were slipping away.

Taking Serena's words at face value, I left my jeans and Chelsea boots on but pulled on a navy wool jumper over my striped shirt. I dabbed some concealer under my eyes, touched up my make-up, fluffed my hair and pushed the little strands that always kinked out back behind my ears. My short hair might now hold more grey than blonde, but it was happening naturally and, in the right light, almost looked deliberate. Having spent the first twenty years of my life under the Australian sun (mostly without sun protection – as was the fashion in those days), my skin would never be as flawless as one whose summers consisted of more cloud and less sun. My jaw might be a tad softer than it used to be, and my blue eyes now crinkled at the sides with lines of laughter (and pain), but the reflection that peered back at me in the mirror would, I thought, do.

Before leaving the room, I closed the curtains against the dying light, noticing with some concern that the snow was falling heavier and now blanketed much of the gravel. The sky was leaden, and the wind whirled the flakes about and whistled through a gap in the window. The fountain had disappeared.

Robbie was already in the hallway waiting for me. He, too, had added a jumper but was otherwise attired as he had been earlier. 'Will we do, Philly?'

'You forget I'm from the colonies and have no time for situations where I might possibly "not do",' I said in an affected drawl that made him laugh. 'Besides which, we're just here as the help.'

'Right you are,' he said. Then his smile slipped. 'Did you notice the snow?'

I nodded. 'It seems to be getting heavier. Is there any danger of us getting snowed in?'

He wrinkled his nose and pulled at his earlobe. 'Let's hope it stops soon.'

'In that case, there's nothing for it but tea and scones – they will have scones, won't they?'

'I certainly hope so, Philly. It's been a while since lunch.'

Shaking my head in exasperation. 'Are you ever not hungry?'

He tilted his head and rubbed at his chin as he pretended to think. 'Probably not,' he finally said with one of his half smiles.

'We'd best get downstairs then.'

Ginny's joy at our appearance was tinged with enough relief to have me wondering about the congeniality of the rest of the company, while Robbie's relief was directed towards the tea trolley, which included not just scones but a Victoria sponge and some cut sandwiches.

After explaining that while they had a housekeeper who supervised the daily help and cooked their meals ('I'm simply hopeless in the kitchen darling'), they had employed the housekeeper's daughter to assist with the catering this weekend, Serena had run off to check that the kitchen was under control. While we'd only known her for a matter of hours, I suspected Serena was always rushing off to check on something or another and briefly pitied the team in the kitchen, who probably found Serena's check-ins a hindrance rather than a help. In her absence, the rest of the company split off into groups. Richard and Robbie stood within reach of the tea trolley, the delicate china cups seeming incongruous in their large hands. With his elbow resting on the mantelpiece, Lord Deverell ('call me Rupert, please') stood chatting to Piers Beaumont-Brown and Wentworth Fitzroy. On the two-seater lounge, Tara Beaumont-Brown was speaking intently with Lucinda Fitzroy.

In a separate armchair, Orlando Stark balanced his teacup casually on one crossed leg, listening to the two women and interjecting with the occasional remark that prompted the sort of loud exclamation of mock outrage from Tara that wouldn't have been out of place in Jane Austen's drawing room. Mallory Stark, however, had drunk half a cup of tea and retired to her room with a headache, announcing she needed to rest up so she wouldn't miss dinner.

Ginny and I found ourselves on the spring-green upholstered window seat, far enough away from the others to talk without fear of being overheard, the crumbs on our tea plates a testimony to our enjoyment of the treats.

'You know what?' I said. 'I think those scones are almost as light as yours.'

'I think they're lighter. In fact,' Ginny said with a complicit grin, 'if I get a chance, I'll be having a word with the cook.' She placed a hand over her mouth to suppress a sudden laugh. 'How do I sound? "I'll be having a word with the cook."'

I giggled at her attempts at an upper-class accent, uncaring that we probably looked (and sounded) like guilty schoolgirls.

'Seriously though, Philly, you have no idea how happy I am to see you. Through Serena, Richard has met the others once or twice, but he feels as awkward with the men as I do with the women. Would you believe that Mallory actually asked me last night whether I felt comfortable being on the other side of the stove?'

'No!'

Ginny nodded once, her usually sunny disposition clouding over. 'Richard told them I run the café at Chipwell Barn, and from that, Mallory assumed I was half a step removed from being the hired help. And when Serena introduced her to me as Mallory Stark, she corrected her and said, "I'm Lady Mallory Stark, and my husband is Lord Stark – he's a viscount." You can tell just by looking at her she wasn't born to this' —her cheeks tinged with pink— 'and I know that makes me sound awfully snobbish. She's trying so hard to speak like them and dress like them – although she manages to make designer brands look cheap – when it's obvious that she's almost as far away from being one of them as I am. I heard Tara referring to her as "not QOC, darling".' When I frowned a silent question, she clarified. 'Not quite our class.'

I struggled to suppress another giggle.

'And that, I suspect,' she added with a meaningful look, 'is the real reason behind her migraine this afternoon. Even though she looked down her nose at me, I can't help feeling sorry for her. Serena was lovely to her last night – Serena is lovely to everyone – but neither of the other women gave her the time of day. Tara was particularly mean, and Lucinda followed her lead. The pair of them were sniggering like teenagers at everything she said. Although' —another meaningful look, this time with a little nod in the direction of the men— 'the men don't seem to have a problem with her. Wentworth Fitzroy – although they call him Wenty' —she rolled her eyes— 'sat beside her at dinner last night and spent quite a lot of the meal looking down her cleavage. And trust me, Philly, her dress was so low and so tight there was plenty of it fighting to escape.'

I couldn't help but chuckle at the image Ginny had conjured up with her words. Glancing across at the women on the sofa, I said, 'Tell me about the other two – Tara and Lucinda. For a start, which is which? Serena made the introductions so quickly I didn't have a chance to take it in.'

'Tara is the brunette in the black turtleneck, channelling Kate Middleton, and Lucinda is the blonde channelling Geri Halliwell's white power dressing vibe. She's Wenty's second wife and almost twenty years younger than him.'

'That's confidence right there,' I said wryly, noting the younger woman's cream funnel-neck jumper with cream pants, and brushed a crumb from my jeans. It was a joke at the barn that cream or white – whether a shirt or a chair – wouldn't stay cream or white for very long around me. I spent my days either up ladders or rummaging in dust and tended not to notice when much of that dust ended up on me.

'She looked amazing at lunch.' Ginny's face held a wistful expression. 'She wore a long cream coat over what she's got on now and teamed it with camel boots and camel bag. Tara looked fabulous too. She wore a tweed belted jacket, and even though we both wore dark jeans, hers looked expensive, and I felt like such a frump in mine.' She swept her hand down her jeans and navy jumper emblazoned with a sequinned star.

'Do we need to have "the talk" again?' I chided gently. 'Besides, can you imagine the cost and effort of maintaining a look like that? And I haven't seen either of them eat yet; how awful must it be to be presented with light as air scones and not allow yourself even one?' Ginny smiled gratefully at my attempt to make her feel better. 'What do you know about them?'

'Well.' She placed her plate and teacup on a side table. 'From what I can gather, the men went to the same school. They're all involved in business in the city and talk endlessly about hedge funds, stocks and investments. Richard could hold his own, but my eyes glazed over. Rupert and Orlando are the only ones with titles, but' —she leant forward conspiratorially— 'Rupert was the second son and not expected to inherit, except his brother died.' She frowned. 'I don't know the details, but Wentworth alluded to it over dinner last night. Orlando and Mallory live on the family estate in Lincolnshire somewhere, and the others are in the Cotswolds – part of that Chipping Norton set you read about in the papers and the social pages.'

I nodded at her reference to the media, show business, political, and general monied set who lived around Chipping Norton in Oxfordshire.

'Rupert seems alright, I suppose,' she said grudgingly. 'Serena is his second wife. I'm not sure what to say about the others; Orlando is the only one who has even acknowledged my existence.' She lifted a shoulder. 'Would anyone notice if I had another piece of cake?'

'It doesn't matter if they do.' I patted her hand and smiled encouragingly. 'I was going to get another piece for myself, so you stay here, and I'll get it.'

Robbie and Richard greeted me with a smile. 'All okay?' Richard asked, his eyes on Ginny rather than me.

'Yes, we're just catching up.'

'Oh Philly …'

At the sound of my name being called, I looked across to the sofa where Tara was beckoning to me. Handing one plate to Richard, I said, 'It seems I've been summoned. Can you take this to Ginny for me?'

CHAPTER SIX

At my approach, Orlando stood and pulled another chair up. 'Thank you,' I said, my nose filled with a sweet, herbal scent that smelt familiar but wasn't any aftershave I'd encountered.

'Serena tells us you're some kind of' —Tara wrinkled her nose— 'what do you call it? A "divvy"?'

People in the antiques business referred to some individuals as 'divvy' because of their innate ability to distinguish antiques from junk and fakes from the real thing. It was sort of like a water diviner but with art and antiques.

I shook my head. 'I wouldn't say that. I have good instincts, but instincts are no good without experience and study – and fortunately, I have both.'

Orlando's smile was smug. 'You're telling us you can tell if, say, a painting is a forgery?'

Refusing to rise to his bait, I swallowed my annoyance and smiled sweetly. 'Perhaps. I can usually tell if something is off with a piece. I mightn't know exactly what's off, but I know enough to investigate further.'

'What do you mean by off?' Lucinda's gaze met mine. There was no sign of mockery in her green eyes.

'When it comes to art, the possibilities are endless – perhaps a signature in the wrong place, a frame that's older than the canvas, and brushstrokes slightly different from the original. It's marginally easier to identify fake china and furniture – if you're familiar with the maker.'

'Give us an example,' demanded Orlando, scepticism in his tone. 'What can you tell us about … that?' His gaze wandered around the room, landing on an oak bookcase. Standing about six feet tall, an open bookshelf with panelled back and sides sat over a latticed cupboard with iron hinges and latches.

Our exchange had attracted the attention of the three men by the fireplace, who ceased their conversation. Robbie's mouth twitched with his amusement at the direction of the conversation.

'Yes.' Tara's smile was more of a smirk. 'I'd like to know what you can tell us about this piece, too.'

I placed the plate of half-eaten cake on a Liberty side table. 'Well,' I mused. 'Furniture isn't my speciality, but' —I tilted my head to the side— 'this is a relatively recent piece, probably made in the late nineteen-thirties – or thereabouts – by Robert Thompson – in the village of Kilburn.'

'How do we know you're not making this up?' Piers stepped forward to take a closer look at the piece.

'If I'm right, there'll be a little carved mouse on the top of the far panel on the right,' I said confidently.

Piers walked across and peered to the side of the bookcase. 'She's right,' he announced. 'How did you know that would be there?'

'Because Robert Thompson signed each of his pieces with a mouse – it's why he's called "the Mouseman."'' They didn't know I'd had cause to research Mouseman pieces last month after finding some in the barn of one of my customers.

'In full disclosure,' I said. 'I've seen this piece before – in the saleroom at Young and Johnsons in York. It was originally one of two made for a' —I searched my memory— 'customer in Slough. That customer paid thirteen pounds for both bookcases. You' —I turned my attention to Rupert— 'paid rather more than that. Almost twenty thousand pounds more if memory serves me correctly.'

Piers clapped slowly and shook his head in amazement at the performance. Wentworth watched me through narrowed eyes, his expression guarded. Rupert, however, was silent, disconcertingly so. I'd need to be on my guard around him.

Serena, who'd watched it unfold from the doorway, laughed out loud. 'Bravo, Philly! Tony told me you never forgot an antique.'

'Just don't ask me to talk about the latest reality TV show or remember a shopping list I haven't written down.' I sighed theatrically to mask my relief. 'It's my business to remember antiques.'

Orlando hadn't finished with me. 'Anyone can fake a carved mouse.'

I shrugged lightly. 'Perhaps, but no one can fake that level of craftsmanship.' I stood and walked across to the bookshelf. 'This cute little fellow has so much personality that it would be easy to imagine him leaping out of the wood and running away into a mouse hole.' I shook my head and looked pointedly at Orlando. 'As I said, you can't fake that kind of craftsmanship.' I returned to my chair and picked up my cake plate. 'The same goes for this Liberty side table – early twentieth century, bone and ebony inlay, arts and crafts design at its best.' I smiled at him, and he smiled back. We both knew the smiles were fake. He'd laid down a challenge, and I'd risen to it – and he didn't like that.

Tara seemed annoyed I'd taken Orlando's attention from her. 'Serena was saying she's hired you. What exactly will you do for her?'

I hid my grin at her blatant attempt to put me back in my place and mulled over my answer as I cut into the cake with my fork.

'She hasn't said yes yet,' Serena jumped in. 'But I'm hoping she'll agree to go through the attic and identify anything important that isn't already catalogued before we clean it out. We're very fortunate she's agreed to consider helping us.'

'And your friend?' asked Lucinda, in a friendlier tone than Tara had used. 'Robbie?'

'I'm nowt important – just the plus one,' said Robbie with a grin. 'I help with the heavy lifting.' I almost laughed aloud at the way he'd deliberately reduced himself to the status of my hired help. What was he playing at?

Before anyone could say more, a younger woman bustled in and gathered the teacups and plates, piling them onto the trolley. I took my plate across to her. 'Were you responsible for that cake and those scones?' I asked.

She straightened in surprise. 'No, that would be my mother.'

'Mrs Phillips is a treasure,' said Serena. 'This is her daughter, Hattie, who we're very grateful to for helping out this weekend.'

Hattie's smile was tight.

'Well, please tell your mother how much we enjoyed them. My friend' —I pointed towards Ginny— 'runs the café where I work, and she says your mother's scones are even lighter than hers – and trust me, that's a big call.'

This time, Hattie's smile was sincere. 'Thank you. Tell your friend she's welcome to come to the kitchen any time – you too, of course. I'm sure Mum would be happy to share her recipe.'

'Thank you, we might just do that.'

As she wheeled the trolley out, Serena took me

aside. 'I'm sorry about before.'

'Serena,' I began. 'Is Rupert okay with me being here and what I'll be doing?'

She reached for my arm, the strength in her grip surprising. 'Absolutely! Rupert can get a bit …' She bit her bottom lip before proceeding. 'Lord of the manor-ish when his friends are around. I fear they're a bad influence on each other.'

While she seemed desperate for me to believe her, I wasn't convinced her husband was as on board as she said he was. That, however, was her problem. 'That's fine. It's forgotten already. I'm looking forward to getting in and rummaging about,' I said. 'I'd also love another look at the Stubbs – although you have some lovely art here, too.' I inclined my head towards a small Gainsborough.

'Yes.' She seemed relieved at my change of subject. 'Feel free to wander around.'

Ginny, Richard, Robbie and I left the drawing room soon after. Rupert smiled as I passed, but the look in his eyes sent a shiver through me.

'What was that about?' Robbie asked as soon as we cleared the drawing room and in the chill of the entrance hall.

'I have no idea, but I don't think whatever game he and the other men are playing is finished.'

'Men like that don't like being shown up,' Richard said sagely, his arm drawing Ginny closer.

'And you certainly weren't bowed by him.' Robbie chuckled at his own understatement.

'And to some men, that's the same thing,' added Ginny. 'I suspect these men aren't used to women challenging them – or responding like you did. When Orlando asked you about that bookcase, my heart was in my throat.'

'I got lucky with that.' I shrugged. 'Whatever. I'm not here for their entertainment; I'm here to look at antiques, and as far as I'm concerned, the sooner I can begin doing that, the better.'

'Maybe,' mused Ginny, 'Lord Rupert has some skeletons in the family closet he doesn't want you to find.'

'Perhaps,' added Richard. 'He was fine with the idea of you coming on board when he thought you were some random Serena had employed, but now you've proven yourself, he's worried about what you'll unearth.'

I looked between the two of them, their faces so serious, and couldn't help but burst into laughter. 'You almost had me there! No, I suspect our host and his friends simply enjoy putting people in their place, and he's still working out what that place is for me.'

'Bloody colonials,' Robbie said wryly.

'Exactly.' I returned his smile and began to head up the stairs. When I turned back to see if the others were following, Robbie was frowning, the furrows in his forehead deeper. 'What's wrong?'

There was the slightest of pauses. 'Nowt. I might just put my head out the door and see how heavy this snow is.'

Nodding, I continued up the stairs, unable to shake the feeling that Robbie had just lied to me – and wondering why he had.

Chapter Seven

At dinner, Orlando and Piers sat on either side of me. Robbie was opposite me and beside Mallory, who seemed to have recovered from her migraine and was now chasing any leftover pain away with gin and tonics. Wentworth was again on her other side, and I had to bite the inside of my lip when his gaze lingered on her tightly restrained breasts, a hint of black lace peeking above the printed fabric of her bodycon dress. Orlando was too occupied with Tara, who sat on his other side, to notice. As Mallory drained her glass and summoned Hattie to mix her another, I wondered what came first – his diminished attention or the alcohol she was numbing the pain with.

Conversation over dinner was light and inconsequential, although as the meal wore on – and more red wine was consumed – Robbie and I came under scrutiny.

'That accent,' began Piers.

'What accent?' I asked. 'Do I have an accent? Now, you have an accent, but me?' I shook my head, and laughter rippled around the table.

'Very funny,' said Piers, who, with Rupert, hadn't joined in the laughter. 'Where are you from? Australia?'

'Yes,' I acknowledged. 'Although I've lived here longer than I lived in Australia.'

'When did you come out here?' asked Lucinda.

'Almost forty years ago. I did what plenty of other Aussies my age did in the eighties – deferred my university admission and came out here on a gap year. I intended to find work in London and then travel. But then I met Stewart, my ex-husband. He was in the police force and had just finished his basic training, so there was no question of him moving to Australia. I didn't know what else I wanted to do, so I joined the force too.'

'You were a police officer?' Tara's wrinkled nose showed her distaste.

'I was a detective in London – at least until my husband began climbing the ranks, and we found ourselves in Yorkshire. The kids were heading into those tricky teenage years, so I resigned from the force and finally completed that fine arts degree I'd skipped all those years ago.'

'How old are your children?' asked Lucinda.

'Ryan is thirty. He lives in York with his husband Jordan and has four-year-old twins, Ada and Alfie. My daughter, Chloe, did the opposite to me – she went to Australia for a gap year, fell in love with Kyle, and stayed. She's twenty-eight now.'

'And your ex-husband?' Tara sent a loaded look towards Robbie.

'He's still in the force – a chief superintendent in York. He's remarried and has another couple of children. We get along.' I shrugged to let her know there was no animosity and nothing more to see here.

'Stewart Barker?' asked Rupert. I nodded. 'We've met at charity events,' he said laconically.

'And where do you fit in, Robbie?' asked Lucinda.

'As I said this afternoon, we're friends. I met Philly when I was investigating some fake antique china. Since then, she's helped me on a couple of cases, and now I've retired, I'm helping her where I can.'

'Cases … investigations … don't tell me we've got another rozzer in the house,' drawled Orlando.

'Aye,' said Robbie, with a hint of a smile. 'Detective Inspector Dawkins, recently retired.'

'Do you know Philly's ex-husband?' Tara seemed determined to get a rise out of us.

Robbie nodded. 'Stewart was my chief super.'

'Well, visiting a house like this as a guest must be a treat for you.' Mallory's patronising comment prompted a hastily muffled giggle from Tara.

Robbie's expression was impassive. 'Happens I've been here before.' He glanced down the table towards Rupert, lingering briefly.

'Oh, really?' Serena sipped her wine. 'How lovely! When was that?'

'Nearly four decades ago,' Robbie said sombrely. 'I was on the other side of the table, though.'

'You were on a case? Do tell more.' Tara leant forward, her eyes wide.

'Aye. We were investigating the disappearance of a local girl. Sad business – she left behind a husband and a bairn.'

The table was silent.

'That's terrible,' Lucinda finally said. 'Did you ever find her?'

Robbie shook his head. 'Not a trace.'

Orlando let out a sardonic snort. 'That's because the little tart ran off with Rupe's brother. *Now* —he emphasised the word with a smirk— 'was heard of him either. It's why Rupe's now Viscount Deverell.'

Lucinda broke in with, 'I'm sure she wasn't … what you said she was.'

'A little tart?' Orlando shared complicit looks with Wentworth and Rupert. 'Trust me, she was.'

'Well, that's all very unfortunate.' Lucinda set her drink down.

'Not for Rupe,' sniggered Orlando in a loud whisper.

Hattie wheeled in a trolley with our desserts – ginger parkin with rhubarb and spiced cider sauce served with ice cream. While Tara and Mallory declined and Lucinda pushed hers around the plate, I tucked into mine with relish and made a mental note to visit the kitchen and ask Mrs Phillips for the syrup recipe.

'Tell me, Philly,' said Rupert. 'What's your plan of attack tomorrow? Will you be rooting around in the attics for all our secrets?'

'I suppose that depends on whether you have any secrets up there. All I'll do this trip is take a cursory look through the attic and anywhere else Serena would like me to look to determine if it's worth undertaking a full catalogue. How long has it been since anyone was up there?'

He waved his hand, the Sauternes slopping over the edge of his glass. 'God only knows. I remember playing up there as a boy – do you remember that Wenty?' Without waiting for an answer, he continued. 'We were always told not to play up there, but that only made us want to go up there more.'

'Why weren't you allowed there?' I wondered aloud.

'Edward used to tell us it was haunted by a witch who placed a curse on the second or third viscount … or was it the fourth? Who can remember details like that?' He shrugged and drained his glass. 'Mary Flounders, her name was, and she'd been a housemaid here.'

'Did she die because she was a witch?' I asked, my mind reaching to grasp what I knew of the history of witch trials in this part of the country.

'No, she died because she murdered my ancestor.' He reached for the bottle and topped up his glass, beckoning for Hattie to fill the empty glasses around the table. 'Poisoned him.'

I shook my head and covered my glass with my hand. 'Why would she haunt the attic?'

'No idea,' he said. 'But it makes for a good story. Apparently, she cursed the house and its firstborn sons.' When he laughed at his joke, his friends joined him. 'You might say that there's no such thing as a cursed house, but history shows you do rather better as the spare than the heir in this family.'

'What a dreadful topic of conversation. Perhaps now would be a good time to tell you I have coffee and petit fours in the drawing room, or, if you prefer, Rupe will serve whisky and cigars in here.' Serena rose from her seat. The other women, plus Robbie and Richard, followed.

'You're not staying for a cigar, Robbie?' There was a hint of a challenge in Orlando's voice.

'I'm right.' Robbie waved his offer away. 'I think I'll check on the weather and join the women in the drawing room.'

'What about you, Richard?' Piers asked sardonically, accepting a whisky from Rupert. 'Surely you don't prefer the company of the women?'

'Thank you, but no, I'll join Robbie in some fresh air.' The men's laughter followed us as we left the room.

Hattie and a woman about my age, who I assumed was her mother, were deep in conversation in the drawing room. 'Is everything alright, Mrs Phillips?' asked Serena.

The housekeeper broke away from her daughter. 'I'm sorry, Lady Deverell. I was telling Hattie that the Tan Hill access road has been closed. It's good she's staying over because there won't be any getting in or out of here tonight.'

'Oh dear. Are many people stuck at the inn?' Serena's expression turned into a concerned frown.

'Aye. There's quite a few there for a band of some sort,' said Mrs Phillips. 'But there's nowt to do about it, and it's not the first time it's happened – and won't be the last.'

'Will we be able to leave tomorrow as planned?' Panic laced Mallory's voice.

Mrs Phillips seemed to enjoy being the bearer of bad news. 'I wouldn't think so, lass – not unless it stops snowing soon, and they don't reckon that will happen until tomorrow – and then they have to get through with the snow ploughs.'

Richard and Robbie entered the room, their cheeks pinched red with the cold, and made directly for the fire to warm their hands. 'It doesn't look like stopping any time soon,' said Robbie with the authority of experience.

'You're from these parts?' Mrs Phillips straightened

the silver coffee pot on the trolley.

'Aye, down the road a bit.' He turned to Serena. 'Do you have a generator?'

'I believe so,' she said uncertainly. 'Mrs Phillips?'

'Aye, we do,' she said. 'In case the lines come down, it's set to switch over automatically, but I've put candles in everyone's rooms in case.'

'Thank you. I think that would be a good idea,' Robbie said.

'What's going on?' asked Mallory tremulously. 'How long are we going to be stuck here?'

'Perhaps another twenty-four hours.' Serena looked sternly in Mrs Phillips' direction. 'Rest assured, we have plenty of food.'

As if on cue, the lights flickered once or twice, and we tilted our heads to look at them, hoping somehow it would make a difference.

'If there's nothing else, Lady Deverell …' Mrs Phillips beckoned to Hattie.

'That will be all. Thank you, Mrs Phillips.'

As the older lady turned to leave, Ginny stopped her. 'That was a lovely dinner, Mrs Phillips, thank you.'

The older lady beamed. 'You're welcome. Hattie mentioned you'd like my scone recipe?' Ginny nodded. 'Come see me in the kitchen after breakfast tomorrow.'

'Thank you, I will.'

Coffee cup in hand, I walked across to where Robbie stood at the fireplace, Richard having joined

Ginny on one of the sofas. 'Is it that bad outside?'

'Aye. It's thick out there and still coming down. No one's coming or going until at least tomorrow afternoon – and that's only if it stops snowing soon.' He pinched his chin between his thumb and forefinger, his frown deep. 'I was afraid of something like this; I just didn't want to worry you.'

'I see,' I said, but the back of my neck prickled with the foreboding that hadn't been far away since setting foot in this house.

Chapter Eight

While my bed had been warm and comfortable, I slept lightly, waking with a start at every creak and groan the old house made as it settled for the night, the wind roaring across the moors and the fells and around the house, the old windows rattling in their frames as it fought for ways to get in. At times, it felt like the whole house could be lifted from its centuries-old bearings and flung into the night. When I did sleep, it was to dream of missing girls, witches in the attic, cursed firstborns and Catherine Earnshaw from *Wuthering Heights* knocking at the window begging to be let inside. I must've fallen into a deeper sleep around dawn but woke around seven, shivering. Nothing happened when I flicked my bedside lamp on and, upon rising, found the radiators were cold.

Dressing quickly in leggings, a jumper and sheepskin boots, I grabbed a scarf and my parka and, using my phone as a torch, hurried downstairs to the kitchen, where the soft glow of hurricane lamps provided dim but adequate light. Robbie was already down there, and Mrs Phillips was telling him where he could find the generator. 'It should've switched over automatically,' she said. 'I can't see why it wouldn't have.'

'Do you want me to come with you?' I asked, pulling my jacket tightly around me.

He shook his head. 'There's no point in two of us freezing. This isn't the first generator I've had to start, and I doubt it will be the last.' Zipping up his anorak and switching on the torch Mrs Phillips had given him, he headed out into the cold.

'Is there anything I can do, Mrs Phillips?' I asked.

'Please call me Susan, dear. And no, there's nothing you can do. I've lit the Aga, so we'll be able to have a brew and a tea cake soon. Hattie is seeing to the fire in the dining room.' A grateful smile spread across her face. 'It was nice of you to offer, though. Why don't you sit down there and keep me company for a bit.'

'Is it still snowing?' I asked. 'I tried to look out my bedroom window, but it's still so dark.'

'Aye,' she said, pulling four cups and saucers from the cupboard and placing them on the table. 'It's not coming down so hard now, so hopefully, they'll be able to get the snow ploughs out to clear the roads later today. I don't think anyone can leave here until tomorrow at the earliest, though.'

'In that case, Ginny and I will happily help you with any meals. Ginny especially will be grateful for the diversion, I expect.'

The housekeeper must've read between the lines. 'Aye, Lady Deverell means well, but I daresay your Ginny is worth more than those other three put together.' She spooned tea leaves into a large ceramic pot.

'Nicely said, Susan.' I chuckled. 'How long have you worked here?'

'It would have to be getting on for over forty years,' she said with a little eye-roll. 'My father was head gardener, and my mother was the housekeeper, so I grew up here.' She turned away to lift the kettle from the stove and pour boiling water over the tea leaves. 'You could say I grew up with the current Lord Deverell and Mister Fitzroy – although they were very different back then.' She wrinkled her nose to let me know the change hadn't been an improvement.

'So you were here when Jenny Black went missing?'

Her face fell, her eyes clouding with remembered pain. 'Aye. She worked here, too. It was a bad business. I remember Robbie from back then; I don't suppose he remembers me, though …' Before she could finish, the lights came on, and with them came the electrical hum of appliances starting up and the ding of the clock on the microwave. 'There we are. With luck, those upstairs won't even know the power's been off.'

The back door swung open, and Robbie's footsteps echoed as he stamped his feet onto the mat in the boot room and hung his anorak before re-entering the kitchen.

'Just in time for a brew,' said Susan, splitting and buttering some hot tea cakes. 'I expect it's proper parky out there.'

'Aye.' Robbie blew into his hands. 'It's raw, but it's hardly snowing now, although the wind hasn't let up.'

'Susan was just telling me she was working here when Jenny Black went missing,' I said as Robbie sat at the table across from me.

'Oh, aye?' said Robbie, nodding slowly. 'I thought I recognised you. You were but a slip of a lass then. You and Jenny were friends, weren't you?'

'Aye. We grew up together, but we'd grown apart a bit by the time she disappeared.' Susan set the teapot and a plate of tea cakes on the table and sat down with us. 'Help yourselves.'

Robbie didn't need to be asked twice and reached for one of the hot, buttered buns. 'Susan,' he said after taking a bite. 'You're a grand woman.'

The other woman's face tinged pink, and she battered his compliment away with her hand. 'Oh, away with you.'

'What do you think happened to Jenny?' I added a drop of milk to my strong tea.

'I don't know.' She leant forward conspiratorially. 'But I'll tell you this much for nothing – that lass did not leave here with Edward Deverell. I never saw any indication of any relationship between her and Teddy.

He was a good man, was Teddy – a better man than Rupert turned out to be any road.'

'Everyone we asked at the time said she wouldn't have cheated on John Black,' said Robbie.

'I wouldn't say that—' Susan began.

'Are you gossiping again, Mum?' Hattie entered the kitchen, sat down with a grin and poured herself a cup of tea. 'You wouldn't want Lady Deverell to hear you blathering about the family.'

'It's a good thing she won't be up for a while yet,' said Susan. 'Robbie here was involved in the original investigation into Jenny's disappearance, and I was about to tell him that while I couldn't believe she'd run off with Edward, there was something between her and Rupert.'

Robbie's eyes widened. 'That didn't come out at the time …'

'Happened as no one asked me,' Susan said with an affronted sniff.

'Do you have any proof about that, Mum?'

'Only what Jenny told me and what I witnessed with my own eyes. We all ran about together when we were kids. Rupert was different then – even Wenty Fitzroy was nicer than he is today. They'd come back from school each holiday and we'd pick up where we left off. The old Lady Deverell – the present viscount's mother – disapproved, but what she didn't know …' Her eyes took on a dreamy gaze. 'That last summer, the year Lord Deverell and Mr Fitzroy finished school, something changed between us. The boys had changed – they were more … entitled. Jenny and I were older, and Jenny had … you know …' She cupped her hands in front of her breasts. 'Both men noticed. I was seeing my Fred, and we were saving to get married, so I didn't go about with them, but Jenny was always skiving off to go on picnics and whatnot. I used to cover for her here, and I told her nothing good would come of it, but she was besotted with Rupert, and Wenty was besotted with her. She'd date local boys when Rupert was away at school, but they'd never last because come the holidays, she'd be mooning about Rupert again. I used to say to her, "Jenny, love. Nothing can ever come of it," and she'd laugh and say, "I know, but it's such fun."'

'But she married John Black,' said Robbie, frowning.

'Aye, she did, not long after the boys went off to Oxford. Sudden-like it was, and then the bairn came along.'

Robbie narrowed his eyes. 'Are you suggesting she married John Black because she was pregnant?'

'I wouldn't like to say.' She lifted her chin, leaving us to think that that was precisely what she wanted us to think. 'All I'm saying is either that bairn arrived early or Jenny had been seeing John that summer. Her father would've killed her if she'd had a bairn out of wedlock, but her father passed away not long after the wedding.'

Robbie absently reached for another buttered half of teacake.

'What about her mother?' I asked.

'Now there's a story,' said Hattie.

'Go on …' I urged.

'Well,' she began. 'Jenny's mother was a healer, as was her mother. In fact' —she sipped at her tea— 'Jenny came from a long line of "healers", and the word is that if Jenny had wanted to lose that baby she was carrying, she would've known what to take to make it happen if you get my drift. Her mother died when Jenny was a bairn herself.'

'When you say healers, do you mean—' I began.

'Witches? Yes. That's what people used to say.' Susan nodded. 'Although Jenny never let on anything of the like to me.'

What was it Rupert had said last night? About one of his ancestors being murdered? Before I could ask about that, though, the bell on the wall marked 'dining room' rang.

Hattie jumped up. 'I'll get that, Mum.'

'That's enough larking. I'd best be getting on with things, too.' Susan stood and straightened her apron. 'Tell your Ginny to come and see me after breakfast, and she can help me with the scones.'

'I'll let her know,' I said.

As we headed back up the stairs to leave our anoraks in our respective bedrooms, Robbie said, 'The generator had been switched off – that's why it didn't switch over automatically.'

'Why would anyone do that?'

He shrugged. 'Maybe it was accidental …'

I paused outside my room and searched his face. 'You don't think it was, though?'

'If it was deliberate, I have no idea why.' He pulled thoughtfully at his chin.

'Did you question Rupert or Wentworth when Jenny went missing?' I asked.

He shook his head. 'No. We didn't know about their involvement, and Rupert was at university when Jenny disappeared. A DC in Oxford checked his alibi.'

'I don't suppose that alibi was Wentworth Fitzroy?'

Robbie looked hard at me, but Ginny and Richard coming out of their room prevented him from answering. 'You two are up early,' said Richard.

'Aye,' said Robbie. 'The power went out.'

'This is from the generator?' Richard waved his finger towards the lights, and Robbie nodded. 'Will we be able to leave here today?' He shot Ginny a look I couldn't decipher.

'I wouldn't bank on it,' said Robbie.

Ginny's eyes filled, and I reached for her arm. 'I'll be busy in the attic, but it's okay – Susan, Mrs Phillips, has said you're welcome to join her in the kitchen.'

'Thank you.' She brightened a little and turned to Richard. 'I'm sorry, darling. I know Serena is your friend, but those other women …' She shuddered.

I didn't blame her.

Chapter Nine

It was easy to see the attraction the attic would've had for a young boy. Sheet-shrouded furniture loomed out of the wood-panelled shadows and provided both places where a tiny body could be concealed in a game of hide and seek and the perfect place to jump out from should one wish to frighten the bejeezus out of one's friend.

On a sunny day, dust motes would dance in the ribbony streams of light from the small, mullioned windows. However, natural light was limited on a morning like this and was, at best, dull and ineffective. Although we'd switched on the single overhead bulb, we needed our torches to illuminate corners. The wind still roared outside, attempting to find a gap through which it could force its way in, and as there was no heating in here, Robbie and I had layered up with jackets over our thick wool jumpers and gloves to protect our fingers from the icy temperatures.

We'd spent the first couple of hours on the large furniture – most of which was readily saleable and some which would bring good prices if taken to auction. Simon could give Serena a better idea of pricing than I could, so if we progressed further with this job, he'd need to be brought in.

Next, we pulled out all the artwork stacked against walls, in boxes and under sheets covering furniture. Again, there were some lovely pieces, but from what I'd seen, the pick of the art was hanging downstairs.

'Anything?' asked Robbie, stretching a kink in his neck.

I'd been kneeling on the floor and struggled to my feet, brushing dust from my jeans. 'No. It's all saleable, and some pieces might fetch a few thousand pounds, but nothing like the Stubbs in the ballroom.' Frowning, I pictured the painting. 'It's just …'

'What?'

'I've seen the Stubbs hanging in the National Gallery, but never seen any in the wild, and I thought it would be …' I struggled to find the right word. 'I thought it would be more exciting. I thought *I* would feel more excited looking at it.' I ran my hand across the smooth mahogany of a long-forgotten hall table. 'I remember the first time I went to the National Gallery; it was my first day in London, and my senses were blown by' —I shrugged— 'everything, really. But when I stepped into the National Gallery' —I shook my head— 'everything made sense, but simultaneously, my senses were overwhelmed. Here they were – all the artists I was heading home to study at university.

Gainsborough, Turner, Constable, Stubbs – all the boys in the band. Looking at Stubb's painting of Whistlejacket made the back of my neck prickle. It was astonishing. It's that prickle I've felt every time I've seen something really important.'

'And you didn't get that prickle yesterday?' Robbie leant against a writing desk, his arms folded against the cold. 'Maybe because we were being rushed through and it was freezing.'

'Maybe,' I conceded with a wry smile. 'There was a prickle, but it wasn't like when I saw the Wilson peeking out of that box.' Late last year, I found a painting of Whitby in a mixed job lot at auction that turned out to be by the nineteenth-century artist JT Wilson that did exceptionally well when I resold it at auction last month. 'It was more of a … warning or foreboding. I know' —I laughed at myself— 'it makes no sense. What also makes no sense is why you would have a painting like that and hide it away in a room no one uses.'

'With a heap of dead relatives and dead animals, you mean?' Robbie finished, bending to lift another box onto the writing desk.

'Exactly. There are some valuable paintings downstairs. Aside from the small Gainsborough, I noticed a Degas and a Sisley in the drawing room, and some of those landscapes in the dining room are valuable, too.' I shrugged. 'But that Stubbs could be the most valuable of the lot. Obviously, Rupert has his reasons, but I don't understand them. Art like that should be seen.'

'Maybe you should ask him,' said Robbie, pulling a brown salt-glazed stoneware pot embellished with a grotesque bearded face and an emblem – or a primitively crafted coat of arms – from the box he'd just opened. 'What do you think this is?'

Under the layers of jumpers I wore, the hairs on my arm stood up, my heart beating faster. Even though I'd only seen one in an auction catalogue and another in a museum, I knew exactly what it was.

'I think there's something in there.' He shook it lightly.

'Yes,' I said, excitement bringing my heart to my throat. 'There'll be a few nails or bent pins in there. Maybe another talisman – something like a felt heart. Anything else will have dried up by now.'

'What is it?' Frowning, he handed me the pot as I switched the torch on to get a better look.

'It's a witch's pot.'

Robbie's eyes widened in fascination. 'Go on…'

After running my fingers across the raised image of the bearded man, I eased the cork stopper out and tipped the bottle's contents into my hand. As I'd suspected, inside was an assortment of bent, rusty nails and a roughly hewn and frayed grey flannel heart. 'These should stay with the pot,' I said, tipping them back in.

'How old is it?'

'Eighteenth century, maybe a little earlier but not much. I wonder where it had been hidden – before it ended up in this box.'

'Would it have been hidden?'

I nodded. 'Yes. For it to do its work, it must've been.'

'Should I ask what you mean by "it's work"?' Robbie's words came out hesitantly as if reluctant to hear the answer.

'Well,' I began. 'Remember how Susan told us this morning that Jenny Black came from a line of healing women?' He nodded. 'This was probably either made up by one of them or,' I mused, 'it might even have been created to throw a curse back on one of them.' When he still looked perplexed, I clarified. 'Back in those days – the sixteenth and seventeenth century and even into the eighteenth century – if there was anything wrong with you, the likelihood was a witch had touched or cursed you. Your cow dies? Witch's curse. Miscarriage? Witch's curse. Bad dreams? Witch's curse. Urinary tract infection? We wouldn't have blamed poor nutrition or insufficient clean water; it was more likely you'd had a curse placed on you.'

The beginning of a disbelieving smile came to his mouth. 'And people believed this?'

'Different times, Robbie. But yes, they did believe it. The local healing woman might advise you to create one of these.' I held the pot up. 'The idea was to send the curse back threefold. The afflicted person would've peed into this pot' —I sniffed the opening suspiciously— 'and filled it with nails. The pot represented the witch's body, the urine represented what should be attacked in the witch's body, and the nails would bring the witch the same pain as the victim was suffering.' I chuckled at his look of distaste. 'I know, it was delightful. The UTI example is just one of the reasons you might feel you were cursed. Once you'd completed this, all you needed was for someone to die suddenly in the village – male or female – or even the next village, and hey presto, they must've been your witch, and you were cured. The key to it working was getting rid of the bottle; it would be buried or hidden or even thrown in a stream, effectively sending the curse back to the witch.' I weighed the pot in my hand. 'Of course, the healer was treading a fine line – get it wrong, and she risked being accused of witchcraft.'

'And being arrested and burnt?' guessed Robbie.

'Especially in Scotland, yes. Not so much here in England. I can't remember the numbers, but I remember reading about how only a quarter of those accused – most of whom were innocent – were convicted and hanged in England. Plus, by the mid-eighteenth century, authorities had repealed most of the legislation against witchcraft – not that it stopped people accusing women of witchcraft. You could be accused for any reason – looking different, behaving differently, curing someone who'd been ill. Some women were accused because they were menopausal and grew hair where women didn't grow hair.' I touched my top lip and my chin. 'And all too often, the accusers were other women. The ultimate mean girls.' I lifted a shoulder. 'So much for the sisterhood.' Turning the pot over in my hand, another thought occurred to me. 'Another possibility is the witch – or healer – felt under threat and used this as a protection for whoever she suspected had it in for her. She might've filled it with pins or nails, wine and maybe rosemary. In that case, the pins or nails were intended to trap anything trying to hurt the witch; the wine "drowned" it or took away its power, and the rosemary banished the danger.'

'Do you think it belonged to Mary Flounders? The one who was executed?'

'Perhaps. Or maybe this housed the curse she placed on the house.' I let out a derisive snort of laughter. 'Although it's easy to make up stories that could fit. If it belonged to her, it would be interesting to know if her ledgers were here somewhere.' When he raised an eyebrow, I clarified. 'Most healers kept a ledger – a journal detailing who they'd treated or provided with herbs or charms. They'd probably call it a Book of Spells in today's era, but most of these women were just an early version of an apothecary or chemist, and many handed their book – and their skills – down the female line.' A small smile twitched at the thought of finding something like that in one of these boxes. 'Although if Mary Flounders was hanged I'm assuming she died childless.'

Robbie chuckled. 'I know that look, Philly Barker.' He dug further into the box and emerged, holding a thick journal bound in worn fabric-covered board. 'Would the ledger look something like this?'

There it was, that ripple of excitement at a truly interesting find. 'Yes, that is exactly what it would look like!'

Impatiently, I pushed aside a vase and some picture frames to clear space on the hall table; Robbie carefully set the book down. Reverently, I opened the cover and carefully turned the brittle pages. 'Damn, I left my reading glasses downstairs.' Patting at the pockets of my parka, I located my loupe and peered through it. 'I'm going to need to take my time and read through this properly, but' —I straightened and beamed— 'this is *quite* the find.' Closing the book, I tucked it under my arm. 'I'll take this downstairs and leave it somewhere safe in my room, but the pot can go back into the box for now and' —I glanced at my watch— 'we'll pick this up after lunch.'

Robbie rubbed his stomach. 'Excellent timing – I'm starved.'

'Are you ever not?' I scoffed.

Calling in at our rooms on the way down, we took turns using the bathroom and cleaning up after our dusty morning. I swapped my thick fisherman's gansey for a lighter wool. A quick glance out the window told me the snow had stopped, and visibility was returning with the fountain and outbuildings now back in view. It really was pristine seeing it like this before anything had had a chance to mark its smooth surface. With a final fluff of my hair, I was ready to head downstairs and face the others. On impulse, I took the ledger from where it lay on my bed, wrapped it in a jumper and put it in my suitcase.

Chapter Ten

'Oh, Philly?' Wentworth Fitzroy called to us from the door of what Serena had pointed out the previous afternoon as being Rupert's library. 'Have you got a second?'

Attempting to hide how much his cold smile unsettled me, I nodded. 'Sure.'

Robbie's eyes narrowed warily as we followed Wentworth into Rupert's library – which was everything I'd have expected it to be. Wood panelling and ceiling-height bookshelves lined the room, complemented by heavy green drapes that framed the windows and a Georgian mahogany partners pedestal desk with brass trimmings that dominated the room.

Rupert sat behind his desk, Wentworth leant casually against a matching mahogany cabinet, and Piers Beaumont-Brown was seated in one of the three burgundy leather-covered wingback armchairs, his legs stretched out in front of him and crossed at the ankles.

'Is that …' I began.

'Go on.' Rupert waved at me to continue.

'I was going to say, is that Chippendale?'

Rupert's mouth twitched into that same unpleasant half smile, half smirk. 'What do you think?'

Approaching the desk, I ran my hand across the beautifully burnished gilt-tooled leather top, my skin prickling in excitement. 'Oh yes,' I murmured. 'This is definitely Chippendale, late eighteenth century, I suspect, and it's spectacular.'

'It's just a desk,' he drawled. After a glance across to Wenty, the smirk grew wider. 'What would you say if I told you it was a fake?'

There was something between the three of them that made me feel uncomfortable, as though I was about to be the butt of some cruel schoolboy prank. 'I'd say whoever had told you it was reproduction wasn't telling the truth.'

Rupert's smiled unpleasantly. 'Did you just call me a liar?'

Wentworth's face held the same cruel smile as Rupert's. Piers lifted a shoulder, his expression clearly saying, 'I dare you.' I imagined the three of them in their dorm back in their respective expensive schools terrorising one of the lower-grade boys – probably one who hadn't yet adapted to life away from his parents and maybe, thanks to their bullying, never would.

Resisting the impulse to look back at Robbie for

support, I squared my chin. 'No, I said whoever told you it was a reproduction was lying.'

He tilted his head to the side, his eyes narrowed. 'Are you sure about that?'

I laid my hand again on the table, the warmth of the rich-grained wood sending a hum through my veins. 'Oh yes,' I breathed. 'I'm positive.'

'I think she knows her stuff, old man,' said Wenty, slapping his friend on the back. Rupert's smirk slipped. 'You're right, it's genuine. How much do you think it's worth?'

Biting at my bottom lip I cast my mind back through auction listings. 'These don't come up for auction often – and certainly not in as good a condition as this one is.' When Rupert raised his brows, my eyes met his. 'If you wanted to sell, Simon, the furniture guy at Chipwell Barn Antiques, could give you a better idea. But, if it were to come up for auction, I'd expect to see an estimate of between fifteen and twenty thousand pounds on it.'

Piers raised his eyebrows and let out a low whistle. 'That much?' He spoke for the first time since we'd entered the room. 'What's so special about it? Surely it's just a desk?'

'A genuine Chippendale is not just a desk,' I said haughtily. 'Aside from the wood – this one is mahogany and chosen for its durability and beauty – the craftsmanship is superb. Every detail from the finest of leather to the quality of the joinery, the brass on the drawers to the silk upholstery and curve of the legs on the chair you're sitting at' —I waved my hand in his direction— 'is taken into consideration.' Sighing my appreciation, I added, 'It's stunning ... and to have the chairs and cabinet as well ...' Simon would love to see these pieces.

Lucinda walked into the room. 'Sorry to interrupt, but Serena has just asked me to let you know lunch is out.' She bit her bottom lip, and I wondered unkindly whether the injectables in her forehead allowed her to frown. 'Also, have any of you seen Orlando? Mallory is just down, and she can't find him anywhere and is beginning to worry.'

Rupert shook his head in exasperation. 'Stupid woman. She's worrying over nothing. He probably went out earlier.'

'In this?' Robbie asked sceptically, looking out at the drifts on the front drive.

'Wouldn't you if you were married to that?' Wentworth said with another of his sneers.

'It didn't seem to stop you ogling her for the last couple of nights,' Lucinda snapped back.

'She's got you there, old man.' Piers rose from his chair with a sigh. 'Come on, chaps, let's go find where Orlando's hidden himself.'

Lucinda followed the men out, leaving Robbie and me alone in the library.

'What is this place, Robbie?' I asked.

'You mean with its missing girls, witch's pots, and curses?' His grin was designed to ease my discomfort.

'And men born with silver spoons so highly polished they haven't matured past puberty and …'

'Now, now now, Philomena Barker, your prejudices are showing,' chuckled Robbie.

'They're arrogant and entitled plonkers – don't tell me you don't think so too!'

'Oh aye, he's a reet berk,' he said, lapsing into Yorkshire slang. 'They all are. And now one of them's gone and got himself lost.' As I would've opened my mouth to say he could stay lost as far as I was concerned, a high-pitched shriek shattered the air.'

Following the direction of the shriek, we caught up with Lucinda and burst into the drawing room where Tara was cradling a hysterical Mallory; Serena, Richard and Ginny were looking on. Tara's impatient eye roll might have been intended for Lucinda, but Richard's was meant for us.

'What's happening here?' asked Robbie.

Serena seemed unfazed by Mallory's distress. 'Mallory came downstairs not long ago – well, we rarely see her before midday – and wondered where Orlando was. We all assumed he was with the other men, but when they told her they hadn't seen him, she got quite … she became a little emotional.' The glare she sent her husband told us the men hadn't been gentle with delivering their message.

'Damn fool has probably gone to the barn for a sneaky smoke,' grumbled Rupert. He reached for a sausage roll and a sandwich from the trolley and retired to stand by the fireplace where Wenty and Piers were already eating.

'Even if he has gone out to smoke one of those funny cigarettes of his' —that explained the sweet herbal smell from yesterday— 'I highly doubt he'd be doing it in this weather.' Serena sent another frown to her husband.

'I do, too,' Robbie said solemnly in a voice low enough not to reach Mallory's ears.

'Maybe he had an accident out there,' sobbed Mallory. 'He might have slipped and bumped his head or sprained an ankle. And now he's freezing. He could already be frozen, and none of you care!' Her voice rose again, and Tara and Lucinda took turns patting her back or rubbing her arms in comfort.

'Alright, we'll head out and ensure he's not there,' Rupert said wearily. 'But we'll finish lunch first – another ten minutes won't make any difference.'

'Have you searched upstairs yet?' asked Robbie, frowning.

'Why would I do that?' snapped Mallory between sobs. 'He wasn't in our room or bathroom when I woke up. They're the only two rooms he'd go into up there. What are you implying? That he'd be visiting someone else's room?'

Robbie held up a hand to indicate he hadn't meant to imply anything. 'And he certainly wasn't in the attic. How about the four of us' —he waved his hand to include Ginny and Richard, who were sitting together on the window seat— 'look around down here?'

Serena, her voice filled with gratitude, clasped Robbie's arm. 'Thank you, Robbie. I should stay here with Mallory. Just make sure you grab something to eat and a hot drink first. See Mrs Phillips for the key to anywhere you can't get into.'

After filling our plates with mini tarts, sausage rolls and sandwiches, we joined Ginny and Richard.

'I'm glad you're here,' said Ginny. 'Things were getting quite out of control.'

'Although no one other than Mallory seems concerned by his absence,' mused Richard. The other three men were idly chatting as they ate.

'Yes, there's a definite lack of urgency.' Robbie placed an entire sandwich triangle into his mouth and chewed thoughtfully. 'Maybe Orlando has done this before?'

'Or, at the very least, has a habit of sneaking out to the barn to smoke his wacky backy,' I mused, reaching for a mini quiche.

Ginny choked on her coffee. 'His what?'

'Wacky backy – marijuana.' I pulled a little piece of bacon from my tart. 'What do the kids call it these days? Dope, pot, weed?' What was it I was missing?

Robbie's lips quirked. 'Weed will do fine, Philly.'

'Having watched them at dinner on Friday night and again yesterday, I wouldn't be surprised if another habit he indulges out there involves Tara Beaumont-Brown,' said Ginny, placing her coffee cup on a coaster and rising to get more sandwiches.

'Have you got any proof?' I asked.

She shook her head, her mouth full of chicken sandwiches. I waited for her to swallow. 'It's more an impression, an ease between them that tells me there's history – whether it's modern or ancient, though, I don't know,' she finally said. 'Mrs Phillips really is a treasure,' she added, picking up a sausage roll.

'Listen to you, "Mrs Phillips is a treasure",' I teased. 'Another day here and you'll be moaning about the availability of good help!'

Once the laughter had died, Ginny said, 'Come to think of it, Susan dropped a comment this morning that made me think they were still at it – Orlando and Tara, that is.' Tapping at the edge of her plate, her eyes went to the ceiling as she thought. 'It was something about how it's fortunate "madam"' —she inclined her head towards Mallory— 'takes a sleeping tablet each night and doesn't hear any comings and goings. Let me tell you, Mallory's not made friends with the staff. She lies in bed until midday, and Hattie says she has a drinking problem too – there was an empty bottle of gin in the garbage bin in their room yesterday.'

'In other words,' I said, 'she wouldn't know what time her husband was up this morning.' What was it I was trying to remember? Walking backwards through my recent movements, it hit me. 'That's it! Remember how we went back to our rooms before coming down?' Robbie nodded, his frown telling me he had no idea where this was going. 'Well, I happened to look out the window to check out the snow and remember noting there were no footprints in the snow in the courtyard – either to the barn or what I assume is the estate office. And given how deep it is, I'd expect to see some if someone had been over there.'

'Maybe they stuck to the edges of the gravel and went that way,' suggested Ginny.

I considered that. 'No, the whole courtyard is covered in snow, and I remember thinking about how pristine it was.'

'Maybe fresh snow covered them,' suggested Richard.

'No, it stopped a few hours ago. Even when I went out to kick the generator started this morning, it was falling too lightly to cover footsteps.' Robbie shook his head. 'I don't think Lord Stark or, indeed, anyone has been to the barn this morning.'

'Why isn't anyone looking for my husband?' Mallory wailed, her eyes casting frantically around the room. 'Someone needs to help me.'

'I really don't see what all the fuss is about,' said Wentworth laconically.

'I'm sure there's nothing to worry about,' said Rupert with a dismissive wave of his hand.

'Waste of effort if you ask me,' grumbled Piers.

'Can you check the estate office while you're out there?' Serena asked. 'I know Robin is away this weekend, but you never know.'

'Why the blazes would he be there?' Rupert reluctantly placed his empty plate on a side table. 'Robin always keeps it locked.'

'Maybe he forgot on this occasion,' Serena said evenly, ignoring Mallory's sobs in the background. 'You'll need to rug up warm; that wind is icy. I'll have Mrs Phillips put on fresh coffee for when you're back.'

'We'd better also get moving.' Robbie gathered our plates and placed them on the trolley. 'Richard and Ginny, if you can cover the reception rooms on this side of the house, we'll take the generator room, the storerooms and the Great Hall.'

'Done.' Richard saluted with his finger to his head.

'I don't know what you expect to find,' I said a few minutes later. Robbie and I were in the boot room off the kitchen, shrugging into our parkas in preparation for going outside. 'Probably nowt,' he said, the line of his jaw saying the opposite.

'But your copper's radar is telling you the opposite?'

'Aye,' he said.

'That's Madam all over – making summat of nowt.' Susan joined us in time to hear Robbie's comment. 'I think you'll find Lord Stark asleep in Madam's bed – and Madam was too out of it to notice.' She pulled a chain, holding a fistful of keys, from around her neck and handed them to Robbie.

'You're probably right,' I said. 'But we'll check anyway – just to be sure.'

CHAPTER ELEVEN

'There's nothing in here.' Robbie cast the light of his torch into the shadows of the generator room. 'It looks like the main power is back on and the generator has switched back. That must have been that flicker when we were in the attic.'

'Does this house have a cellar?' I rubbed my arms against the cold that streamed in through the ventilation shafts.

'No one has mentioned one,' he said. 'But it's worth asking Susan about.'

Back in the house, there was just the ballroom to search, but when I turned the bronze doorhandle, nothing happened. 'It's locked.' I turned back to Robbie. 'It wasn't locked yesterday when Serena showed us through, was it?'

Robbie shook his head solemnly. 'No, it wasn't.' Reaching into his pocket, he pulled out the housekeeper's keys and selected the largest and oldest to try in the keyhole.

A chill ran through my body even before the door swung fully open, leaving me on edge. Although the room had been closed, the air felt unsettled, as if it had recently been disturbed. Robbie must have felt it, too. 'Why don't you stay out here, Philly, and I'll check inside.'

'I'll come with you.' My heart was already racing with fear, dreading what was behind these doors.

With a nod, he pushed the doors open.

At first, the hall seemed as it had been yesterday – vast and empty – until we noticed a figure-shaped lump lying on the wooden floor near the fireplace. Robbie instinctively pulled a handkerchief from his pocket and placed it over his fingers before pushing the doors shut behind him and locking them, taking care not to touch the knob. I immediately understood – if that lump was Orlando Stark, we didn't want anyone else disturbing the scene.

'Is it …?' I asked.

'Aye, I think so,' he said soberly. 'You right?' I nodded, and we began the long walk down the hall to where the body lay.

It was, indeed, Orlando Stark. He lay sprawled on his back, with his eyes open, gazing sightlessly at the ceiling rising above him. His arms were flung out to the side, his left leg twisted at an awkward right angle, and a dark stain lay on the floor beside him.

'Is he dead?' I asked as Robbie crouched down and rested two fingers against Orlando's throat.

'Aye, and has been for some time. Most of the night, I'd wager.' Touching the blood on the floor with his index finger, he added, 'It's still tacky, but it is cold in here. I'm no pathologist, but I'd be surprised if he were still alive past two am.'

Orlando had clearly changed after dinner, now dressed in loose jogging pants, trainers and an olive-green anorak over a grey sweatshirt drenched in blood. With the hanky again over his fingers, Robbie gingerly opened the anorak, then sat back on his haunches. 'He's been stabbed. While I call this in, can you do a scout around for the murder weapon?'

I nodded, unable to move my eyes from the lifeless body on the floor and reconcile it with the smirking, flirting, arrogant Lord Stark we'd met not twenty-four hours earlier.

'Philly?' Concern filled Robbie's voice. 'I know this is a shock, but I need you to hold it together for me, okay?' He stood and, gripping my shoulders firmly, gazed down into my eyes. 'Take a few deep breaths.'

I nodded again, my heart racing, my breath coming in short gasps. While I'd seen my share of dead bodies during my years on the force and, more recently, last month, it was something I'd never got used to.

'I'll be fine,' I finally said, my voice catching, my attention still on Lord Stark's body.

'I know you will.' His grim half smile was reassuring. He stood and pulled his phone from his back pocket, then grimaced at the screen. 'This is not a call the chief super will be happy to get on a Sunday.'

'Knowing my ex-husband, he'll be at a pub somewhere halfway through lunch. No, he won't be pleased.' Despite the scene, I managed to chuckle at the thought. Sunday lunch had always been sacred for Stewart.

Scrolling through his contacts, Robbie selected Stewart's number, waited for a few seconds, and then looked back at me. 'I've got no reception in here.' He sighed. 'It's these walls. You'll need to call while I stay with him.' He inclined his head towards Orlando. 'Probably best if you make the call from your room so no one can overhear you, and if you do come across anyone, not a word until after you've spoken to Stewart.' He placed his hands on my shoulders again and met my eyes, his mouth in a grim line. 'Will you be alright to do that?'

Again, I nodded. While I wasn't superstitious, there was no way I wanted to stay here alone with a dead body. 'I'm sure I still have silicon gloves at the bottom of my bag from last time, so I'll bring those back with me.'

'That's grand. Before you go, though, we need photos of the body and the scene – and we'll do the same when you get back.' When my eyebrows rose, he clarified, 'In case a defence lawyer wants to argue about scene disturbance while I'm alone.' The thought hadn't occurred to me. He paused. 'I'll also need you to lock me in with him.'

Reluctantly, I took the keys he offered. 'Really?'

'Aye. I don't want anyone in here other than you or I.' A quick glance at the corpse and, 'I don't like the idea any better than you do, so don't hang about out there for a brew and a scone.' His attempted smile took any severity from his words. 'Now, let's take these photos so you can call this lot in.'

I roamed around the space for the next few minutes, taking photographs. We also quickly searched the bench chairs, the floor under them, and the fireplace without success. There was, as far as we could tell, no sign of the murder weapon.

As I began the long walk down the hall towards the doors, I turned back to see Robbie settling onto one of the bench seats to wait. 'Mind how you go, Philly,' he called.

I raised a hand in acknowledgement, letting myself out and closing the door behind me. The pins in the lock fell into place with a crunch that sounded overly loud in the foyer's quiet. After pausing to listen for any sound of conversation behind the door to the drawing room, I scampered up the stairs to the sanctuary of my bedroom.

•

'Philly! How are you?' Despite my calling his number, Stewart's wife, Alison, answered. 'Stewart's just gone to the bar. We're at this fabulous family pub just outside Bingley – best tasting roast beef we've had in a long time. What about you? You've gone away this weekend, haven't you? Ryan mentioned it when I was over there yesterday. The storm hit quite badly up there, didn't it? We got a light dusting down here, but I heard Tan Hill was snowed in again.'

I closed my eyes briefly to temper my impatience at Alison's incessant chatter. 'I'm well, Alison, and I'm sorry to disturb you today, but I need to talk to Stewart – urgently.'

'Philly … are you sure you're alright?' Alison sounded worried.

'Yes, yes, I'm fine, but I have a situation that Stewart needs to know about.' I paced back and forth on the soft carpet in my bedroom, my free hand tapping against my denim-clad thigh.

Alison had been Stewart's wife for long enough to know the phrase 'a situation' was code for police business. 'Hold on, Philly, I'll be right back.'

True to her word, Stewart was on the phone before I'd had time to stride the length of my bedroom twice. 'What's this about?' He cut straight to the chase with no preamble.

'Robbie and I have found a body,' I blurted out.

'You've what?' His voice rose, and I immediately bristled at the way I always did when Stewart's voice rose. Alison must have given him 'the look' she'd been perfecting as his tone lowered. 'Alison said you're away – where are you?'

'We're at Deverell Grange, it's …'

'I know where it is – it's out in the middle of nowhere. I also know Rupert, Lord Deverell; he's a generous supporter of the Police Foundation. Are you sure?'

'Am I sure it's a body?' I took a breath and deliberately moderated my tone. 'Of course I'm sure. It's got a stab wound in the middle of its chest, and there's quite a lot of blood involved.'

Stewart's groan was audible. 'Okay, let's start from the beginning. Do you know who the victim is?'

'We do – it's Orlando Stark, Viscount of somewhere or another – you know what I'm like with titles.' In my anxiety, I was rambling.

'Lord Stark? It gets better.' I imagined him squeezing his eyes shut and rubbing his face like always when exasperation warred with frustration over a problem I was at the centre of. 'What else?'

'His wife reported him missing at around midday today, and Robbie and I searched the Great Hall and found him there. Robbie thinks he's probably been dead since the early hours. We've had a look around but haven't found a weapon. His clothes have absorbed a lot of blood, and while there's some on the floor, there's not enough to indicate he was alive for long after the injury.'

'Is the scene secure?'

'Yes. We haven't touched anything other than the outside of the doorknob, and Robbie is locked in there with him now while I make this call. Oh, and the door was locked when we found him, although I suppose the murderer could've locked it after they'd finished.' I made a mental note to ask Mrs Phillips who else might have keys to the room.

'Right.' I could hear the cogs in Stewart's brain turning. 'I'll get DI Whitely onto it; it will take him a couple of hours to get there, though.'

Pulling the curtain aside, I peered out the window. While the sky was still grey, the snow had stopped, the previously pristine scene now marred by deep footprints leading to the barn and across to the estate office. Lord Rupert, Piers and Wentworth emerged from the estate office, zipped their anoraks against the cold and stood huddled. What could they be talking about? 'That's the other thing – the roads are closed, and we're snowed in. It's stopped falling now, but the housekeeper said earlier it will be a while yet before the snow plough can get through. And it's still blowing a gale.'

'You're telling me that in the meantime, you and Robbie are stuck in a house with a murderer?' His voice grew louder, and in the background, Alison gasped.

'I hadn't thought about it that way.' But now that I had …

'Here's what I need you to do, Philly. With your help, Robbie will have to run the investigation and hand it over to DI Whitely when he can get through. Check in with me every hour. I'm assuming the body is safe where it is?'

'Yes – it's not much above freezing in there, and we can lock the door.'

'Good. Leave it there, and as hard as it sounds, don't cover it – we can't disturb the scene further. Who else is in the house? For that matter, what are you and Robbie doing there?'

'It's a long story, but Ginny's boyfriend Richard is friends with Serena – Lady Deverell – and she asked me to look through a few things she might want to sell. Other than Ginny and Richard – and Robbie and me, of course – there's the deceased's wife, Mallory, Lady Stark; Piers and Tara Beaumont-Brown; and Wentworth and Lucinda Fitzroy. Also in the house are the housekeeper, Susan Phillips, and her daughter, Hattie. The estate manager, Robin someone-or-other is away.' The three men began to trudge back to the house, the snow about mid-calf height.

'Alright. The deceased's wife must be told, but I suggest you talk to Lord Deverell first and let him know what's happening. Don't wait for DI Whitely to get there before you take statements, and if Lord

Deverell causes a fuss, you can put him through to me. Tread carefully with him though – you know what that lot can be like … especially if it's one of their own.'

'Okay,' I said, Stewart's instructions helping my mind to settle back into procedure. As long as I could follow the processes I'd been trained in, I'd be able to support Robbie.

'And Philly?'

'Yes, Stewart?'

'Until you prove otherwise, everyone in that house is a suspect.'

'Even us?' I forced a chuckle.

'Did you or Robbie kill him?'

'Well, no, but neither of us have alibis either, and I thought he was a pompous—'

'I'm sure you did. For now, let's assume you and Robbie are innocent – although DI Whitely will want your statements, too, when he gets there.'

'Unless we've solved it before he does,' I said cheekily. To say DI Whitely and I had gotten off to a friendly start when we met last month would be overstating the situation.

A snort of laughter came down the line. 'Right you are. Just mind how you go, Philly, and keep me updated.'

CHAPTER TWELVE

While I'd avoided seeing anyone on my ascent to my room, I wasn't as fortunate on the descent, encountering Ginny and Richard at the foot of the stairs.

'There you are,' said Ginny with a laugh. 'We were beginning to think we'd need to send out a search party for you and Robbie. Any sign of Orlando?'

Pausing, I reached into my pocket for the keys to the Great Hall and closed my fist around them, their solidity helping me stay focused.

'Philly?' Her smile faded. 'What's wrong?'

I took a deep breath to calm my nerves. 'Ginny darling, I can't talk about it yet, but I need you to do something for me. Can you please get Lord Rupert and bring him to the Great Hall? Just Lord Rupert. It's urgent.'

'What's going on, Philly?' Richard instinctively placed his arm protectively around Ginny's waist.

'I'm sorry, Richard, I can't say just yet, but I need you to do this for me.' When Ginny nodded, I kissed her cheek. 'Thank you. I promise I'll explain everything as soon as I can.'

Without waiting for either to say more, I pulled on a pair of silicon gloves and let myself into the Great Hall, locking the door behind me.

Robbie rose to his feet and stretched his arms out wide to loosen his shoulders. 'All okay?'

'Yes,' I said, slightly out of breath and tossed him the keys, which he caught in one hand. 'Stewart will send DI Whitely up' —Robbie grinned at my grimace— 'but he won't be here until the roads open – although knowing Stewart, he'll pull whatever strings he needs to pull to make that happen quickly. In the meantime, you're to take charge. He said we should let him know if we have any fuss from Rupert. I've asked Ginny and Richard to bring him to us now.'

Robbie nodded grimly.

'And I've brought down a notebook, some silicon gloves I still had in my bag from last month – and I even found a couple of Ziplock plastic bags.'

Robbie brightened and pulled on the gloves I offered him. 'Good job.'

Crouching beside the body, Robbie carefully checked the pockets of Orlando's jacket. 'There's no phone but …' Robbie opened the jacket and slid his hand into the inside pocket. 'What have we here?' Using the floor to help him stand, Robbie held out a buff-coloured card the size of a business card. With a puzzled expression, he asked, 'What do you make of this?'

I pulled on a pair of gloves and examined the card. While one side was blank, the other was printed with a symbol – a circle enclosing six petals radiating from a central point. 'This is a daisy wheel.'

'A what?'

'A daisy wheel – or a hexafoil, depending on how technical you want to be.' I traced the design with my gloved finger. 'They were often called "witch's marks".'

'Because they were made by witches?'

With a casual gesture, I lifted a shoulder, unsure of how to respond. 'Mainly, they were used to ward away evil' —I looked up and met Robbie's eyes— 'much like the pot we found upstairs. But what it's got to do with this, I don't know.' I took a photo of the card and placed it into one of the bags.

'Hmmm.' Robbie folded his arms and turned away, his attention on the fireplace, before swivelling back to face me. 'After we've spoken to Lord Deverell and broken the news to Lady Stark' —Robbie had moved into more formal territory with reference to titles— 'we'll need to find out who else had access to the keys. Then—'

A pounding on the door interrupted whatever Robbie was about to say.

'I say, man, why is this door locked?' Lord Rupert began to bluster when Robbie finally let him in, his brows rising when Robbie relocked the door behind him. About to say more, he stopped as he saw the body on the floor at the opposite end of the room. 'Is that …?'

'I'm afraid so,' Robbie said sombrely.

'Did he … did he have a heart attack or something?' His gaze skated around the room until it finally landed on me.

'No, he didn't,' I replied in a hushed tone, my voice filled with apprehension about how he would react.

'Lord Stark has been murdered,' Robbie said bluntly.

'Murdered? Are you saying someone has broken in here today and murdered Orlando? That's a preposterous idea.' Rupert stood taller, his chin high and firm, his expression one that would brook no arguments under different circumstances.

Robbie, however, was unmoved. 'No, Lord Deverell, that's not what I'm saying. I believe Lord Stark was killed in the early hours of this morning – not long after midnight and, if I'm any judge, certainly no later than around two. He was found locked in this room, no sign of forced entry, his body quite cold.' He laid out the facts almost as a challenge.

'That's impossible.' Our host looked down his haughty nose at Robbie. 'This room is always kept locked.'

'It was open yesterday when Serena showed us through,' I pointed out.

He waved my words away like one would shoo a bee. 'Serena likes to let visitors through, but Mrs

Phillips would've locked it before she turned in last night. She always checks it's locked at night – some valuable paintings are in here.'

'Yes.' I nodded towards the painting on the wall. 'Like the Stubbs.'

'Quite.'

'Who else has keys?' Robbie folded his arms.

'Are you insinuating someone in the house is responsible for this?' He pointed towards the body of his friend.

'Please answer the question.'

Lord Rupert stared at Robbie until he realised Robbie was serious. 'Just Mrs Phillips and myself. And before you ask, mine are locked in the safe in the library, and Mrs Phillips normally wears hers around her neck during the day or keeps them in her pocket – although you'd have to ask her what she does with them at night.' He took a few uncertain steps towards the body before stopping, unable to move closer. 'What happens now?'

'We've already called it in; an investigation team and the pathologist will be up as soon as the roads are clear. In the meantime, I'll need statements from everyone. This room is a crime scene, so it will remain locked.' Robbie spoke matter-of-factly. 'We'll also need to break the news to Lady Stark; it would assist us greatly if your wife could support us with that.'

'Yes, of course.' He rubbed the back of his neck. 'Do you mean to treat my friends as suspects?'

'I will require statements from everyone,' Robbie said again. 'I understand you know Chief Superintendent Barker personally' —I hid a smile at the way Robbie pre-empted the other man's protests— 'and he said he's happy to talk you through the process should you be concerned at any stage but trusts you'll do all in your power to ensure everyone cooperates with the enquiry.'

'Hmph. Very well.' He made it sound like he was giving Robbie permission to proceed. 'What about you two – who will be questioning you?'

Robbie didn't miss a beat. 'DI Whitely will take our statement when he gets here. In the meantime, the chief super has asked me to proceed – with Philly assisting.'

Rupert turned back towards the body, his finger tapping against his cheek. 'How long ago did you retire?'

'Just two weeks ago – and that was after over forty years of service, so in any other circumstances, I'd be heading up the enquiry.'

'Right. Good. And you've dealt with people of our class in the past?'

I bit the inside of my mouth to suppress a smile. Robbie's expression was unchanged. 'On numerous occasions,' he said. 'Unfortunately, though, in a murder enquiry, we're forced to ask questions that may seem impertinent. However, I assure you, all information is potentially relevant.'

'Right. Good.' He straightened his back and clasped his hands behind his back. 'Well, I don't suppose I have any choice in the matter, so I will naturally provide all the cooperation and resources you require.' He allowed himself a tight smile. 'Starting with my wife. And where would you like to speak with Mallory? In my library?'

'If that's convenient, thank you.' Robbie unlocked the door to let us out.

'Consider it your domain for the length of the investigation.' Once in the entrance hall, Rupert said, 'Will he be okay in there?'

I laid a hand on his arm. 'It's the safest place for him.'

When Robbie turned the key in the lock, the click of the levers falling into place jolted Rupert back into action. 'I'll gather Mallory and Serena and see you shortly.' He paused slightly and then, with none of his usual arrogance, said, 'The killer really is in the house, aren't they?'

Robbie hesitated for half a beat and nodded. 'Yes, sir, in all likelihood they are. There's no sign that anyone other than us has entered or left the house since yesterday.'

A grimace and then, 'I was Rupert earlier; now you're calling me sir.'

Robbie nodded again. 'In the circumstances, I think that's best, don't you?'

Chapter Thirteen

'What do you think?' I asked, walking across to peer out the library window. Outside, the sky was leaden, the wind still hurling itself against the house. While Rupert had gone to get Serena and Mallory, Robbie and I had gone straight to Rupert's library.

Robbie pulled out Rupert's chair and sat behind the desk, his back straight, his hands splayed against the leather top, said, 'Is this really worth twenty thousand quid?' I nodded. 'And the chairs?'

'You don't want to know.'

He shook his head in disbelief and stood, walking across to join me at the window. 'I think we need to know when Lady Stark last saw her husband and whether Mrs Phillips locked the Great Hall last night.' His lips twisted. 'And that's just for starters. How are you holding up?'

'I'm fine.' I tapped my notebook against my thigh, my reading glasses dangling from the other hand. 'It's amazing how quickly the training returns, right?'

He laid a supportive hand on my shoulder before 'You had a sneak preview last month with that business over at Albert Horsley's. By the time DI Whitely shows up, you'll probably feel you've been back on the force for years.'

I snorted a laugh. 'God forbid.'

A single knock and Rupert led Serena and Mallory into the library. Serena looked slightly apprehensive, her arm linked through Mallory's. Mallory's eyes were red-rimmed and swollen, and her nose was pink.

'Have you found him?' Mallory's voice cracked with emotion.

Serena's eyes met mine, an unspoken understanding between us that Mallory needed to be handled gently. 'Here, Mallory, why don't you sit down.' The two women sat in the chairs we'd pulled away from the desk, Mallory gripping Serena's hand tightly.

'Why?' Mallory's eyes wildly searched our faces. 'What's happened?'

After a slight nod from Robbie, I pulled another chair opposite the two women. 'We've located your husband, but I'm really sorry, Lady Stark' —a quick glance at Robbie for reassurance— 'your husband has been murdered.'

'Murdered?' Her voice rose. 'Are you telling me he's been … he's dead?'

Serena's eyes widened and filled with tears, and she

put an arm around Mallory to hold her.

'Yes, Lady Stark, that is what we're saying.' Robbie sat on the edge of the desk, his hands clasped in his lap.

'Surely you mean he's had an accident?' Serena frowned, her eyes meeting mine.

'I'm afraid not,' I said.

Robbie cleared his throat. 'I know this is a difficult time for you, but we have questions we need to ask you that I'm afraid can't wait.'

'But who would kill Orlando? Everyone loved him. Are you saying someone broke in and murdered him? If people had searched for him when I said he was missing, he might still be alive.' She managed to glare at us through her tears.

'I'm sorry, but that wouldn't have made any difference. We believe your husband has been dead for several hours,' I gently informed her.

'I don't understand. You must have it wrong; I would've known if he'd been killed.' She punched her chest. 'I would have felt it *here*.' She raised her eyes to Serena. 'Serena, tell them how everyone loved Orlando.'

'Mallory ...' I began.

'Lady Stark,' she corrected, drawing herself upright and sniffing. 'If you're going to interrogate me, you can refer to me by my rank. I'm the wife of a viscount; therefore, I am Lady Stark.'

'Mallory, I really don't think ...' said Serena, raising apologetic eyes to me.

'No, Serena, she's quite right.'

'Well, I don't want you Lady Deverelling me,' Serena said firmly.

Across from me, Robbie raised his eyebrows but said nothing. The tiniest twitch of his hand was an indication for me to continue. 'Lady Stark, please tell me when you last saw your husband?'

'Are they allowed to ask me these questions?' Mallory directed the query towards Rupert.

'Yes,' he said. 'They have the authority of the chief superintendent.'

'And what sort of man is he? Didn't she say at dinner last night that he's her ex-husband?' I kept my expression impassive as she spoke about me as if I wasn't there. 'And the other one's retired. Aren't the police taking this seriously?' Again, her voice grew in volume.

'I know Chief Superintendent Barker socially,' said Rupert. 'He's a good sort of man. And they are taking this very seriously, but remember, Mallory, we're snowed in. No one can get in or out. Robbie, Detective Inspector Dawkins, was a senior member of the Yorkshire CID for forty years until his retirement just two weeks ago. Until the team can get through, we're in safe hands.' My eyes widened at this show of support.

'And the questions are necessary if they're to find out who killed Orlando,' Serena said gently. 'I'm sure Robbie and Philly will question everyone – even us.'

'That's right,' said Robbie. 'We'll be taking

statements from everyone.'

'Well, it can't be one of us.' Mallory sniffed. 'And it certainly wasn't me. I wouldn't look any further than that housekeeper and her rude daughter. Will you be questioning them too?'

'As I said, Lady Stark, we'll be talking to everyone,' Robbie said firmly. 'Now, when was the last time you saw your husband?'

'At dinner last night.' Lady Stark's voice diminished to a mere whisper.

'You didn't see him afterwards?' I asked.

She shook her head, her eyes cast down to her lap. 'No, I sometimes take a sleeping tablet – these old houses do creak so – and I'm afraid it put me out for the count. I know he was in the room after dinner, though, as he left the clothes he wore last night on the floor for that useless maid to pick up. I woke briefly at around ten this morning, but he wasn't there, and I assumed he'd got up already – he usually rises much earlier than me. I suffer terribly from headaches, you see.' She crossed and recrossed her legs awkwardly.

'So you didn't know he was missing until the other men mentioned they hadn't seen him?' I asked gently.

She shook her head, her eyes filling again. 'No. Who would do such a terrible thing to him? Everyone loves Orlando; you have to find out who did it!'

'Do you know why he might dress and go out again? Would he be meeting somebody?' Robbie's expression didn't show it, but I detected some impatience in his voice.

'Of course not! Are you implying he was having a' —her voice caught— 'an assignation? Orlando wouldn't do that – he was faithful to me.'

'It might not have been a woman he was meeting.' I gave a reassuring smile. 'We didn't find his phone – do you know where it is?'

'No.' She waved my question away as if swatting a fly. 'Feel free to search his things – you might find it there. Now' —she stood and straightened the skirt of the tight printed dress she was wearing – a day version of the one she wore to dinner last night— 'if you've quite finished with me, I'd suggest you get on with searching our room for Orlando's phone and question that dreadful woman and her daughter.'

'Would you like to be present while we search?' asked Robbie, tapping notes into his phone.

'No,' she said haughtily. 'But I expect a receipt for anything you take away. If you need me, I'll be in the drawing room.' The hand Serena put out to support her as she stumbled in her strappy sandals was pushed away, and with her head held high, Mallory left the room. Robbie stood as she left.

'I'm so sorry she was like that,' Serena said, worried eyes on the door Mallory had just walked through.

'Don't be,' I said. 'She's grieving.'

'Even if she weren't, she still would've been like

that,' grumbled Rupert. 'She's hung up on Landy's title; God knows who's next in line now Orlando's gone. He has no son – just a daughter with his first wife, and she can't inherit.'

'I assume Lady Stark would be the main beneficiary in Lord Stark's will, though?' Robbie strolled around the desk and sat behind it, Rupert's eyebrows raising as he did.

Rupert shook his head. 'Not necessarily. Orlando has sisters but no brothers, so the title and the estate will probably go to whoever is next in line – a cousin or nephew. Mallory will have to move out when they move in, and she'll hate someone else usurping her. As for the money, well, there's not much of that. Orlando was always good at spending the stuff but not so good at making it. By the time debts are paid and provisions made for his daughter, there won't be much, if anything, left for Mallory – and certainly not enough to keep her in the style she's become accustomed to since marrying him.' He snorted a short laugh. 'So if you're looking for motives, Inspector, I wouldn't be looking at Mallory. He was worth far more alive than dead to her.'

'Poor Mallory,' Serena whispered.

'Do you know who he might've met last night?' I asked.

Rupert shoved his hands into his pockets and kept his eyes on the carpet. 'Sorry. Maybe if you find his phone?'

'I'm sorry to have to ask,' said Robbie, 'but where were you between midnight and two this morning?'

'Is that when he died?' Serena asked in a small voice, her pale face now chalky. When Robbie nodded, she said, 'I was in bed asleep, but I'm afraid Rupe and I slept apart last night – we do sometimes. I don't sleep well these days, especially not when I've had a late night. I get so…' She fanned her face. 'You know how it is.' She directed her grimace at me.

'I certainly do,' I said.

'I'm afraid that means neither of us have an alibi, Robbie.' Rupert shrugged his shoulders. 'You'll just have to take us at our word when we say we didn't kill poor Landy.'

'Do you know of any reason someone would want him dead?' Robbie asked.

'No,' he said. 'None at all. Now, if you'll excuse me …' He turned to his wife. 'Darling, we should return to our guests.'

Robbie's expression was unreadable. 'Before you go, I'll need your set of keys.'

'Of course.' Rupert walked across the room to where an eighteenth-century pastoral scene was hanging and swung it away from the wall to display a safe. He entered his code into the pin pad, opened the door and drew out a matching set to the keys Susan had given us. 'And before you ask, I haven't shared this combination with anyone.'

'Thank you,' said Robbie as Rupert handed the keys to him, relocked the safe and swung the painting back into place.

'Is that all?' Rupert asked, his straight-backed posture again that of a master impatiently dismissing an annoying servant.

'Oh, one more thing …' I held out the plastic bag containing the card we'd found. 'Does this mean anything to you?'

Rupert took his reading glasses out of his top pocket and, after putting them on, took the bag from me. 'No.' He handed it back. 'It doesn't mean anything.' Replacing his glasses in his top pocket, he said, '*Now*, is that all?'

Robbie nodded and placed the keys in the pocket of his jeans. 'For now, thank you.'

Once they'd left and Robbie had shut the door behind them, I said, 'You don't believe him when he said he'd never seen that daisy wheel before.'

'I certainly do not – nor did I believe him when he said he doesn't know who Orlando met.'

'And you don't think we'll find his phone in their room either, do you?'

Robbie shook his head, then suddenly smiled. 'But Lady Stark has told us we can search the room, so that's what we'll do – after we talk to the others.'

Chapter Fourteen

In a replay of the scene just a few hours ago, when we re-entered the drawing room, Mallory Stark was sobbing in the arms of Tara Beaumont-Brown and Lucinda Fitzroy – both women having forgotten their dislike of Mallory in the face of her grief. Ginny and Richard, I assumed, must be in the kitchen.

Wentworth Fitzroy stepped forward. 'I say, man, what is this business about poor Orlando? Mallory says he's been murdered, and Rupert doesn't seem to know any details.'

'Lord Stark has, indeed, been murdered,' said Robbie firmly.

'In the Great Hall by the butler with the candlestick,' muttered Piers under his breath, earning him a glare from Serena.

Robbie glanced across at Piers, his brows raised. 'He was found in the Great Hall, and it appears he has been stabbed, although a final cause of death won't be determined until the pathologist arrives – and that won't be until the roads open and the weather improves.

In the meantime, the Great Hall is a crime scene, and the doors will remain locked.' Robbie cast his eyes around the room, his gaze briefly meeting that of each of the friends before moving on to the next. 'Chief Superintendent Barker has charged me to commence the investigation pending the arrival of DI Whitely and his team, so I will call each of you into the library to provide me with your statement.' He paused and added, 'I must ask that no one leaves this room alone.'

'You can't possibly think it was one of us,' sputtered Wentworth.

'Given that no one has entered or left this house, I'm afraid it follows that the murderer is someone in this house,' Robbie pointed out.

'But surely not one of us. It's more likely to be one of the staff or ...' Tara looked meaningfully at Serena.

'Or one of my friends?' Serena's eyes flashed their anger. My hand balled into a fist, fingernails digging into my palm as I comprehended Tara's meaning.

Robbie held his hand up. 'We're keeping all possibilities open, but if anyone has any firm ideas about what may have happened to Lord Stark, please let us know.'

'You're telling us we're stuck in this house with a murderer on the loose?' Lucinda's voice had a hysterical edge.

'We will be safe as long as we all do as I ask – and that means don't wander anywhere alone. Now,' Robbie said, the authority of countless murder investigations in his voice, 'who would like to be the first to give their statement?'

Piers Beaumont-Brown stood. 'Someone has to go first, and it might as well be me. Let's get this over and done with.'

Piers raised his eyebrows as Robbie sat behind Rupert's desk but did not comment. We'd angled the two chairs on the other side of the desk so it didn't feel quite so much like an inquisition, and Piers waited only until I'd taken my seat beside him to say, 'I'll keep it simple for you. The last time I saw Orlando was last night after dinner.'

'Do you know what would've made him go to the Great Hall?' Robbie rested his elbows on the desk and leant forward.

'By which I assume you mean did I know who he was going there to meet?' Robbie inclined his head. 'Normally, I'd tell you not to look any further than my wife – or, at a pinch, Lucinda, although I think she woke up to herself as far as he was concerned some time ago.'

'You know about Lord Stark and your wife?' Robbie's voice was even, his expression unreadable.

'Of course I do.' Piers scoffed at the gasp of surprise I'd been unable to suppress. 'Good God, you're not going to come over all middle class and judgemental on me, are you? Orlando wanted whatever someone else had; something is always worth more if someone else owns it. In this case, it was my wife – and, for that matter, Wenty's.' He paused and smiled wryly. 'If she were going to play around, I'd rather she kept it in the family, so to speak, and Wenty will probably say the same. It's much more discreet, and Tara has always been discreet.'

Unable to believe he could be so blasé about it, I pushed my glasses back onto the bridge of my nose and focused my attention on my notebook. 'You said that normally you'd tell us not to look further than at your wife … Do you know if your wife met Orlando last night?'

'You'll have to ask her; I'd had rather a lot to drink, so the house could've fallen down around me and I wouldn't have heard a thing. My wife was in bed beside me when I woke up this morning, wearing exactly what she'd gone to bed in – which is nothing.' He grinned wickedly. 'Tara likes to sleep in the nude – especially when we're away from home. I think she likes the idea of being caught.'

'Were there any other clothes left out? Something she might've changed out of?' Robbie's elbows rested on the leather desktop, his hands steepled under his chin.

Piers shook his head. 'Not unless she wore what she'd had on yesterday afternoon.'

'I see.' Robbie tapped his forefingers together. 'Can you think of any reason someone would want to kill Lord Stark?'

He shook his head, frowning, his eyes clouding with … grief? Or perhaps regret? 'No. Poor old Landy. He never entirely fitted in – which was never more evident than when he married Mallory. I don't know what possessed him to do that. Women like her …' He shook his head again, his voice trailing away.

'Not QOC?' I said wryly.

'Quite. He knew it too – how could he not? The women weren't exactly subtle about it, were they?' He stretched out in the chair, crossing one ankle over the other, his hand patting idly at the side of his thigh, a show of nonchalance I wasn't convinced he felt. 'He was gearing up to divorce her, you know.' Robbie's eyes widened. 'She hadn't delivered him an heir, and while everyone enjoyed looking at Mallory, he realised that she'd never be accepted. She tried, but she would never be one of us. People like us don't marry women like Mallory.'

Despite her attitude towards us, I couldn't help but feel sorry for Mallory. She desperately wanted to be accepted by these people, this clique she'd married into, but instead, they were all laughing at her behind her back. 'Her title was important to her—' I began.

'I'll say!' Piers snorted a laugh. 'She liked nothing more than putting Tara and Lucinda in their places. Serena, as you would have noticed, isn't big on ceremony, but on Friday night, Mallory insisted she and Landy walk into the dining room behind Serena and

Rupert. She then said that Richard and your friend – Ginny, isn't it? – had to go last because they had no rank. Even Landy was embarrassed by that, and I could tell Serena was furious, but' —he shrugged— 'that's Mallory for you.'

Pushing down the anger I felt on behalf of Ginny and Richard, I completed the question I'd begun to ask. 'If Orlando divorced her, where would that leave her? Would she retain her title?'

He rubbed at his receding hairline. 'She could use the courtesy title but would rank below any new wife. And if she remarried, these days, the practice is to lose any reference to her previous husband's title. It's why we laughed when Mallory tried the whole precedence thing on with us – after all, Tara was almost Lady Deverell.'

I flashed Robbie a quick glance. 'Was Tara married to Edward?'

'No.' His eyes narrowed. 'You haven't heard this story?' I shook my head. 'She was briefly engaged to Rupert.'

'When was this?' I asked.

'Not long before I met her – thirty years ago, I suppose. She called it off when she realised there was nothing in it for her. Rupe was the spare – everyone still assumed Teddy would return from whatever European rock he was hiding under. And it wasn't as if there would ever be any money. It wasn't until the old baronet fell ill that they did what they needed to do to have Teddy declared dead.'

'How did they manage that?' Robbie settled back in his chair as though he was settling in for a long, drawn-out story.

Piers gave a dismissive shrug. 'The usual. They employed private investigators – no expense spared – but no one turned up anything on him. Teddy had been gone for almost twenty years by then.'

Robbie's eyes were on the ceiling, his finger tapping on the table, his expression one I knew well – his brain searching for connections. 'Did Mallory know Tara had been engaged to Rupert?'

'Probably,' said Piers. 'It was never a secret.'

'Were you worried that if Lord Stark divorced his wife, he might marry yours?'

There was a brief silence before he laughed. 'Are you looking for a reason I might want to kill Landy? Tara would never marry Orlando – to her, he's a diversion and, if I'm honest, a way of getting back at me.'

'But he has a title,' I pressed on.

'Your theory being she missed out on a title when she finished with Rupe? While I admit she'd get some enjoyment out of watching Mallory kowtow to her, Tara cares more about money than she does titles. I could probably buy and sell Rupert and Orlando twice over – and there are no messy entailments as there are with their estates. What I have is mine – or, I suppose, ours.'

'She'd get a share of that if she divorced you,

though?' Robbie said.

'True, but we have a tight prenup. She knows how hopeless Landy is with money and is intelligent enough to know that what she'd get from me would have to last a lifetime. I wouldn't be surprised if there's anything left for anyone to inherit once Landy's debts are settled. In any case, Landy needs – needed – an heir, and Tara's well past being able to provide one. No, you're barking up the wrong tree there. If he were planning on replacing her with anyone, it would be Lucinda – or Serena even – they're both a similar age to Mallory, so still young enough to have more children.'

His self-satisfied smirk rankled me. 'Did Lord Stark ever … keep it in the family with Serena?'

A snort of laughter escaped him. 'He wouldn't dare touch Serena.'

'So Lady Deverell is off limits?' Robbie asked.

'She adores Rupe,' said Piers. 'And they haven't been together long enough for …'

'Him not to mind if she strayed?' I guessed.

'Quite.'

'Did you ever loan Lord Stark money?' I asked, shuffling in my seat and re-crossing my legs.

He shrugged. 'From time to time I might've helped him out. Fifty thousand here or there, sometimes more, to get him through a tight patch.'

'Did he repay you?' asked Robbie.

'No, but before you start looking at that as a

motive, I knew that before I gave it to him. The amounts were never large enough for me to miss.' He glanced at his watch. 'Is that all? Shall I send Wenty in to tell you the same thing?'

'One more question, sir,' Robbie referred to the notes on his phone. 'Did Mallory know about her husband's affair with your wife?'

For the first time since he sat down, Piers Beaumont-Brown appeared unsure. 'I don't know,' he finally said. 'But no, I don't think she did. Mallory isn't the type to have been able to ignore it if she had.' His lips twitched. 'There would've been a hell of a row, I imagine.'

'Did she know about Lord Stark's financial situation?' Robbie asked.

'What are you getting at?'

'Just that Lady Stark may have decided she'd get more out of Lord Stark if he died before he could divorce her.' Robbie's gaze held the other man's. 'You say there's very little for her to inherit, but that only holds up as a lack of motive if she was unaware of her husband's financial situation. So I'll ask you again, was Lady Stark aware of her husband's financial situation?'

Piers dropped his gaze from Robbie's. 'No,' he finally said. 'I don't think so. She spent as though the money pit was bottomless. I can't imagine he would've confided in her – they didn't have that sort of relationship.'

'Thank you. If you'd like to send Mr Fitzroy in now. Philly will accompany you back to the drawing room.'

'In case someone murders me between here and there?' Piers asked, a self-confident smirk back in place.

'You can't be too safe, sir,' Robbie said, a twitch at the corner of his mouth showing his attempt to suppress a smile.

Chapter Fifteen

At first, Wentworth Fitzroy's answers correlated with his friend's.

He, too, had been aware of Orlando's fling with his wife but wasn't as accepting of it as Piers had been.

'Were you concerned that if Lord Stark divorced his wife, he might turn his attention to yours?' I asked. 'After all, Lucinda is still young enough to give him an heir – and she'd get a title out of it.'

'Don't be ridiculous,' he snapped, his face reddening. 'Lucinda doesn't care about any of that. Her fling with Landy was her way of getting back at me for …'

'An indiscretion she found out about?' Robbie finished the other man's sentence.

'Quite.'

'Did either of you arrange to meet Lord Stark last night?' I asked.

'Of course not! Why are you haranguing us about this?'

'We're asking everybody the same questions, sir,'

Robbie said evenly, sitting forward in his chair. 'Would you say you're a deep sleeper?'

A wave of uncertainty crossed his face. 'Well, I had rather a lot to drink last night. I must have been snoring because my wife elbowed me during the night to push me over.' His expression brightened. 'There you go – we both have alibis! I even noted the time – it was one-thirty. Thank heavens for my snoring.'

'How long have you known Lord Stark?' I asked.

On safer ground, his shoulders relaxed, and he crossed his legs, one ankle on the opposite knee. 'Since school, although we only became friends in our final year. Landy was always a bit of a wet sap, and Rupe and I were into sports and girls.' He sighed heavily. 'Looking back, he didn't really fit in with us … he didn't really fit anywhere. His father expected a lot – as fathers do – and constantly reminded Landy that the family's future was his responsibility. It was different for Rupe and me: Rupe was a second son, and my father had made rather a lot of money; no one was relying on us.

'Landy, though, was expected to keep the family name going and rescue the family coffers. We felt a bit sorry for the poor sod, though, and he was … useful.' A secretive smile crept over his lips. 'Landy knew how to … procure things. Cigarettes, weed and alcohol when we were at school, and … well, other things when we left. He knew everyone – that was his natural talent – knowing people, charming people. He might never have had money, but you'd never know that; he was always making connections. If you needed anything done, Landy would know someone who could help – I guess we all owed him, and every so often, he'd remind us of that. It would be subtle, but in a way that you knew you were being reminded.'

'Is that why you tolerated his behaviour with your wives?' Robbie asked. 'Because you owed him? What had he done for you?'

Wentworth frowned, sat up straighter and uncrossed his legs. 'Of course not. That was just … Landy always wanted what we had.' He shrugged as if it didn't matter. 'And his flirtations didn't last long.'

'What about Lady Stark – did she know?' I asked. Orlando Stark was turning out to be more complex than we'd assumed.

'I wouldn't think so.' He snorted laughter.

'What would she have done if she did find out?' Robbie asked idly, standing to walk over to the bookcase, his back to Wentworth and me.

'Aside from causing a fuss, what could she do? She wouldn't divorce him – appearances matter much more to her than the rest of us, and I think she really did love him.' He sounded surprised. 'I remember when he first married her – none of us met her until the deed was done – but he was quite besotted. She's good to look at – and he liked that we enjoyed looking at her – but she's not the type you'd marry, if you know what I mean. It took some time for him to realise what we all thought of her.'

'Not QOC,' I murmured.

'Exactly.'

'What would Lady Stark have done if she knew her husband was planning to divorce her?' Robbie perched on the edge of the desk.

'She …' He frowned and bit his bottom lip. 'She wouldn't have killed him.'

'Are you sure about that?' Robbie pushed on without giving him time to answer. 'Mr Beaumont-Brown mentioned Lord Stark had financial problems. Were you aware of those?'

He scoffed. 'Problems? He was almost skint. His father had sold anything that could be sold, and while Landy had made some lucky investments in the nineties and early two thousands, there'd been nothing for a while. He'd borrowed money from Piers, you know – and me.'

'What about Lord Deverell – did he borrow from him too?' I looked up from my notebook and caught Wenty's eye.

'Perhaps … from time to time … You'd have to ask him.' Wentworth's eyes skittered away from mine. What was he hiding?

'Were you ever repaid?' Robbie asked.

'Landy was going through some bad luck, but I'm sure we would've been.'

'Did Mallory know about his financial problems?'

Wentworth considered Robbie's question. 'No,' he finally said. 'I don't think so.'

'Did she know he was intending to divorce her?' I pushed my glasses down to the snub of my nose to see over them.

He shook his head, the beginnings of a smirk on his lips. 'We would've heard about it if she had. Is that all?'

'For now,' said Robbie, closing the notes on his phone.

'Who do you want me to send up next?' Wentworth stood, his sardonic smile back in place now the questions were done.

'Philly will go back with you. We'd like to see your wife next.'

Other than further insights into the character of Orlando Stark, neither Lucinda nor Tara had anything new to offer – although both women admitted to having had an affair with Orlando.

'You'll have heard by now that Orlando and I were … close. We still meet occasionally, but I haven't slept with him in a while,' said Tara. 'He's very … grateful.' Her smile was smug. 'Piers is very generous financially, but Landy appreciated me. Sometimes, it felt like he couldn't quite believe his luck. At other times, I think he got off on knowing I was sleeping with him even though I was married to Piers.' She laughed derisively. 'You're probably terribly shocked, but no harm was done, and it was all kept in the family, as it were.' There was that phrase again: kept in the family. 'Besides, Piers knows all about it and is hardly in a position to say anything.'

'If Lord Stark had divorced Mallory, would you have left Piers for him?' I asked.

'God no! Landy was fun, but he didn't have a bean – or, rather, not enough beans. And that mausoleum of his – it's not quite as depressingly gothic as this one, but I couldn't imagine living in it.' She shivered at the thought. 'That was one of the reasons I finished things with Rupe – this place. I much prefer the Cotswolds, sweetie. No, Mallory is welcome to him.'

'What would Mallory do if she thought he intended to divorce her and marry you instead?' Robbie's voice was deceptively casual.

'Well, he'd hardly divorce Mallory for me. Landy needs an heir, so he'd be more likely to get one of those from Lucinda. That boat, as it were, has sailed for me. As for what she'd do? Do you want me to say she'd probably kill him? Because I think she'd be capable of it – especially if she knew Lucinda and I had been fooling around behind her back with him. Appearances mean everything to Mallory. It would be one thing to know he'd been unfaithful and another entirely to know it was with us.'

'Even though it's keeping it in the family?' Robbie drawled.

Tara let out a short laugh. 'Yes, well, Mallory comes from a different background to us. She came from nothing, you know, and the idea of going back there is not something she'd countenance.' There was a long pause before she continued. 'I think Mallory would do whatever she needed to do to preserve her lifestyle.'

'Tara' —Robbie held her gaze— 'did you meet Lord Stark last night?'

'No. I was in bed beside my husband all night – not that he could attest to that; he was out like a light as soon as his head hit the pillow.'

Lucinda, however, was horrified we'd found out about her fling. 'I wouldn't call it an affair,' she said, her cheeks tinged with pink. 'At first, it was fun, but then it became clear he only wanted me because it gave him something over Wenty, and I'd hate Wenty to find out about it. You don't have to tell him, do you?'

Robbie and I exchanged glances. 'Not unless it's pertinent to the case,' Robbie said.

She placed two fingers on her smooth forehead and tapped. 'Who told you? Piers probably – Landy would've boasted about it to him and Rupe. He wouldn't have been able to help himself. Maybe he's already told Wenty – he used to threaten me he would.' In her anxiety, her clipped accent slipped; there was more to Lucinda Fitzroy than met the eye.

'He threatened you?' The furrows on Robbie's forehead deepened.

She ducked her head, a silvery curtain of hair hiding her face. 'Never overtly. But it was always implied.'

'Did you give him money?' Robbie asked.

'He never asked for money.'

A moment of silent communication passed between Robbie and me. 'He pressured you into sex?' My tone was gentle.

She looked up, her eyes clouded with an emotion I couldn't pinpoint. Embarrassment, perhaps? Or shame? Maybe a combination of both. 'After the first time, yes. But soon, that didn't do it for him. He only wanted me if he thought I preferred him to Wenty. It's been over for ages.'

'Did Tara know about your involvement with Lord Stark?'

'Yes, Piers told her. She knows I want to forget it happened, but she'd never tell Wenty.' She chewed at her bottom lip. 'What if he already knows and hasn't said anything to me about it?'

'Did you know Lord Stark was considering divorcing Mallory?' Robbie's eyes observed Lucinda's face for a reaction.

'No.' While her face betrayed no emotion, in her lap, her nails left little half-moons in her palms. 'I shouldn't be surprised, though. Landy always made out that he was confident and one of the boys, but there were times he was just as out of place as Mallory was – even though he was born into it. He got a kick out of her parading about in those tight dresses and high heels – he loved that they all wanted to sleep with her. But when he realised his friends were laughing about Mallory behind his back, he wasn't happy. It mattered to him, you see, what they all thought of him. Maybe he thought we'd get used to her, and she'd get used to us, but the harder she tried to fit in, the more out of place she was.' She wrinkled her nose in self-deprecation. 'None of us were pleasant to Mallory, and she was unravelling – probably because of that.'

'What do you mean by unravelling?' I asked.

Lucinda lifted a shoulder. Again today, she was dressed head to toe in cream. It gave her an elegance that screamed money and class in a way that Mallory's too-tight dresses and spindly heels never could – despite their designer labels. Poor Mallory never stood a chance with this lot.

'She was drinking too much and pushing home the correct protocols – who ranked higher than who and who should go into dinner first, things nobody else cared about. Those headaches she has in the afternoon – that's her going upstairs to drink, and her long lie-ins each morning is her sleeping it off.' Lucinda twirled her wedding rings on her finger. 'Part of me felt sorry for her, but I knew they could turn on me just as easily. Unlike Tara, I didn't go to the right schools, and my parents don't have money.' My eyes widened. 'I've probably come from a similar background to Mallory; the only difference is I've been working towards being one of them for years. I watched how they dressed; I listened to how they spoke and behaved, and I practised and practised until I could pass for one of them.

'Fifteen years ago, I met Wenty and became one of them for real. Sleeping with Landy is the only time I've slipped up – and Landy knew it. Landy always seemed to know things about people – who they were, what they needed, skeletons they wanted to keep locked away. It was like a game to him.'

'What skeletons did your husband have to hide?' Robbie asked, leaning forward, his hands open.

She shook her head and lowered her gaze. 'It was a figure of speech.'

'Did Mallory know her husband was unfaithful?' I asked quietly.

Lucinda shook her head. 'No, at least I don't think so.' She smiled tightly. 'I suppose you want to know what she would do if she found out – or if she found out he was planning to divorce her?' Robbie gave a little nod. 'Well' —she dragged in a breath— 'she'd do whatever it took to maintain the lifestyle and the title.'

'I see.' Robbie steepled his fingers under his bottom lip. 'Did you meet Orlando last night?'

'No. Although, I didn't sleep well. There are too many creaks and groans in this house and all that talk about it being cursed.' She shuddered. 'And that's before you factor in my snoring husband.' She chuckled lightly. 'At one point, I must've elbowed him too hard as he woke with such a start.' She drew her shoulders up. 'Is that all?'

'Yes, thank you.' Robbie sighed his frustration.

We stood and watched as she left the room. Robbie shut the door behind her and sat on the edge of the desk.

'What do you think?' I asked.

'I think,' he began slowly, standing at the window and peering out. 'I think they want us to think Mallory killed her husband. Besides Rupert, each has given us a narrative where she'd do anything to hold onto her lifestyle.'

'But according to Rupert and Serena, Orlando was worth more alive than dead to her.' I stood and joined him at the window. Despite it being midafternoon, the light was dimming; the snow still piled high on the drive. 'And there was no time for them to confer before we brought Piers in.'

'Aye, but they all know each other well, and it wouldn't take much for the others to fall in line.'

'True,' I conceded. 'But if we're looking for motives, Lucinda could have one. The way she tells it, she was essentially blackmailed into continuing an affair with him and was petrified in case her husband found out.'

'Even though he already knows,' said Robbie. 'But the affair had finished, and she has an alibi – as does her husband.'

'What I found interesting was the idea that everyone owed Orlando something. It seemed he actively looked for knowledge he could use to control others – or am I jumping too far with that?'

Robbie shook his head. 'I don't think you are. I can't believe Piers and Wentworth were as relaxed about the money they lent him as they'd like us to believe.'

'Or about his affairs with their wives – regardless of that "in the family" crap they fed us.'

'Nor do I. I think Lord Stark had something on both men that they wouldn't want to be exposed.'

'It would have to be something big if they were prepared to give him that sort of money and tolerate him sleeping with their wives,' I said sardonically. 'I think they both have reasons they'd like to see him dead.'

'I agree. Serena seems to be the only one of the wives he hasn't attempted to sleep with.'

'Maybe he has nothing on Rupert?'

'Perhaps. I would, however, like to know how much Lord Deverell also lent him. Lord Stark "borrowed" money from the other two, I can't believe he didn't also ask Lord Deverell for funds. After all, he and Serena don't have alibis either.' Robbie turned to me. 'We might have a better understanding of why someone would want to see Lord Stark dead, but we're still no closer to understanding how he could have been killed in a locked room.'

'Or who he arranged to meet in there.'

'Right,' Robbie said decisively. 'Let's quickly search Lord Stark's room – not that I think we'll find anything in there – and then head to the kitchen and talk to Susan and Hattie.'

'And Ginny and Richard,' I reminded him. 'We have to dot all the i's. I'll message Stewart and let him know what we're up to.'

Chapter Sixteen

We found nothing in the Stark's room to further our investigation. Where my room was comfortably decorated in chintz and plaid, this one was more opulent with bold damask stripes in the upholstery and bed linen, and heavy damask curtains tied back with gold rope at both the windows and on the bed canopy. Touches of gold throughout gave the room heaviness and import.

'Mallory would love this,' I commented. 'It would suit her sense of precedence.'

'Aye.' Robbie wrinkled his nose. 'It's not to my taste though.'

Discarded clothes littered the floor, and in the ensuite towels had been left on the floor. 'Do you think she expects Susan and Hattie to refold and rehang all of this?'

Robbie lifted a shoulder, pulled on silicon gloves, opened the suitcase lying on the window seat, and began to rifle through its contents carefully. Pulling on my own set of gloves, I set about checking the pockets of the clothes hanging in the wardrobe.

'Well, well, well.' I turned at the tone in Robbie's voice. He was holding a ziplock bag full of what appeared to be lawn clippings. Opening it, he sniffed, a grin spreading across his face. 'I think we've found Lord Stark's stash.' He handed me the bag.

'I know I smelt it on him last night, but he didn't exactly seem the type, did he?' I tapped each side of my nose in illustration.

Robbie chuckled and turned back to the suitcase. 'Oh aye, what have we here?' He held up a black woollen sock, reached into it and pulled out another small plastic bag. This one contained a small amount of white powder. 'Is this more what you'd expect?'

'It certainly is.' After photographing where we found it, I took the bag from him and placed it with the marijuana in a larger ziplock bag and continued my own search.

'Anything?' Robbie had moved into the bathroom.

'Just gin bottles,' I called back. 'One empty, one almost empty and another unopened. You?'

'Only her sleeping tablets. They're prescription and, washed down with what was in those bottles' — he inclined his head towards the empty gin bottles— 'would certainly be enough to knock her out.'

'But no phone?' I asked.

Robbie shook his head. 'No. Photograph those

bottles, but you can put them back where you found them. This, however' —he held up the ziplock bag containing the drugs— 'I'll lock in my suitcase until Whitely gets here.'

Ginny, Richard, Susan and Hattie sat around the kitchen table enjoying tea and buttered teacakes served on a vintage Doulton plate. Judging by the way Ginny's cheeks flashed pink when we interrupted them, the subject of their discussion was the murder.

'Is it true?' asked Susan, automatically rising to switch the kettle on to make tea for us. 'Has Lord Stark been murdered?'

Robbie pulled up a chair and sat down. 'It certainly is. Philly and I found him in the Great Hall.'

'How was he killed?' asked Hattie.

Robbie ignored the question and instead turned his attention to Susan. 'Have you noticed if any of your kitchen knives are missing?'

'Was he stabbed?' Hattie's eyes were wide with interest. 'Mum was saying how she locked that room last night before bed.'

'What time was that?' I asked, my pen poised over my notebook.

'Not long after Lady Stark went to bed, so not much past eleven.' Susan grabbed another two teacups and saucers from the dresser. 'I did what I always do when we have company – check there's no one in there and lock the doors.' Her eyes narrowed, her mind stepping through the previous night's events. 'Happens I saw Lord Stark at about that time. I'd come out of the Great Hall and locked the door, and he scuttled past me, furtive-like, his attention on his phone. He smiled how people smile when they're up to no good and think no one's watching them, and then he went upstairs. So he definitely wasn't in that room before I locked it.' She spooned tea into a pot and poured hot water over it. 'And before you ask, the keys stay with me, and I sleep with my door locked. Lord Deverell has the only other set, and he keeps them locked in a safe in the library.'

'Did you hear anything after you went to bed?' I smiled my thanks as she passed the tea to me.

She shook her head. 'No. I was out like a light, I was. Hattie, did you hear anything?'

'With Robin away this weekend, I stayed in his quarters and didn't hear a thing – other than the wind howling like a banshee. The first thing I knew was when I woke and realised the power was off – around six this morning. Would he have been dead by then?'

'Almost certainly,' said Robbie, adding sugar to his tea and helping himself to one of the buttered teacakes.

'What I did see,' began Hattie hesitantly, her eyes flicking between Robbie and me as if deciding whether to tell us what was on her mind, 'was Orlando with Tara Beaumont-Brown. It was yesterday morning before everyone went out to lunch. All I saw was his hand reaching out and pulling her into the dining room, and then I heard her giggling.'

'I see,' I said thoughtfully.

Ginny nudged Richard. 'You need to tell them,' she said.

'But what if it was nothing?' Richard frowned, his finger tracing patterns on the coaster his mug sat on.

'Everything is relevant in a murder investigation,' Robbie said. 'Even if it mightn't seem to be.' When Richard remained silent, he said, 'How about we start with whether either of you saw Lord Stark last night after dinner.'

'No,' said Ginny. 'We went straight upstairs.' She glanced at Richard and blushed. 'And almost straight to sleep.'

I didn't even attempt to hide my grin. Lucky Ginny. 'Did you hear anything afterwards?'

'No, but …' She sat back in her chair, twisting her fingers into a knot. 'I thought I heard a door open or close or something.' She shook her head. 'I don't know what I heard, but I thought it might've been a door – you know what it's like when you're in a strange house, and this one is very strange. Sorry, Susan, but it is.'

'That's alright, lass. If I hadn't lived here for most of my life, I'd probably think the same.'

'Do you know which direction the noise came from?' I didn't look up from my notebook, not wanting to interfere with Ginny's train of thought.

'No, I couldn't be sure. I know it was around half past twelve – I noticed the time on my bedside clock – but I couldn't tell you whether it was the room beside us or one across the hall.'

Robbie chewed at his bottom lip. Having just searched the Stark's room, we knew they and the Fitzroys were across the corridor from Ginny and Richard, with the Beaumont-Browns in the adjacent room. 'Richard,' Robbie began, 'you said you heard nothing last night, but what do you have to tell us? It mightn't seem important to you …'

Richard took a mouthful of tea, looked across at Ginny and sighed. 'As I said, it's probably nothing, but yesterday we were all getting ready to go over to East Witton for lunch, and I realised I'd left my jacket hanging over the back of the chair in the dining room at breakfast. Ginny was already in the car, so I returned to the house, but I couldn't get my jacket because Rupert and Wentworth were in the dining room arguing with Orlando. I don't know what it was about, but Rupert told him it was none of his business and he'd better keep quiet. Orlando then said something about how the market hadn't been kind to him and said he'd helped them out when they needed it, but now it was his turn. He asked for something to tide him over until he could get the divorce business finalised. His words, not mine. I didn't hear anything after that, as it sounded like they were coming my way, so I ran upstairs and got another jacket. By the time I got downstairs, Orlando was also heading out; I don't know where the other two were.'

'Serena mentioned when we arrived that everyone had gone to lunch, but Rupert and Wentworth had business to take care of,' I reminded Robbie.

'How did Orlando seem at lunch?' Robbie asked.

Richard shrugged. 'Smug, arrogant, pleased with himself. I figured Rupert had given him the loan – or whatever it was he'd asked for.'

'Thanks, Richard.' Robbie's brow furrowed as he played with the information.

'See.' Ginny playfully punched his arm. 'I told you it was important. I know you're loyal to Serena, but you don't owe the others anything.'

I reached for a teacake. 'Susan, you mentioned that Wentworth was a frequent visitor here when he was younger – what about the others? Orlando and Piers?'

Susan sipped at her tea, her expression thoughtful. 'Mr Beaumont-Brown is relatively new to their set – he's only been here half a dozen times. Lord Stark, though … While Mr Fitzroy virtually grew up here, I recall Lord Stark coming on the scene during the current Lord Deverell's last year at school. He was here that final summer before Jenny got married – how had I forgotten that?'

'Did he know Jenny too?' I asked, unsure why I was taking my questions down this track. Robbie's eyebrows lifted ever so slightly. He mightn't know what I was trying to get at, but he was interested in the answers. 'You said earlier she was besotted with Rupert, and Wenty was besotted with her; where did Orlando fit into the mix?'

'As far as I can remember, Jenny paid him no attention. He might be the ladies' man now.' Susan grimaced as she realised what she'd said. 'Sorry, he used to fancy himself as a ladies' man, but back then, where the other two had a sportsman's build, he was gangly and pimply and acted the clown to get attention. I think he might've had a thing for Jenny too – it was like she'd cast a spell on them all – but she didn't know he existed.'

'Susan, is there any other way in or out of the Great Hall except through those doors?' Robbie asked, brushing crumbs from the front of his jumper.

Susan shook her head. 'Nay. And when I locked that door, I swear there was no one in there – dead or alive.' She glanced at her watch. 'I'm late with getting the tea things out, so is that all you need to ask me?'

'For now,' said Robbie.

'Do you need our help?' Ginny stood and started clearing the empty plates.

'Bless you, lass,' said Susan. 'You've helped me with the baking today, so it's just about putting things out now.'

'Will you two come in for tea?' asked Richard.

'Shortly,' said Robbie. 'We need to check in with the chief super, and I've had a missed call from DI Whitely that I'd better return.' He rolled his eyes. When he'd taken over from Robbie last month, the younger, more ambitious detective had made no bones about what he thought of Robbie's more traditional investigative methods. 'You two get in there and listen to what's said when we're not there. And please, do your best to keep everyone together.'

Ginny's eyes glowed with a cheeky gleam. 'We'll be helping with the investigation, Richard,' she said as they left the kitchen.

'We can be just like … Morse and Lewis,' Richard said.

'Or Scott and Bailey.' Ginny's voice grew faint.

'I think we've made their day,' I quipped as we returned to the library.

'I'm glad someone's day has been made.' Robbie frowned as his phone beeped an incoming message. 'Although it worries me that even Richard and Ginny don't seem to understand that there's still a murderer in the house.'

The smile slipped from my face as a chill ran up my spine. 'You're right. And unless Orlando was the only intended victim, we could all be in danger.'

'Aye.' He nodded. 'You need to call Stewart and I'd better ring Chris Whitely back. Will you be alright in here if I duck outside to talk to Chris?'

I nodded. 'Rather you than me out in that.'

'I'll rug up.'

Chapter Seventeen

Sunday 4.30 pm

'You're telling me Lord Stark somehow got into a locked room with his killer who then escaped from said locked room with the murder weapon?' I pictured Stewart shaking his head in disbelief. 'How do you manage to get yourself involved in these messes, Philly?' Stewart's tone held a mix of incredulity and frustration with a sliver of exasperation that somehow his ex-wife had again landed herself in the middle of a murder enquiry.

'It's not as if I've done it deliberately, Stewart.' It took all my effort to keep my voice calm. 'Trust me, I'd prefer not to be stuck in a house with a murderer at large and no way of leaving. Any word about when the roads will be reopened?'

Stewart sighed in disgust at his inability to control the weather. 'Apparently, the snow is still in drifts around Tan Hill – it was very heavy there – so they're saying not until tomorrow morning. I looked at getting a chopper in, but flying in this weather is too dangerous.' He paused. 'Seriously, Philly, how are you coping?'

'I'm fine.' I waved my hand dismissively, even though he couldn't see it. 'We're so busy I've not had time to think about it. So far, we've searched the victim's room and spoken to everyone who was here last night, but' —I shrugged— 'I'm stumped. I can't help wondering whether it has anything to do with the disappearance of a local girl from here forty years ago, but it's only a feeling – I've got no evidence to support it.'

'You know how it works, Philly – instincts are well and good, but without evidence, they mean nothing. Unless there are any clear links, take my advice and leave the cold case in the past. Have you identified any motives so far?'

It was my turn to let out a heavy sigh. 'The victim sounds like a real charmer. He'd slept with two of the other wives here – which could've been a motive, except their husbands knew all about it. Keeping it in the family, they say.' Stewart snorted. 'Almost everyone wants to point the finger at the wife.'

'Does she have a motive?'

'According to Lord and Lady Deverell, no. She's very motivated by her social standing as a viscount's wife, and she'd lose that as a widow. The house and estate would go to the next in line, and she'd lose her ranking. Plus, as he apparently has no money – or very little – to leave her, she'd be broke and homeless.'

'That sounds like he would've been worth more to her alive.'

'Yes, but according to the rest of them, the victim was preparing to divorce her, and everyone we spoke to said she'd do anything to retain her status.'

'Even murder her husband? But as you say, she'd be left with nothing.'

'The general consensus is Lady Stark had no idea about her husband's financial problems and may have thought she'd be better off financially with an inheritance rather than a divorce settlement. It all sounds a bit flimsy to me, though.'

He must have been mulling it over and, after a long pause, said, 'I agree. You'll need to talk to her again, though. What else have you got?'

'He blackmailed one of the wives – Lucinda Fitzroy – into continuing an affair with him. Apparently, he threatened to tell her husband about it if she didn't.'

'Charming … but didn't you say the husbands both knew?'

'Exactly. In any case, the affair has been over for a while, and the Fitzroys have provided alibis for each other. Other than that, what I knew of Orlando Stark I didn't like – and I'm sure I'm not on my own there. One of the guests heard him arguing with both Lord Deverell and Mr Fitzroy yesterday, and the others hinted he liked to gather knowledge on people to use when he most needed it. And he owed both Piers

Beaumont-Brown and Wentworth Fitzroy sizeable sums of money – even though they both dismissed it as being not enough to murder for.'

Stewart chuckled. 'You're telling me that being a pompous pratt these days is sufficient motive for murder?'

'I don't see why not.' I said haughtily, only half-joking.

I could picture him shaking his head in exasperation. 'You said you searched the victim's room?'

'We did – and before DI Whitely has kittens about following procedure, we had Lady Stark's permission to do so, and we used gloves. We found nothing, though – just his stash. I thought I'd smelt marijuana on him yesterday afternoon, but you expect a man like that to be more of a white powder-up-the-nose type of guy rather than a sneaky roll-your-own-in-the-barn type of lad – and then we found that too – the white powder – hidden in socks would you believe.' Stewart laughed. 'We took that and put it into evidence bags, aka Ziplock plastic bags I happened to have in my handbag.'

'That's my Philly, always prepared.' His laughter was loud through the phone.

'I usually carry them to transport any leftovers from lunch home for Bally, but needs must. Anyway, Lady Stark was adamant she wanted receipts for everything we took away, so we'll give her one for his drugs.' Another snort of laughter from Stewart. 'Lady Stark, on the other hand, is a little more obvious about her means of escaping reality. We found a couple of bottles of gin at the back of the wardrobe, and the housekeeper's daughter had told us she cleared away an empty yesterday as well. With the sleeping tablets she said she took, she would've passed out last night. You could've stampeded a herd of elephants through their bedroom and she wouldn't have noticed. She certainly wouldn't have noticed her husband changing his clothes and sneaking out to meet someone else.'

'So while she might have had a motive, you don't think she had the means?'

'I saw what she drank over dinner, and if she'd also had another half bottle of gin upstairs before dinner – or after, who can tell – she would've been in no state to murder anyone. She certainly wouldn't have been able to do it in a locked room in a house unfamiliar to her.' I paused, then added, 'I know those so-called friends of hers are pointing the finger at her, but I really don't think she did it.'

'Alright, what are your priorities now?'

'We need to talk to Lady Stark again. Robbie wants to find out whether Lord Deverell also lent the victim money, and I'd like to have another look at the scene. There was something about it I couldn't quite grasp. Then I suppose we'll need to join the others at dinner. We've asked everyone to stay in pairs, and so far, there's no panic or hysteria – other than from Lady Stark and if you ask me, that's weird in itself. It's almost like it hasn't occurred to them that there's a murderer in the house. They're pointing the finger at one of the staff or, at the very least, Richard and Ginny.'

'Unless they know who did it,' Stewart said flatly. 'I know Robbie will keep DI Whitely updated—'

'On a scale of one to ten, how annoyed is he that we're on the ground and he can't get here to save the day?'

'He's a good detective, Philly,' Stewart warned. 'He reminds me a lot of myself at that age.'

'I rest my case.'

Stewart laughed one of the belly laughs he used to laugh when we were younger and happily married – in the years before kids, work stress, and Alison took his laughs away from me. 'If it makes you feel better, he didn't like you getting a result before he did last time, so he was less than ecstatic when he found out you two were there and had a head start on him.'

'We'll just need to solve it before he gets here – and on that note, we'd better get on with it.'

'Mind how you go, Philly, and ring me if you need to.'

'Thanks, Stewart, I will.'

Robbie walked back in a few seconds later, rubbing his hands together to bring warmth back into them.

'Stewart said DI Hotshot isn't happy.'

'After talking to him, I'd say that's an understatement.' With a cheeky grin that matched mine, Robbie shed his jacket and sat down in the chair behind Rupert's desk. 'At least now, though, I have a complete set of instructions from him on how to conduct the interviews and run the investigation.'

'Phew.' I rolled my eyes. 'After all, it's not that you've never done this before.' I wandered across to the bookcase behind the desk, running my eyes over the leather-bound titles.

'Robbie,' I began slowly, something from the conversation with Stewart returning to me. 'If Orlando wanted what his friends had, why do you think he hasn't slept with Serena? Aside from the fact that I credit Serena with more taste.'

When he didn't immediately answer, I turned to face him.

'Who's to say he hasn't?' Robbie finally said.

'If he had, he would've told someone. From what we've heard, he wouldn't have been able to help himself. Yet Piers said Serena was off limits, and he didn't even flirt with her last night.' I turned back to the bookcase. 'I think Lucinda's right; it's not about the women but who "owns" them. Yet,' I mused, my fingers running along the titles on the shelf, 'from what Richard said, Rupert owed Orlando for something.'

'There seemed to be a lot of that hinted – that people owed Orlando … and that's how he liked it.' He pushed his chair back and stood beside me. 'Are you looking for anything specific in those books?'

'I was hoping there might be something about the house's history, but it would probably be easier if I asked Rupert or Serena.' In the hallway, the grandfather clock chimed five times. 'I'd like to have another look at the scene before dinner. It feels as though we've missed something.'

'Okay. Let's do that now.' A pause. 'Why did you ask Susan whether Orlando knew Jenny Black?'

Pulling out a volume, I flicked through the pages before replacing it on the shelf. 'I don't know, but I have this feeling that the two events are connected – although, as I said to Stewart – I have no evidence, so it's probably just fanciful thinking.' I pulled out another book that appeared to be about the dissolution of the monasteries during the Civil War. 'Robbie, would it be worthwhile asking DS Stanley to find out who supplied the information about Rupert being in college when she went missing?'

'Well,' he drawled, with that familiar wry half smile. 'When I mentioned the Jenny Black case, DI Whitely ordered me not to go raking up ancient history that has nothing to do with the here and now.' I grinned as he parodied the younger man's tone. 'So I've asked Lewis to do it as a favour for me and not let on to Whitely. Do you think Wentworth Fitzroy provided the alibi?'

'No.' I flicked through the pages, a fragment of

a thought hiding behind other thoughts. 'I think we'll find it was Orlando Stark.'

'And if it is, are you saying the two cases might be connected?'

I shrugged. 'Not necessarily, although it could be what Rupert "owes" Orlando.'

'And potentially, a motive for his murder,' he said grimly.

Chapter Eighteen

When we ducked into the kitchen to retrieve the parka and scarf I'd left in there – and would need in the Great Hall – Ginny and Richard were in there too.

'How was tea in the drawing room?' I asked.

'No one said anything interesting.' Ginny sounded disappointed.

'They were all just talking about Good Old Landy and how they don't believe it could possibly have been one of them who did for him,' added Richard. 'The implication being it must have been one of us.'

'We knew we weren't welcome so had our tea and came back here,' said Ginny.

'I don't blame you,' said Robbie.

Serena was in the hallway when Robbie and I emerged twenty minutes later. 'Oh good, you're here. I was beginning to think we needed to send out a search party for you, too.' Her laugh was high-pitched, but under it I detected concern.

'You shouldn't be out here on your own, Serena,' Robbie said sternly, shaking the keys to the Great Hall in his hand.

Her pale skin flushed pink. 'You don't really believe the rest of us are in danger?'

'We don't know.' I touched her arm. 'And that's the problem. Is everyone else in the drawing room?'

'Yes, well, not really.'

Robbie shook his head and sighed heavily. 'Lady Deverell—'

'I thought I asked you not to call me Lady Deverell,' she chided, her smile attempting to return lightness to the situation.

'And I thought I asked everyone to stay in the drawing room and, if they had to move about the house, to do so in pairs.' His expression was stony as he met and held her eyes. 'I'm serious, Serena. We don't know who we're dealing with here or what the motive was in murdering Lord Stark. All we know is we're safer in a group until help arrives tomorrow morning. Now, where is everyone?'

She tightened the cashmere wrap around her shoulders. 'You're right, Robbie, and I'm sorry. We haven't taken it seriously, and we should have. Richard and Ginny are in the kitchen helping Mrs Phillips; Rupe and Wenty are in the library, I think; Tara has ducked outside to make a call, although I think she's probably sneaking a cigarette – no one is supposed to know she occasionally smokes; Lucinda is upstairs; and—'

The lights flickered once before going off. And then a scream filled the sudden darkness.

The front door swung open, and Tara appeared, her figure outlined by what light there was remaining from the setting sun. The wind rushed in with her. 'Where did that scream come from?' Tara's eyes were wide with fright, her voice trembling. 'Where's Piers? Piers?'

Serena grabbed her arm as she would've run into the drawing room. 'We need to stay together,' she said with a sheepish glance in Robbie's direction.

From the kitchen, Richard and Ginny and the Phillips' ran in; Mallory and Piers appeared from the drawing room, and Rupert strode through from the library. 'What the blazes is going on?' he demanded, shutting the front door and pitching us all back into darkness. Susan had already grabbed a torch and was busy lighting candles.

Robbie held up his hands in a calm gesture. 'Who are we missing?'

Worried glances were cast around the room. 'Wenty and Lucinda,' Rupert said finally. 'They're probably in their bedroom.'

'I think the scream came from that direction.' I pointed up the stairs.

With that, another cry came. 'Somebody help me!'

'That's Lucinda!' Tara grabbed at my jacket. 'You have to get up there!'

Robbie nodded grimly. 'I want all of you in the drawing room now – and this time, stay there.'

'I say—' began Rupert.

'I mean it,' Robbie said firmly, waiting until Rupert nodded before turning his attention to Susan. 'I'm happy for you four to remain in the kitchen as long as you all stay together. Philly? You and I are heading upstairs.'

'But the generator …' Susan began.

Frowning as he realised the generator hadn't kicked straight in, Robbie said, 'I'll see to that after we've seen to upstairs. There are plenty of candles and torches, so no one is to go out there.' He met each person's eyes. 'Am I clear?' Without waiting for a response, he selected two torches from the hall table, tossing one to me. 'Philly?'

Robbie climbed the stairs slowly, clinging to the right-hand side to maximise visibility. The torch swung in a wide arc before each step. My heart was beating so hard I thought it would fly out of my chest.

At the top of the staircase, we proceeded at the same speed along the hall to the open door of the Fitzroy's room where Lucinda stood, hands braced against the doorframe. 'Thank goodness,' she said, rubbing her hands against her thighs, her chest rising and falling with emotion. 'I came up to get changed and found him like this.'

She stood aside to allow Robbie to rush into the room, turning her tear-ravaged face towards me. 'I don't know if he's alive,' she said tremulously, her eyes wild with panic, smears of what I assumed were blood on her cheeks and staining the front of her cream jumper and cream wool slacks. Holding her hands towards me, she said, 'There's blood and …'

Unable to continue speaking, her face crumpled, tears spilling from her eyes. Putting my arm around her, I guided her back into the room where Robbie was crouched on the floor beside the supine form of Wentworth Fitzroy. Lucinda turned away from the sight of her husband; I mouthed to Robbie, 'Is he alive?'

He nodded and mouthed back, 'There's a pulse.'

'Lucinda,' I said gently, willing my pulse to slow, 'your husband is alive, so we'll do what we can to stop the bleeding. While I do that, Robbie has some questions for you. Is that okay?' When she nodded, I guided her to the winged-back chair in the corner of the room. 'Are you comfortable?' When she nodded again, I poured her a glass of sherry from the decanter on the dressing table. 'You've had a nasty shock. This will help.'

Robbie pulled the chair out from the dressing table and sat opposite her, his smile showing a calm I was sure he didn't feel. 'I know this is hard, Mrs Fitzroy …' When her eyes flew to her husband, he said, 'Philly will call it in and check him over.' She nodded, so I turned away to concentrate on Wentworth.

'Can you tell me exactly what happened this afternoon? From the beginning, please.'

As Robbie asked his question, I quickly examined Wentworth's body for signs of injury. As far as I could tell, the blood was coming from a wound to the side of his head. I laid my ear close to his mouth, my eyes on his chest. He was breathing, and his airways were clear. I ducked into the ensuite and pulled a hand towel from the sink. That would have to do as a makeshift dressing.

'Not long after tea was served, Wenty and Rupe went into the library. Serena said something about how the library was now your domain, but Rupe said it would be fine; they'd be done before you knew they'd been in there,' Lucinda said.

'Where was everyone else when this happened?'

A short silence, and then, 'Mallory and Piers were on the sofa. She got quite hysterical when Rupe and Wenty left the room, and Tara told her to snap out of it.'

'So Mrs Beaumont-Brown was there?' Robbie asked.

'Yes, she was then, but soon after this, she said she needed to make a phone call, so she left too.'

'Where did Mrs Beaumont-Brown go?'

The room fell quiet again momentarily. 'I don't know. I don't remember hearing the front door shut, so I don't think she immediately went outside. She might have done, though.'

Pulling my phone out of my pocket, I tapped on Stewart's number, frowning when it didn't connect. Without wi-fi, I had just one bar of signal.

'Would she have had to go upstairs to get a jacket?' Robbie asked.

Lucinda shook her head. 'You don't think Tara did this, do you?' Lucinda sounded disbelieving.

Robbie ignored her question. 'How long had she been gone before Lord Deverell and your husband returned to the drawing room?'

'Oh,' she said. 'They didn't come back. Didn't I say? That's why I decided to get changed upstairs. I thought Wenty was still in with Rupe.'

Hoping there was enough signal for a text to get through, I tapped out a message to Stewart:

Wentworth Fitzroy attacked – blunt force trauma to the head. He's alive but needs medical care. Power down, no wi-fi.

'And that's when you found your husband?' Robbie asked her.

'Yes.' Her voice broke with emotion. 'Someone has hit him, haven't they?'

'It certainly looks that way. Can you think of anyone who would want to harm your husband?'

On impulse, I pulled my gloves on, reached into Wentworth's jacket pocket and pulled out a mobile phone and what appeared to be a business card. I clicked the side button, and the screen filled with a photo of Mallory Stark. Why would Wentworth Fitzroy have a photo of Mallory Stark as his screensaver? The answer was so obvious that I almost hit myself on the forehead at my obtuseness. He would if it was Orlando Stark's phone. I turned the card over in my hand. On one side was a hexafoil similar to the symbols on the wooden frame in the barn. It was the same card we'd found on the body of Orlando Stark.

'Robbie,' I said, straightening. 'Can I interrupt you for a sec?'

'Of course. Please excuse me, Mrs Fitzroy.'

'Is Wenty okay?' Lucinda asked, her voice rising again in panic.

'He's fine,' I said vaguely, my mind racing with all the reasons why Wentworth would have Orland Stark's phone – and why they'd both have this card in their pocket.

Robbie was soon beside me. I held out my phone with my message to Stewart that was still attempting to send. With only a single bar of reception, I wasn't confident the message would get through. 'And …' I showed him the phone I'd found in Wentworth's pocket. 'There was this' —Robbie's eyebrows flew up— 'and this.' I handed him the card.

'Is that …?'

'Blood?' He nodded. 'I think so. The card was with it and also has blood on it.'

With another nod, he got to his feet. 'Mrs Fitzroy, do you recognise this phone?'

Lucinda shook her head. 'I don't think that's Wenty's phone. Wenty's phone is on the bed.' When

Robbie tapped the screen and the screenshot opened, her eyes widened, her hand flew to her mouth. 'That's … that's Landy's phone. But what was Wenty doing with it? Is that … blood?'

Again, Robbie ignored her question. 'Have you seen this before?' He showed her the card.

She took just a cursory look before shaking her head. 'No, I have no idea what it is.'

'Are you sure? Take another look.' Robbie extended the card towards her once more.

'No … maybe …' She looked up at the ceiling, squeezing at the fingers on her left hand between the thumb and index finger of her right. 'I might have seen something similar yesterday, but I didn't get a good look at it.'

'Where did you see the card, Mrs Fitzroy?'

'Landy had it. He was showing Wenty and Rupe.' She paused and frowned slightly. 'Whatever it was, it meant something to Wenty and Rupert. I could be wrong, but I'm quite sure they were arguing about it.'

'When was this?' I asked.

'Umm, yesterday morning. It was definitely after breakfast, but before we went out for lunch.'

On the ground, Wentworth groaned, his eyes fluttering open. 'Wenty! Darling!' In a flash, Lucinda sprung from her seat and crouched by her husband's side.

Lucinda and I helped him sit up, manoeuvring him

slightly so he could rest back against the bed. 'Is he going to be okay?' she asked.

'I think so,' I assured her. 'Although he could have a concussion.' I attempted to remember my first aid training from a long time ago.

Robbie nodded. 'He'll have a headache, and we'll need to keep an eye on him until we can get him looked at by a doctor. Try and keep him awake and have nothing to eat or drink.'

'Did you see who did this to you?' Lucinda asked, fussing around him.

Wentworth grimaced as he attempted to shake his head, his hand holding the towel against the bleeding. 'No, he must've been waiting in the bathroom, and when I stooped to take my shoes off, that's when I was hit.'

'You said "he",' commented Robbie. 'Why do you think it was a man?'

Wentworth struggled to his feet, leaning on his wife. 'Because whoever it was hit me hard!' He frowned. 'I also recall seeing a flash of khaki, like an anorak.'

'I see.' Robbie held out the phone I'd taken from his pocket. 'Have you seen this before?'

Placing a hand on his forehead, he frowned. 'Yes, it's Landy's. Where did you find it?'

'In your pocket. Do you have any idea how it got there?'

Wentworth's eyes widened, panic coming into

them. 'No, of course I don't! Whoever it was who clocked me must've put it there.'

'And this?' I showed him the card I'd taken from his pocket.

'I say, you shouldn't be rifling through a man's pockets,' he said feebly.

'This *is* a murder investigation, Mr Fitzroy,' Robbie said sternly.

Wentworth nodded slowly, his hand again on his forehead. 'It was left in an envelope on my pillow. I have no idea who put it there.'

'I think you've questioned him enough,' Lucinda said tearfully. 'He needs to rest now.'

Robbie inclined his head to acknowledge her point. 'Do you think you can manage to make it downstairs? I need everyone to be together.'

With Robbie on one side and Lucinda on the other, Wentworth gingerly made his way out of the room, Robbie's torch lighting the way.

The wind whistled through a chink where the window hadn't been closed properly, the frame rattling. I shivered as last night's dream returned to me and automatically closed it shut, noting it immediately sprang back up by an inch or so. This time, when I closed it, I locked it.

Chapter Nineteen

Following Robbie's instructions, Rupert and his guests had gathered in the drawing room, candlelight casting a gentle glow over the party.

At our entrance, Rupert and Piers sprang up, Piers replacing Robbie and helping Wentworth into an armchair.

'Good God, man! What's happened?' Rupert turned to us, seeking answers.

'Someone knocked him out,' said Robbie. 'But they could've killed him.' He cast his eyes around the room, lingering on each person. 'This is why I asked you all to stay together. Now I have to ask where each of you was when Mr Fitzroy was attacked.'

'What about the housekeeper and her daughter and those other people?' Tara demanded. 'Are you going to ask them?'

'No, I'm not.' Robbie's voice was low and steady. 'Because I already know all four of them were together.

You, however, were not. When we believe Mr Fitzroy was attacked, Lady Stark and Mr Beaumont-Brown were the only ones still in this room. Where were you, Mrs Beaumont-Brown?'

'I can't believe you think it's one of us,' she sputtered.

'I'm not saying it is,' Robbie answered carefully. 'But I need to know where you all were. So I'll ask again, Mrs Beaumont-Brown, you came in from outside; where had you been?'

'So now I'm not allowed to go outside for fresh air?' Her voice was full of indignation, her eyes darting between Robbie and her friends for support.

'Not alone while there's a murderer at large,' Piers said. 'No one is begrudging you a sneaky cigarette, darling – just not alone.'

'I'm afraid I have no alibi,' Rupert volunteered. 'Wenty and I had some business to discuss in the library, and he left me just before six. I assumed he was going to get changed. I remained in the library until the power went off and Lucinda screamed – not that we knew it was Lucinda screaming, of course.'

'I was with Mallory and Piers until I came looking for you two,' said Serena.

'Obviously, I could never harm my husband,' Lucinda said with a forced laugh. 'But I left at the same time as Tara and made a phone call from the dining room. One of the horses has been poorly, and I wanted to check on them.'

'Make of that what you will, Inspector,' said Piers, pouring himself a whisky from the drinks trolley in the corner. 'But I don't see how that's given you any more information than you had previously.'

Robbie's mouth twitched. 'You'd be surprised.' He glanced at his watch. 'It's now almost seven. Philly and I will check the generator and see if we can't get power restored, but first, can I have a quick word, please, Lord Deverell?'

'Of course.'

Robbie inclined his head towards the window seat indicating where he wanted to have the quick word. Rupert and I followed him over.

'What's this about?' Rupert asked.

Robbie pulled out the card we'd found in Wentworth's pocket. 'Yesterday, when we showed you this, you said you'd never seen it before – is that still your position?'

Rupert's eyes narrowed. 'Where did you get this?'

Robbie hesitated briefly. 'It was in Mr Fitzroy's pocket.'

'What does he say about it?'

'He said it was left in his room in an envelope,' Robbie admitted. 'He wasn't fit to say more than that.' As Rupert's hand tapped at his thigh, Robbie added, 'We did ask Mrs Fitzroy, and she mentioned she thought she saw Lord Stark show you a similar card yesterday.'

'I see.' Rupert bit at his top lip and seemed to make a decision. 'Orlando did have one – it was left in his room.' His scoff was high-pitched. 'As for what it means, I wouldn't have the faintest idea. How strange Wenty had one too.'

'Do you still say you've never seen it before?' Robbie asked.

Rupert pursed his lips and shook his head.

'You don't think it's a coincidence that Lord Stark and Mr Fitzroy both had these cards?'

'Not at all.' A little pulse beat in his jaw, but Rupert's eyes remained on me as he answered Robbie's question. He turned his attention to Robbie. 'It could be anything – a club they both frequent, a business consultant they're both using …' He shrugged. 'You'd need to ask Wenty about that.'

'We'll do that, but one last question, if I may. Both Mr Fitzroy and Mr Beaumont-Brown have told us they loaned Lord Stark money – funds he hadn't repaid. Did you also loan him money?'

This time, Rupert's eyes narrowed on Robbie. I could almost see the wheels turning in his head as he calculated how much we knew. 'Yes, I did – thankfully not as much as Piers and Wenty.' He let out a short laugh. 'We've all seen the last of that money, I suspect. There was no paperwork involved, and even if we had formalised the arrangements, I doubt Landy's estate could afford to repay us. Is that all?'

'It is,' Robbie said sombrely. 'Philly and I will try to get the generator going again; we'll check in with the kitchen about food, and then after dinner, I'll have more questions. In the meantime, no one will leave this room unless they need the bathroom – and then only in pairs. Is that understood?'

Rupert nodded. 'Perfectly, Inspector.'

Once Rupert was safely at the other end of the room Robbie wearily rubbed at the back of his neck. 'Why do I feel we're fighting this on too many fronts? Keeping that lot' —he pointed his thumb back towards the drawing room— 'in one place is like herding kittens. Plus, there are only two legitimate reasons for Wentworth Fitzroy to have Lord Stark's blood-stained phone: if he murdered Lord Stark and removed it from the body—'

'In which case he was attacked by someone else,' I finished.

'Exactly, or if Lord Stark was murdered by someone else who tried to kill Mr Fitzroy and make it appear as though he was the murderer.'

'Which makes no sense. Why would you try and pin a murder on someone and then attack them? Instead of making the case appear closed, it underlines that it's absolutely not.' It felt like every time we answered one question, another was asked. We were getting nowhere.

'Unless,' Robbie said slowly, 'you want to make

it clear that whatever this is about also involves Wentworth Fitzroy.'

Robbie stepped back from the generator and scratched his head. 'The auto control has been left in the off position again.' He flicked the switch back on.

'Who would know how to do this?' I swung my torch around the space. 'There's no sign of anyone having been in here.'

'If you know what you're doing, it's quick. It could've been switched off any time since the main power came back on,' Robbie explained. 'Flick the switch from on to off, and then, when you're ready, switch off the mains power, knowing the generator won't kick into action. It's the same reason it didn't come on automatically this morning. I paid no attention to it when we checked in here for Lord Stark earlier.'

'Tara was outside, and you would've noticed she never did explain what she was doing,' I said. 'Piers deflected that for her.'

'It could've been any of them.' Robbie sounded as weary as she felt. 'Each of them went missing at some point during the afternoon, and no one was paying attention to who was doing what this morning.'

My phone beeped to remind me the message I'd attempted to send from the Fitzroy's bedroom had failed. 'I've got a few bars out here,' I said. 'I'll try Stewart again.'

Pinning myself against the stone wall in a feeble effort to stay out of the wind, I clicked on Stewart's number.

He picked up on the first ring. 'Thank goodness,' he said. 'I've been trying to call you and was beginning to get worried.'

'The power went off again, which means no wi-fi. And the walls in this monstrosity of a place are about a million feet thick, so there's no hope of reception inside without wi-fi.' Cold from the stone was making its way through my layers, but suddenly, I was too tired to care. 'We lost power, and someone deliberately switched the generator off auto.' I sighed as I attempted to organise my thoughts.

'Who could've done that?'

'Any of them.' A yawn escaped, and I stamped my feet to try and wake up a little.

'What do you mean by "any of them"? Surely you were watching them all?'

'Really, Stewart?' My temper flared at the criticism in his voice. 'You're giving me a bollocking about this? While we've been busy with interviews, Lord Deverell's lot has been roaming around willy-nilly. There are two of us, Stewart, and somehow we have to keep an eye on a set of over-privileged pratts who think the whole thing is some joke perpetrated by obviously a servant or someone who broke in while we're actually trying to investigate a crime. "You can't imagine it was one of us, darling."' I parodied Tara Beaumont-Brown. 'Then Wentworth Fitzroy was attacked and—' My voice wavered.

'Christ, Philly! What's been going on up there? Are you okay?'

I took a deep breath. 'I'm fine, just …' Mind on the job, Philly, Mind on the job. 'I'm fine, Stewart,' I said firmly. 'Alright, to bring you up to date, Wentworth Fitzroy was attacked in his bedroom with some blunt instrument – which we haven't found yet. I think he'll be okay, but he could have a concussion, so he will need medical attention as soon as anyone can get through. I tried to message you, but it failed.' Again, my voice broke, but I swallowed hard and continued. There'd be plenty of time to break down when this was over. 'We found Orlando Stark's blood-stained phone in Wentworth's pocket.'

'Do you think he killed Lord Stark?'

'No, but someone wants us to think he did. We believe it was placed in his pocket by his attacker.'

'Right.'

'There's one more thing. We found a business card in Orlando's pocket with a pinwheel symbol on it—'

'Like a daisy wheel?'

'Yes. We found the same card in Wentworth Fitzroy's pocket. Lucinda Fitzroy thinks she saw her husband show Rupert, but when we asked him, he denied having seen it.'

'Did you believe him?'

'No. He knows more about that symbol, I'm sure of it. We'll question him again about that.' I paused, and then my throat suddenly thickened. 'Stewart? When can you get someone here?'

'If the wind keeps dropping, we may be able to get a chopper in – even if it's just with a forensic crew to take away the body – leave that with me. It will be morning, though, for any road transport.' He paused. 'A few more hours, Philly,' he said. 'Hold on for a few more hours.'

I nodded.

'Philly?'

'I'm nodding. Robbie's speaking to Chris Whitely now, but going forward, can you do me a favour and update him? We're dealing with too much here to do double debriefs.'

Stewart was silent for so long that I thought he was about to argue with me on this point. 'Understood,' he finally said. 'Just make sure one of you updates one of us regularly. Oh, and Philly?'

'Yes …'

'Why has Robbie asked DS Stanley to dig out the alibis in the Jenny Black case? I thought I said you needed to stick to the case you have in front of you – you don't have time for larking about in cold cases.'

'We're not – it was just something we were wondering about.' I crossed my fingers behind my back. 'Don't worry, we don't have time to do anything but focus on the evidence in front of us.'

'Hmmm.' He didn't sound as though he entirely believed me. 'See that you do – and mind how you go, Philly. I don't want the next victim to be you or Robbie.'

A chill ran up my spine. 'Surprisingly, Stewart, nor do I.'

Chapter Twenty

With the power restored and DI Whitely updated, Robbie let out a weary exhale, his hands on his hips. 'That's done. How did you fare with Stewart?'

'Fine. He thinks they'll be able to get someone here later tonight.'

'Are the roads open?' Robbie's frown was doubtful.

'No – it will be tomorrow for road access, but if the wind conditions continue to improve, they may be able to get a helicopter out here tonight. The priority is for the forensic crew to secure the body and the scene. The rest of the team will come by road.'

Robbie nodded. 'That makes sense. Now, as for our next moves—' A ping alerted him to an incoming message. 'Lewis has sent through the witness statements confirming Lord Deverell's alibi for when Jenny Black went missing.' He reached under his anorak and jumper to retrieve his glasses from the top pocket of his shirt. 'You were right, Philly. Orlando Stark stated that Rupert

Deverell had attended a party with him in Oxford the night before Jenny went missing.'

'And the day she went missing?'

'Rupert was hungover and capable of very little.' He read some more. 'Orlando confirmed he checked on him at midday. Wentworth Fitzroy corroborated the story … in fact, all three stories match exactly – almost to the letter.' His half smile was wry. 'And that's something I always find interesting.'

'Stewart reminded me we're to focus on the investigation in front of us,' I warned.

'And so we will, but my gut tells me this is connected, so this is useful information to keep in my back pocket.' He replaced his glasses. 'As I was saying, I want to talk again to Lady Stark, Lord Deverell and Wentworth Fitzroy.'

'Okay, but before we go back in, can we look at the garden outside the Fitzroy's room? The bedroom window wasn't closed properly, and I can't imagine Lucinda would've slept with it open last night.'

'You're thinking whoever assaulted Wentworth Fitzroy escaped through the window?'

I nodded. 'Or, at the very least, tossed the weapon out there. Although,' I mused, 'I'm still not sure whether the attack on Wentworth was designed to kill or frighten him.' Another thought struck me. 'Could he have done this to himself?'

'To make it look as though he was being framed

while simultaneously making it obvious he was being framed?' He mulled over the idea. 'Maybe, but I don't think so. After all, whatever hit him wasn't in that room.' Slapping his hands against his jeans, he added, 'Alright, let's look at this garden bed so we can get inside and get warm.'

Although the snow beside the house had begun to thaw, the outline of boot prints could be seen – deep in the sludge immediately below the window and less clear leading away towards the front door.

I trained my torch on the prints as Robbie squatted and took photos. 'It looks to be a man's size boot, probably a size ten, I'd say.' He straightened and looked up at the window with his hands on his hips. 'It's too far to jump, and that vine wouldn't take the weight of a grown man.'

I poked about in the bushes. 'This would, though.' A wooden ladder was lying on its side behind the still bare stems of a clump of hydrangeas. 'And this' —I pulled my silicon gloves on and picked up an empty gin bottle— 'I'd wager, is what was used on Wentworth Fitzroy.'

'A gin bottle.' Robbie rubbed the back of his neck. 'The same brand we found in the Stark's room.'

'Hattie said she'd cleared an empty bottle from there yesterday,' I said. 'We'd need to check the recycling, but anyone could've lifted it from there.'

'If it's the same bottle – and I assume it is – the

intention is presumably to point the finger again at Mallory.'

'But it couldn't have been Mallory. She and Piers Beaumont-Brown are the only ones we know for sure were in the drawing room at the time of the attack on Wentworth.' A wave of despair crashed over me. 'What's going on here, Robbie? It seems that everywhere we look, the evidence is pointing in different directions, and I don't know about you, but I can't make any sense of it. And there's still the matter of a missing murder weapon and a body in a locked room.'

'I know, Philly, but there is an answer in here somewhere.' He threw an arm around me. 'Look, how about we head back in, bag this, and ask those follow-up questions we need to ask? I know you still want another look at the murder scene so we'll do that too. Then, and I know it's late, we'll do our best to document it and see if we can't see a pattern. Even though it feels as though almost everyone is involved, I still feel we're pursuing one killer.'

Even though his arm rested lightly on my shoulders, its weight was calming. 'You're right, and faffing about here in the cold isn't getting us anywhere,' I said.

He removed his arm, and I immediately missed the comfort it had given me. 'I don't know about you, but I'm hoping Lord Deverell has a decent whisky open.' He hunched his shoulders against the cold. 'It's raw out here.'

•

Besides Susan and Hattie, the entire party was gathered in the drawing room. Richard and Ginny huddled together on the window seat; Piers and Rupert stood beside the fireplace; Mallory and Wentworth slouched into either end of one of the two-seater lounges while Tara and Lucinda sat opposite. Serena was beside the drinks trolley, yesterday's bustling energy absent.

'There you are,' she said, a spark of light coming to her eyes. 'You must both be frozen. What can I get you? We have everything here – wine, sherry, whisky … Although' —she held up a bottle, her glance flicking briefly to Mallory— 'I'll need to ring for more gin. We seem to have gone through it today.'

'I'd love a whisky, thanks, Serena,' I said. 'Don't worry about the water or ice, though – I feel as though I'm frozen inside.'

'A neat whisky will be fine for me too, thank you,' said Robbie. 'Is that the brand of gin you usually buy?'

'Yes,' she said, frowning as she poured a healthy measure of amber liquid into a crystal tumbler. 'Why do you ask?'

Robbie nodded his thanks as Serena passed him a glass, his expression otherwise unreadable. 'We found an empty bottle in the garden that we believe was used to assault Mr Fitzroy.'

He spoke loudly enough that everyone looked up.

'Was it the same brand as this one?' Rupert asked.

'No. It was' —he pretended to consult the notes on his phone— 'The Botanist.' As Mallory struggled to sit upright, I sipped my whisky, closing my eyes briefly as the spirit slipped down my throat, warmth spreading through my chest.

'We've checked with Hattie,' he continued. 'She told us she'd removed a similar bottle from your room yesterday, Lady Stark, but it's no longer in the recycling bin.'

'Are you saying I hurt Wenty?' Mallory's voice rose with her outrage. 'I've been here all afternoon.'

'No, Lady Stark, that's not what we're saying. Anyone could've removed that bottle at any time before Mr Fitzroy's assault.' He turned the glass idly so the amber liquid gleamed in the light. 'I'm saying someone in this room wanted us to think you had something to do with it.'

A gasp came from the lounge where Tara and Lucinda sat, although I couldn't tell who had uttered it.

'Have you spoken to that rude maid? I wouldn't be surprised if she did it,' Mallory sputtered.

'We have,' Robbie said calmly. 'Like you, she has an alibi for the time of the assault. If you don't mind, I want to talk to you again about your husband, Lady Stark.'

'Does it matter if I do mind?' she asked, her chin jutting indignantly.

'No,' said Robbie. 'I was being polite.' He drained his glass. 'In the library?' As Mallory used the arm of the lounge to struggle to her feet, Robbie said with a frown, 'Are you sure you're up to this Lady Stark? Perhaps you might like some coffee; we can talk later when you're feeling more … alert.'

'I'm perfectly capable,' she said haughtily. 'What are you implying?'

Meeting Robbie's eyes briefly I attempted to defuse the situation. 'He's not implying anything Lady Stark. You're bound to be a little … tired and … emotional after your shock. We do need to talk to you, but we can wait until you've had some coffee.'

'I. Don't. Need. Coffee,' she said through gritted teeth. 'What I need is to get these questions over and done with.'

With the smallest of shrugs Robbie turned to Serena. 'What are the arrangements for dinner tonight?'

'Mrs Phillips will serve it buffet style in the dining room,' she said absently, her eyes on Mallory who had picked up her now empty glass and was making her way carefully across to the drinks trolley. 'Would you like me to have places set for her and Hattie too?'

'I hardly think that's necessary—' began Rupert.

'It's more about making sure they feel safe, Lord Deverell,' Robbie said sternly. 'However, if they want to eat together in the kitchen, I believe they'll be safe there too.' Lowering his voice, he added, 'I've got a few more questions I'd like to ask you, too.'

Rupert nodded once. 'If you think it will help.'

Serena took Mallory's glass and while the other woman had her head turned, filled it with tonic water. 'Robbie, can I get you and Philly another whisky?'

Robbie shook his head. 'No, thank you, Serena. Lady Stark, if you're ready?'

Swaying slightly on her heels, the liquid in her glass sloshing dangerously. 'How about I take that through for you?' I offered.

'Ish fine,' she said, again holding onto the arm of the chair. Raising her chin defiantly, she followed Robbie from the room.

Robbie asked Mallory to sit in one of the armchairs before taking a seat in the other. I perched on the edge of the Chippendale desk. With a glance towards me, Robbie indicated I should begin.

'I know this is hard to talk about, Mallory, but we do need to ask ... We've been made aware of Lord Stark's ... ummm ... dalliances with other women. Were you aware of these?'

Mallory choked on her drink. 'Landy loved me. How dare you suggest he was unfaithful!'

'As Philly said, we're sorry to have to ask, but we do have evidence that he'd been having an affair and may have arranged to meet someone last night,' Robbie said gently.

'No!' She shook her head emphatically. 'I trusted Landy implish … inplishitly.' She took another large swallow, not seeming to notice the absence of gin.

I raised my eyebrows in Robbie's direction and tried another tack. 'Does this mean anything to you?' I handed across the plastic bag containing the card we'd found in Wentworth's pocket.

She took it, frowned and gave it back to me. 'No, should I have?'

'We found a card similar to this on your husband's body, Lady Stark,' said Robbie. 'Are you sure you haven't seen it before?'

'Thatsh what I shaid.'

'One last question.' Robbie clasped his hands on the table. 'Were you aware your husband was having financial difficulties?'

'Landy?' She scoffed. 'Of coursh he wasn't having finansh … money problems. I would've known about it. Landy was clever with money – everyone knowsh that.' She waved her glass, the contents splashing onto her dress. Mallory didn't seem to notice. 'Necks you'll be shaying he was divorshing me.' She stood suddenly, spilling her drink as she stumbled. 'I've had enough of thish and would like to return to the drawing room now.' She lifted her head and attempted to look down her nose at Robbie.

Meeting Robbie's eyes I squirmed in my seat. The longer we'd talked, the more her speech had slurred.

With her state of inebriation nothing she said now would be admissible in any case. Any further questions would need to wait until she was sober.

He nodded and inclined his head in my direction. 'Very well, Lady Stark. We'll take you back.' As she tottered off ahead of us Robbie touched my arm lightly, 'And then we'll have another look at the murder scene before forensics arrive.'

Chapter Twenty-One

Sunday 7.30 pm

The heavy doors closed with a thud that echoed through the Great Hall. Shivering, I wrapped my scarf tighter around my neck and zipped up the parka I'd donned. Wrinkling my nose, I couldn't help but wonder if I imagined the faint smell of death that hung in the cold, still air.

'It's too soon in this temperature for decay to have begun,' said Robbie, correctly interpreting my crinkled nose.

'It's hard to believe it was only a few hours ago that we found him,' I said. 'It feels like it was days.' I bit at my lower lip. 'That first time we came in, it felt like something was still in here; the air was … I don't know … disturbed. But now…' I let out a snorted laugh. 'That sounds ridiculous. Next thing I'll be saying, it felt like his soul was still here, but now it's gone.'

'I felt it before, too – the presence of … something. But there's nothing here now,' he said bluntly.

'It seems wrong – not moving him or covering him with something, but I understand why we can't.'

'I have to say that after forty years, this is a new one for me, too – the body lying here while we clodhop around it.'

We were silent as we approached the corpse, each nodding a silent acknowledgement of respect for the departed as we stood over it before heading to the back of the room and the fireplace.

'What is it we're looking for, Philly?' Robbie stepped into the man-sized fireplace and shone his torch up into the dark of the chimney.

'I don't know.' Closing my eyes, I forced in a few deep breaths. What was it I was missing?

Opening my eyes again, I allowed them to roam around the room, ignoring – for now – the pull of the Stubbs. What was it about that painting? There was a prickle across the back of my neck, but it wasn't the usual prickle of excitement I felt when looking at a painting as important as this one was. Perhaps it was the body of Orlando and the need to resolve that before I could indulge in the art.

With my hands on my hips, I turned towards the fireplace. What was it about that book I'd flipped through in the library? That fragment of thought poked its head out. 'Robbie, do you know if the Deverells were a Catholic family?'

'I wouldn't have a clue. Why is that important?'

Standing beside me, his attention was also on the fireplace, and the beginning of a smile played on his lips. 'You're thinking there might be a priest-hole in here – somewhere a priest can hide or escape from the building without being seen?'

I lifted a shoulder. 'The house is the right age.'

'Aye, it is. I recall another case near Ripon where a priest-hole was used to get from one wing of the house to another.' He tapped at the wooden panel beside the fireplace. 'A cupboard accessed a tunnel that brought you into the library.' He continued prodding the carved panel. 'In that case, there was a button in the centre of the family crest …' He pressed into one of the carved crevices and stood back with a wide grin as the lever clicked into place and the panel swung open.

Using the torches on our phones, we squinted into the narrow stone-lined opening and the darkness beyond. My throat closed up in fear at the thought of the darkness beyond that thin stream of light. Swallowing it back, I took a deep breath, pushing aside thoughts of the tunnel closing in on me, suffocating me. 'I'm going in.'

Robbie shook his head. 'We don't know that it's safe. We should go in together.'

'What if we're unable to open the door again? We have both sets of keys, so no one can get into this room, and no one would know we're in there.' I touched his arm in reassurance. 'I understand what you're saying, and trust me, I don't want to go down there either, but it makes more sense for one of us to stay here and the other to go in. And' —I forced a grin and looked him up and down— 'back when this entrance was built, people were a little … more my size than yours.'

About to argue, he nodded reluctantly, his brow furrowed. 'Alright, but be careful and don't hang about down there.'

'There's no chance of that,' I muttered. With my heart in my mouth and the torch in my hand, I gingerly stepped over the threshold and onto flattened earth, closing my eyes briefly as I imagined the walls of the tunnel closing in around me.

'Are you okay, Philly?' called Robbie.

Swallowing hard, I shook my head to free the images of the roof caving in. 'Yes,' I managed. The faint light of my torch illuminated narrow steps down. With one hand on the wall for support, I turned my feet to inch my way down sideways.

At the bottom of the stairs, the tunnel widened slightly, although there were parts where someone Robbie's height would've had to walk with their shoulders stooped. After what seemed like ages – but was probably only a few minutes – I came to another set of stairs, which ended in a wooden panel. Pushing hard against it with my shoulder, I stumbled into what I assumed was the barn. After blinking a few times as my eyes adjusted to the torchlight, I took in the hard-packed dirt floor, the exposed wooden rafters and the matching support beams. While the space had been emptied of whatever animal-related use it might once have had, resting against the walls were an assortment of agricultural implements. Could one of these be the murder weapon?

Even though I knew Robbie would be getting anxious, I took some time to quickly search the space. There was, however, nothing in here that could have been used to stab Orlando Stark. When the beam of the torch landed on the designs carved into the wooden support beams and the frame that marked the door I'd come through, my heart began beating faster. After snapping some photos of the entrance, lingering on the shapes carved into the wooden supports, I made my way carefully back down the stairs, my progress through the tunnel more confident on the return trip, the light from the entrance reaching down as I got closer.

Robbie had been waiting for me, peering anxiously into the tunnel. 'Can you shut the door?' I called from the bottom of the stairs. 'I want to see whether it can be opened from this side.'

The stairs were again plunged into darkness, with the narrow beam from my torch the only light. At the top of the stairs, I pushed against the panel with my hands, and while it budged, it wasn't enough to open the door. Turning side on, I put my shoulder into it,

Robbie catching and steadying me as I spat out into the ballroom.

After dusting down my jeans and jacket, I straightened, my hands on my hips as I dragged in fresh air, my heart settling quickly into its normal rhythm. 'I've never been good with enclosed spaces,' I said with a relieved laugh. 'I wouldn't want to do that too often.'

'I'd prefer you didn't either.' Robbie reached out to brush dirt or something else I'd prefer not to think about from my cheek. 'You've got some in your hair too,' he said, his touch gentle, the look in his eyes undecipherable but making me feel warm despite the chill in the room. His hand dropped from my hair, and whatever had been in his eyes was gone. 'I would've hated having to explain that one to Stewart.' His trademark wry smile was back in place. 'Where does the tunnel come out? The barn is right behind here, isn't it?'

'Yes, the tunnel brings you out into the barn,' I said. 'So I think we can safely say we know how Orlando got into the room and the murderer got out. I didn't hang about for a look, but I took photos of some marks on the timber supports beside where it opens.' Opening the photo app, I handed my phone to him.

'Are these…?' His eyes widened.

'The same marks on the cards Orlando and Wentworth had? Yes.'

He looked up from my phone. 'That can't be a coincidence. Whoever is responsible for this knows about this tunnel – and can fit down it. How tight would it be for a man of my height?'

'The tunnel is wider than the entrance, and there are places where you'd need to stoop, but you could do it.' I shuddered as the darkness closed in around my head again. 'Wentworth is about your height, but Rupert would be a couple of inches shorter – maybe five foot ten or thereabouts?'

'Any sign of the murder weapon in there?' he asked. 'Or is that too much to hope for?'

I shook my head. 'Sorry, no.' My gaze lingered on the portraits on the walls, the dado rails framing the wooden panels below. Maybe … 'It's a long shot, but …'

'Any ideas at this stage would be good; we've nothing else.' After his elation at finding the tunnel, Robbie was beginning to sound defeated.

I turned back to him. 'I recall seeing a documentary not that long ago – one of those year in the life of a stately home type of things. This one was about Blenheim Palace … or was it Chatsworth?' As I spoke, my hand ran slowly along the wooden rail that framed the panelling below. 'The woman they interviewed – she was about eighty but had grown up there, so must have been one of the previous Duke's daughters – spoke about how when they played in the ballroom, they weren't allowed to touch the knife hidden in there.'

'A knife hidden in a ballroom? What for? In case

someone stepped on someone else's toes too often?'

I chuckled. 'No, in case they needed to get the paintings out in a hurry. In a fire, the staff needed to cut the canvases from their frames to save them. Rolling and carrying multiple canvases is easier than dealing with unwieldy frames.'

'And you think there might be something similar in here that was used as the murder weapon?' Even though his voice held scepticism, Robbie was prepared to go with me on this.

I shrugged. 'I said it was a long shot.'

'Okay, well, we don't have any other ideas. What am I looking for?'

'It will be a piece of the picture rail that hinges open, so perhaps a join or a break in the wood. It will be easier to feel for it. I'll take this side, and you take the other. Because staff would need to access the knife easily, I don't think it will be near the bench seats, so concentrate your search away from them.'

Robbie broke the silence just as I thought my long shot was a waste of effort. 'Philly,' he called, excitement in his voice. 'I think I've found something. Have you got those gloves with you?'

He'd found a piece of dado rail substantially shorter than the others, above which were faint smudge lines on the paintwork. 'This looks fresh.' I rubbed at it with my gloved hand before jiggling the wood until it swung up. Inside was a small compartment – and a wooden-handled knife covered in blood. 'Would this fit the wound?'

Robbie's eyes were wide as I pulled the knife from its hiding spot. 'Well, I've seen it all now. We would never have found that – which is what I suspect the murderer was banking on.' He pulled a plastic bag from his pocket and handed it to me to place the knife inside. 'We'll have to wait for confirmation, but yes, I'd say this is the murder weapon.' He tapped the bag. 'This narrows our list of suspects to those who know the house well.'

'And places Rupert at the top of that list,' I said grimly.

'Along with Wentworth Fitzroy and possibly even Susan Phillips.'

'Susan? What motive would she have for murdering Orlando?' I couldn't imagine the housekeeper being able to hurt anyone. 'Plus, we were with her when Wentworth was assaulted.'

'True, but she said Jenny was the centre of attention all those years ago; perhaps she was jealous?' When he saw the sceptical look on my face, he grimaced. 'I know, I don't believe it either, but she said she and Jenny ran wild through the house with Rupert and Wentworth when they were all kids. They must have known every nook and cranny of this house.' Robbie traced the carved handle of the knife through the plastic. 'I'd like to know whether she knew about this.'

A pounding on the Great Hall door interrupted our musings. Glancing at his watch, Robbie said, 'It's getting on – they're probably waiting dinner on us.'

'How much do you want to say?' I asked as we began walking back to the door. 'Are you going to disclose that we've found the murder weapon and the tunnel?' Rubbing my hands against the cold, I cursed my failure to remember to pop gloves – other than silicon – in my pocket.

'I'm not sure.' Robbie placed the knife inside the pocket of his jacket. 'Let's play it by ear.' Robbie rubbed at his forehead and around to the back of his neck. Finally, he nodded. 'Actually, yes, I think so. I want to see the expressions on people's faces when we mention it.'

Robbie unlocked the door to find Rupert standing outside, his fist raised as if ready to pound on the door one more time.

'Lord Deverell,' said Robbie. 'Do you mind if we have a quick word?'

Chapter Twenty-Two

'Do you want to take a seat?' Robbie asked as we entered the library with Rupert.

'I'm comfortable standing,' said Rupert. 'Unless there's something you think I need to be sitting down to hear?' When Robbie shrugged, he added, 'What's this about? Do I need my lawyer?'

'That's up to you Lord Deverell, although at this stage we're trying to fill in the gaps and I don't think you've been entirely honest with us.' Robbie sat in the armchair, casually crossing one leg over the other.

'Of course I have! What are you getting at, man?' Rupert strode across to the bookshelf, opened a cupboard below it and removed a bottle of whisky and a tumbler. He held it up. 'Would you like one?'

'No, thank you,' said Robbie. He waited for Lord Deverell to pour his drink. 'I got the impression that you recognised the card we showed you earlier.'

He stiffened and turned. 'I told you I'd recognised

the design.'

'Are you sure you haven't seen the card before?' Robbie's eyes held the other man's.

Rupert lowered his gaze to his glass, pursing his lips as if deciding how much to tell us. He downed the whisky in one mouthful, set the glass on the desk with a thud, shoved his hands in his pockets and looked away briefly. 'I received one too.' When he turned back to face us, he was frowning, a mix of worry and fear in his eyes. 'It was left on my desk in the library.'

'When?' Robbie's voice held all his impatience at being told of this now.

'Yesterday. Sometime after breakfast.'

'Is that what the three of you were arguing about before everyone else went for lunch yesterday?' I asked quietly.

His eyes widened. 'How do you—? Yes, it was. Wenty's was in an envelope in his room, and Landy found his in the pocket of his jacket.'

'Does the design mean anything to you?' Robbie asked.

Rupert pursed his lips and shook his head. 'No, other than on the cards I've never seen it before.'

Inhaling deeply, I steeled myself for Rupert's reaction. 'Aside from in the barn, of course.'

His eyes were wary. 'I'm sorry?'

Frowning in mock confusion, I said, 'It's just that I noticed the same marks on the beams in the barn.'

'You've been in the barn?'

Somehow I resisted looking across at Robbie. 'Yes, and I saw these pinwheels in there. Surely you recognise them?' I showed him the photos I'd taken. 'It's a witch's mark – although I imagine you knew that.'

He narrowed his eyes and met mine. 'So it is. I hadn't put the two together. And yes, I knew they were called witch's marks …' He smiled unpleasantly. 'What are you suggesting? That this has something to do with the curse placed on this house generations ago?'

'Not at all.' I kept my voice even. 'Merely to point out that you had, in fact, seen the design before.'

'Well, you've done that.'

Taking a deep breath, I said, 'Aside from being the markings on the barn beams, what is the significance of the design? There is a significance, isn't there?'

'Lord Deverell,' warned Robbie. 'One man has been murdered and another assaulted. I think it's time you were honest with us.'

Rupert turned back to the bookcase, picked up the whisky bottle and set it back down again. 'Yes,' he finally said in a small voice. 'It has a significance.'

Spinning back to face us he squeezed his eyes shut, wrinkled his nose and rubbed at his forehead. 'It's a code we used to use when we were kids when we wanted to meet …' He opened his eyes, his knuckles resting under his chin, the index finger tapping against his lips.

'We?' Robbie's eyebrows shot up.

'When you wanted to meet Jenny Black,' I guessed.

He nodded, his shoulders sagging, all the defensiveness and bluster we'd seen from him slipping away. 'Jenny and I used to meet in the barn.'

'But why would Lord Stark and Mr Fitzroy also receive a card?' Robbie's voice held his puzzlement.

'There was a time …' Rupert screwed his nose again and looked down at his feet. 'That last summer … There was one night … We'd all been drinking and, well, there may have been some weed Landy had been able to get.' He raised his head and grimaced. 'Don't make me spell it out.'

'All three of you?' I couldn't keep the surprise from my voice.

'Just Wenty and me, but Landy was there – he wanted to watch.' His forced smile held a mix of embarrassment and shame. 'Afterwards, well … Jenny got a bit funny about it.'

I tasted the bitterness of bile in the back of my throat. 'You're saying it wasn't consensual?'

'Don't look at me like that,' he said. 'It wasn't rape or anything.' He turned and poured himself another whisky. 'Jenny and I had been seeing each other on and off.'

'Presumably, the "on" was whenever you were home from school, and the "off" was when you were away,' guessed Robbie. While his face held no expression, there was a faint tinge of disgust in his voice.

Rupert nodded. 'It was just a bit of fun between us; Jenny always understood it could never be serious. She knew I couldn't marry the help. Wenty always had a thing about her, and Landy knew about that, so one night after we'd all been drinking … it seemed like a good idea, and she agreed. She seemed really into it; only afterwards she said she felt … used.'

'I wonder why,' I muttered.

'Did it happen again?' Robbie asked.

'Me and her, yes … once or twice … it was never the same, though.' He sounded regretful.

'What about with Lord Stark and Mr Fitzroy?' I asked.

He shook his head. 'No, Wenty may have been all over her, but it was me she was in love with. I don't think she had anything to do with either of them after that night – although I don't think Landy stopped trying.'

I exchanged glances with Robbie at Rupert's conceit. 'Is that why she said yes to the … um … threesome? Because she was in love with you?'

'Probably.' He was staring out the window rather than us, his gaze on a summer evening four decades ago. 'What can I say? We were young and stupid. Anyway, she married John Black a few months after that.' He shrugged as though none of it mattered. My heart ached for poor Jenny Black.

'Who else knew about what had happened between

the four of you?' Robbie stood and leant against the desk.

Rupert raised his eyebrows, surprised by the question. 'No one, I think. We made a pact to keep quiet, and it wasn't in Jenny's interests to make a fuss. Besides, we …' He looked away again.

'You paid her off to stay quiet?' Their lack of consideration towards Jenny had made me feel ill.

'Something like that. Even though it was above board and we were all having fun, it mightn't have looked good if word had got out. People might've taken the wrong end of the stick.'

Somehow I managed not to say anything about how the three of them had acted like entitled prats and instead said, 'You mean if it was deemed she'd been intoxicated and therefore unable to consent?'

Rupert glared at me, but when I refused to drop my stare, he mumbled, 'Something like that.'

'Is that what Lord Stark had on the pair of you? Why you couldn't say no to him?'

'It wasn't like that,' Rupert protested weakly.

'Why did none of this come out during the investigation into Jenny's disappearance?' Robbie asked.

He shrugged lightly. 'No one asked. Besides, I was away when that all happened – someone or another took our statements. Anyway, Jenny was married by then and had a baby.' He turned away to pour himself another whisky.

'Lord Deverell,' began Robbie. 'How did you arrange to meet Jenny?'

Rupert's shoulders relaxed as if knowing he was on safer ground. 'I'd leave a note or a card with the daisy wheel on it and a time.' Cradling his glass, he turned back to face us.

'Where would you leave it?'

Rupert took his time replying to Robbie's question.

'Can I take a guess?' I asked.

A small smile curved on his lips. 'Go ahead.'

'You left messages for each other in the secret compartment in the Grand Hall.'

His eyebrows flew up. 'You know about that?'

'We found the knife that killed Lord Stark in there,' Robbie said calmly.

Rupert's eyes narrowed and flitted between Robbie and me. 'Now, hang on, are you accusing me of killing Landy?'

'Not at all, sir,' drawled Robbie. 'But we do need to know who else knew about that hiding place. Did Mr Fitzroy know about it?'

Rupert nodded. 'He's been coming here for years and knows almost as much about the house as I do.'

'Lord Stark?'

Rupert pursed his lips and finally said, 'I don't think so.'

'What about your wife? Have you told Serena?' I asked.

He shook his head.

'Did anyone else know of this system of messaging you had?' Robbie asked.

Rupert shook his head. 'No. Just the three of us – and Jenny. Our argument yesterday morning was about that, but Landy and Wenty swore they'd never told anyone else.'

'What about Mrs Phillips?' Robbie uncrossed and recrossed his arms. 'Would she have known?'

'About the knife compartment, probably, but about Jenny and me using it for messaging, I doubt it. She and Jenny were friends, but she used to warn Jenny about hanging out with me – and then Wenty and me. Jenny wouldn't have told her – she would've been …' Unable to finish, he shook his head.

An unwelcome thought flitted through my brain. 'Could the cards have been a warning?'

'For what?' asked Rupert warily.

'For what you did to Jenny all those years ago – unless there's something else equally shameful you're not telling us.'

'There was nothing shameful about …' Rupert began to bluster. 'Anyway, that argument doesn't hold – Landy didn't participate, he only watched.'

'And, as you'd told us, was the instigator. From what we've been led to believe, Lord Stark has a history of blackmailing women into bed with him. How sure are you that didn't happen with Jenny?' Robbie crossed the room to the window. The wind had finally died down and outside, all was still.

'It's possible,' Rupert conceded, his eyes wary.

'Is it also possible,' I tentatively began, 'that Jenny Black has returned?'

Rupert's whisky glass hit the carpet, the remnants of its contents spreading darkly across it.

Robbie whirled around at the sound. 'Are you saying you think Jenny is alive?'

'That's impossible.' Rupert's mouth fell open, his head shaking in denial.

'Is it? It's not as if her body was ever found,' I pointed out.

'No, but—' Rupert went to say something and thought better of it. He closed his eyes briefly and when they opened again he'd regained control of himself. Straightening his shoulders, he lifted his nose into the air, his usual imperious expression back in place. 'Is now the point where you ask me politely not to leave the village, Inspector?' Rupert's smile was wry.

'Something like that,' said Robbie. 'You have no alibi for either the murder or the assault.'

'I have no motive for either.' Rupert chuckled mirthlessly. 'If you're basing this case on Jenny Black returning to wreak revenge for what was a harmless albeit regrettable threesome, you must really have no idea about what happened to Landy. How would it go? Jenny has somehow snuck back into the country and is now holed up in this house somewhere?' He lifted his hands and looked around the room. 'No, it's quite impossible.' He bent down to pick up his glass and placed it on a coaster on the desk. 'If that's quite all, Inspector' —he glanced at his watch— 'I'll leave you to it. Dinner should be out by now, so take a break from all of this and get yourselves something to eat – it might make you … think more clearly.'

'One last question,' I said as Rupert turned to leave the room. 'Where are all the outside jackets and boots kept?'

'We have two boot rooms – one for staff at the kitchen entrance and one at the back door for family and guests.' A look of confusion crossed his face, causing him to frown. 'Why do you ask?'

'I'm not sure yet,' I conceded, my glasses dangling from my fingers.

He lifted his eyebrows and left.

'Why did you ask about the jackets?' Robbie asked.

I closed my notebook and slid it and the pen into the back pocket of my jeans. 'It was too cold last night to be in the Great Hall or the barn – let alone that godforsaken tunnel – without a jacket, and there's no way that jacket wouldn't have ended up as dusty as I was.' I paused and gripped his arm, steering him out of the library and in the direction of the boot room. 'There's something else I've been thinking about. Now we know about the tunnel and the access through the barn, the body is no longer secure in the Great Hall.'

He stopped walking and turned to face me. 'You're right.'

Robbie covered his face with his hands, and I felt like doing the same. 'On the bright side, we now know there's a connection between Jenny Black's disappearance and the murder of Orlando Stark,' I pointed out. 'Those cards.'

Robbie shook his head. 'She can't be back. I know we never found her body, but I would've staked my career on her being dead.'

'Maybe she is,' I said quietly. 'Maybe someone wants us to think she's alive.'

'Or they want Deverell and Fitzroy to think she's alive – which means whoever it is knows more about what happened to Jenny Black than they've let on.' Robbie sighed and shook his head. 'Deverell is right, we need food.'

I nodded absently 'What if the murderer knows what happened to Jenny and is now taking revenge on the people they believe responsible?'

Robbie groaned. 'That's all we need – and not just because it means we missed something the first time.' He met my eyes. 'It means whoever it is won't stop until Fitzroy and Deverell die, too.'

The shiver that ran up my spine had nothing to do with the temperature. 'Here we are – check each of these anoraks for dust,' I said, taking the first one off its hook.

'Like this one,' said Robbie, taking an olive-green anorak down. The back and sleeves were covered with the same dust that had covered my clothes when I emerged out of the tunnel. As Robbie placed it over his arm, the inside flew open, displaying an unsightly rusty stain.

'Is that ...?' I whispered.

'Blood? Aye,' he said grimly. 'I rather think it is.'

'Does it have a name on it?' I asked.

Robbie checked the collar and shook his head. 'No. I'll take this upstairs for safekeeping.'

'Before you do, Susan might know...' I suggested.

We took the jacket into the kitchen where Susan had taken a Bakewell tart from the oven and Hattie was pouring custard into jugs.

'I know you're busy,' I began. 'But have either of you seen this jacket before?'

Susan barely needed to look at it. 'Aye, that's Lord Deverell's jacket.'

'Are you sure?' Robbie asked.

'As sure as I can be,' she said, her eyes narrowing.

Before she could say more about it, Robbie smiled tightly and left the room, his grip on my elbow pulling me along with him.

'It doesn't prove anything, Robbie,' I said as I followed him up the stairs, panting as I tried to keep up with him.

'I know, but it's all we've got.' He paused outside my room. 'Philly, did you leave your bedroom door open?'

'No.' Robbie motioned me to wait where I was while he checked the room.

'It's clear,' he said, standing aside for me to walk in. 'But unless you left it like this' —he waved his hand at the jumble of clothes on the floor— 'someone has been looking for something.'

Rushing across to where my suitcase sat I sighed my relief to see the lock had not been tampered with. Twirling the combination, I released the zip toggles and unzipped the case.

Holding up the jumper-wrapped ledger we'd found in the attic, I said, 'I think this is what they were looking for,' and slumped onto the bed clasping it to my chest.

Chapter Twenty-Three

The ringing of my phone in the ensuing silence made me jump.

'Stewart,' I answered wearily.

'I'm just letting you know we've got clearance for a helicopter and there should be a forensic team with you in a couple of hours.' My shoulders sagged in relief. 'What's happening up there?'

'Well,' I began, wondering what information to prioritise, 'we've found the murder weapon …'

'Good work! Where was it?'

'Hidden behind a dado rail in the Great Hall where the body was found. It looks to be one of those knives houses like this kept handy in case canvases needed to be cut from frames in a hurry.'

'How did you know to …? Actually, don't answer that question.' I imagined him shaking his head in that mix of exasperation and wonder at how I could forget to buy milk yet remember trivial tidbits that Stewart used to refer to laughingly as Philly's Useless Book of Knowledge.

'We also know how the killer managed to leave the locked room – a priest-hole in the Great Hall leads you into a tunnel and brings you out in the barn.'

A snort of laughter came down the line. 'Oh, Philly, only you could find that. You've never liked confined spaces, though. Did you send Robbie down?'

I shuddered as a memory of the closeness of the tunnel flitted through my brain. 'No. When it was dug out, people were more my size than Robbie's.' I attempted to push the memory away. 'I coped.'

Silence, and then he asked gently, 'Are you? Coping?'

'I'm fine.' My voice broke, and I blinked feverishly to keep the tears at bay.

Robbie's face filled with concern, and as he would have crossed the floor to comfort me, I shook my head. Pressing the heel of my hand into my eye, I took a deep breath. 'Sorry, Stewart, I'm having a moment.' I brushed away a tear and recovered myself. 'And now it seems someone has searched my bedroom.'

'What for? Evidence you've recovered?'

'No, Robbie hasn't had a chance to lock away the murder weapon yet; it's still in his jacket pocket. I think they were looking for a witch's ledger we found in the attic.'

Stewart was silent for a second; I swore I heard the

cogs in his brain turning. 'What has that got to do with anything?'

'I have no idea. I'm wondering if it could be a connection to Jenny Black.' I shrugged as the possibility occurred to me.

'That cold case? I don't think so, Philly. Is Robbie with you?'

'He is. Do you want me to put you on speaker?'

'Please.'

Placing the ledger back on the bed I walked across to where Robbie sat on the chair I'd contemplated curling up and reading in when we arrived. Was that only yesterday?

'Hello, Sir,' said Robbie.

'You're not on the force anymore, Robbie; Stewart will do just fine. Now, who else knows you found the ledger?'

'Well … no one,' I conceded. 'We haven't had an opportunity to tell anyone.'

'There you go,' Stewart said, a hint of triumph in his voice. 'I think it's more likely whoever searched your room was looking for any evidence you'd found.'

I glanced at Robbie who shrugged. 'I do too.' At my frown he added, 'Only because no one knows we have the ledger. I agree with Philly though – every instinct tells me this is something to do with Jenny Black, but we have no evidence to back that up.'

'Then you need to focus on what you do have,'

Stewart reminded him. 'Do you have anyone at the top of your list yet? Who would know about the tunnel?'

'Only people familiar with the house. Lord Deverell knew but said he hasn't told his wife about it and didn't believe Lord Stark knew about it, so that removes Lucinda and Mallory from the equation. Tara would've been a frequent visitor when she was engaged to Rupert—'

'Tara Beaumont-Brown was involved with Lord Deverell?'

'Yes,' I said. 'Years and years ago. She might know, but I doubt that Piers would. They don't strike me as having the type of relationship where they spend much time actually talking to each other. Plus, the housekeeper told us Piers Beaumont-Brown had only visited a handful of times. I think we can probably exclude him.'

'What about the housekeeper?' asked Stewart.

'Susan? Lord Deverell thought she might be aware of where the knife was hidden, but didn't think she knew about the tunnel.' Robbie flashed a look at me. 'But we'll check with her.'

'She doesn't have a motive for killing Lord Stark,' I said. 'At least not that we've been able to find. She was in the kitchen with her daughter and Ginny and Richard – and us – at the time Wentworth Fitzroy was attacked. There's one more thing. That business card we found with the daisy wheel on it …'

'Yes.' Stewart encouraged me to continue.

'I saw the same symbol in the barn at the end of the tunnel. Rupert said it's where he used to meet Jenny Black and that they'd arrange their meetings by leaving a card with that symbol on it.'

'Philly…' Stewart began.

'We've also found an anorak covered in dirt from the tunnel and something that appears to be a bloodstain.' Robbie must have sensed Stewart was about to warn me away from any links to the cold case and brought the conversation back to this one.

'Who does it belong to?'

'Lord Deverell. The only problem is any of them could have worn it, so we'll wait for forensics to test it,' said Robbie.

'And they'll be there very soon,' said Stewart. 'It will be morning, though, for any road transport.' He paused. 'A few more hours, Philly,' he said. 'Hold on for a few more hours.'

Again, a tear snuck out, and my throat began to close. Damn my weakness.

As if knowing any kindness would bring me undone, Robbie quickly touched my hand, flashed me a smile and stood with his back to me, giving me the space I needed to compose myself.

'We need to get downstairs and get something to eat,' I said.

'Okay Philly. Mind how you go – and ring me at any time tonight if you need to.'

'Thanks,' I managed thickly.

'I'm sorry,' I said to Robbie once I'd hung up. 'For … you know … and, well, thanks for not being nice.'

'For not being nice? I'll take that.' Robbie grinned. 'Don't be too hard on yourself, Philly. It's been a tough day and I couldn't do it without you although,' he mused, 'I wouldn't be here in the first place if it wasn't for you.'

'I think we can safely blame Richard and Ginny for that,' I quipped, grateful he'd lightened the moment.

'Yes, let's blame them. Now' –he unwrapped the ledger and picked it and the anorak up— 'let's get these and the murder weapon locked away in my suitcase with the gin bottle and get ourselves something to eat. I'm starved.'

'Now, that makes a change …'

CHAPTER TWENTY-FOUR

The chatter around the dining table ceased as Robbie and I entered the room. Serena and Rupert both made to stand, but Robbie waved them back to their seats. 'Don't worry about us.'

'Heavens, Philly.' Serena took in my bedraggled appearance. 'What have you been doing?'

Making a show at dusting down my jeans, I said ruefully, 'I'm sorry, I should have changed. I've been crawling about on the floor looking for the murder weapon.' I brushed my hair with my hand. 'And had my head up the chimney as well.' I forced a laugh. 'And now you know why I can never wear white.'

Taking plates from the sideboard, we lifted lids on dishes. Susan had provided a soup of some description – parsnip, perhaps – shepherd's pie and some mixed vegetables. It all looked lovely, but while Robbie piled his plate high with the fare – his appetite appearing to be unaffected by the afternoon we'd had, I'd lost mine.

'You need to eat, Philly.' His tone was hushed. 'I know your brain is tired, and you're overwhelmed, but you need to eat.'

Without saying a word, I nodded and dolloped shepherd's pie and a spoonful of carrots and peas onto my plate, my eyes alighting on spare seats at the end of the table near Ginny and Richard. As I sat beside her, Ginny clasped my arm briefly, her eyes conveying all her unspoken words.

'Have you weeded out the murderer yet, Inspector?' Piers asked, passing a bottle of red wine down the table towards us.

'Not yet.' Robbie poured us each a glass.

'Is there anything you can tell us?' Wentworth seemed to have recovered his normal form but was, I noticed, drinking water and (thankfully) displaying no outward signs of concussion.

Robbie tilted his head as if deliberating over how much to disclose. 'Well,' he began slowly. 'What we can tell you is that Lord Stark was murdered, most probably stabbed and most probably in the ballroom somewhere between midnight and two this morning.'

'You say "most probably",' drawled Piers. 'Surely there can't be any doubt.'

Robbie finished chewing, a wry smile pulling at the corner of his lips. 'It's only a probability until the pathologist confirms it – speaking of which, we're hopeful the forensic team will be here soon to secure the body and the scene and begin gathering physical evidence.' Mallory let out a small sob. 'My apologies, Lady Stark. Perhaps this discussion isn't appropriate …'

'No.' She sniffed. 'It'sh alright.'

'Do you know what he was killed with?' Tara asked. Despite the seriousness of her question, her demeanour was one of casual disregard.

'We do.' As Robbie paused, I glanced at Rupert, whose attention was on the contents of his glass. 'He was killed with a knife that was kept in a secret compartment in the ballroom.'

'A what?' Serena asked, a frown marring her smooth features. 'Hidden where?'

At Robbie's nod, I took up the story. 'It was common in houses like this one. A knife was secreted away in case the staff needed to cut canvases from their frames in the event of a fire.' What was it that was niggling in my brain? Canvases? Frames? Unable to catch hold of the niggle, I continued. 'There was a little compartment hidden behind one of the shorter pieces of dado rail.'

'Well!' exclaimed Serena. 'I've been here for five years and didn't know such a thing existed. You said earlier the room was locked – how did Landy get in and the killer get out?'

'Oooh, a locked room mystery,' Piers said sardonically. 'To complete the cliche, maybe the butler did it.'

No one laughed with him.

'So tell us,' urged Tara. 'How was it done?'

Rupert and Wentworth exchanged glances as if they knew what Robbie's answer would be.

'There's a priest-hole in the ballroom. We believe Lord Stark and his killer entered the Great Hall via the tunnel, and the killer exited by the same means.'

As Robbie made the announcement, I watched each of the party for their reaction. Serena gasped her surprise; Wentworth and Rupert lowered their eyes; Mallory seemed to have tuned out and would, I suspected, need to be put to bed at some point soon; Lucinda and Tara frowned as much as they were able, and Piers sat back in his chair and laughed.

'It runs from behind the fireplace to a tunnel that emerges in the barn,' I added. 'It's narrow in parts but would be accessible by anyone here.'

'*If* they knew of its existence,' said Lucinda. 'Which' —she spread her arms to encompass the rest of the table— 'rules most of us out. Did you know about it, Serena?'

Serena shook her head. 'No.' She glared down the table at her husband. 'I thought I knew everything about this house – other than' —she smiled complicitly at me— 'what's in the attic, of course. Now I'm wondering what else my husband hasn't told me about.'

'I didn't tell you because it's been forty years since I used it,' Rupert said through gritted teeth. 'I haven't even considered it in years. What did you expect me to do? Show you around the house and say "Oh, by the way, darling, we have a priest-hole with a hidden tunnel that would be perfect for murdering someone?"' Rather than raising his voice, Rupert said it with a sneer. 'So you see, Inspector, Wenty obviously hasn't told Lucinda, so that leaves just two people in the house who would know about it – Wenty and me.'

'What about Mrs Phillips?' Robbie lowered his fork to the table. 'Would she know? She said you all used to run about together.'

'I doubt it. I don't even think my parents knew about it,' Rupert said. 'Until Jenny found it, I don't think anyone knew about the tunnel. The only way Susan would know would be if Jenny told her.'

'Jenny Black?' Robbie's ears pricked at the name.

Rupert nodded. 'Yes, she was the one who found it. There was a reference to it in some old book.' Robbie and I glanced at each other. My heart began to beat faster. 'It was our secret.'

'One you presumably shared with Mr Fitzroy,' I said glibly, my stare holding his.

'Quite.' Another undecipherable look was exchanged between the two men.

'Did Lord Stark know about it?' Robbie asked.

Rupert considered the question. 'Maybe.' Another pause. 'Possibly.'

'He used to disappear out to the barn for a secret

cigarette – or whatever it was he did out there – whenever we were here,' said Piers with a meaningful look towards Tara. 'Maybe he was going there for another reason.'

'Why would Jenny Black tell you about it?' asked Serena. 'Isn't she the cleaner who went missing when you were at university?'

'I wouldn't say she went missing,' said Wentworth. 'She ran away with Rupe's brother, and nobody ever heard of her again.'

'That sounds like another mystery for you to solve, Inspector,' said Piers. 'Now, if no one minds, I'd like to take my drink through to the drawing room where it's more comfortable.'

Serena was quick to her feet and back in hostess mode. 'Yes, I think we all should.' She pressed the buzzer for the kitchen.

When Hattie came through to clear the plates away, Serena said, 'We'll have coffee and tea in the drawing room, but there's no need for you or your mother to stay up any later.' She turned to us. 'Robbie, Philly, I think Mallory needs some sleep. Will she be safe upstairs if I stay with her?'

Robbie nodded. 'I don't believe either of you are in danger, so yes, if you're sure you don't mind. As for the rest of you—'

Whatever Robbie was about to say next was drowned out by a loud and rhythmic wop-wop, headlights beaming through the drawing room into the dining room.

Piers was the first to the drawing room window. 'It's a helicopter,' he said needlessly.

My shoulders sagged in relief. 'And the forensic team.' I watched as a group of figures climbed out of the chopper and walked up the drive. Each held bags within which would be their scene-of-crime suits, slippers and other evidentiary tools.

I hurried to open the door before the bell could be rung.

'Philly Barker.' A trim woman in her early sixties stepped through the door. 'And Robbie Dawkins too.'

'It's good to see you, Pen.' I embraced the other woman in a warm hug that contained as much relief as it did affection. Penny Chan had been the primary forensic pathologist attached to the department for years. Back when I was still married to Stewart, there had been many a gathering where we'd be found in a corner drinking wine and gossiping – or on the dance floor dancing like no one was watching.

'You two are making a habit of this,' she said. It had been Pen who had led the forensic team last month when I discovered a body at a nearby farm.

'Trust me,' I said. 'That wasn't the intention.'

'I'm sure it wasn't.' She placed her bags on the floor, unwrapped a scene-of-crime suit, and began pulling it on. 'What have you got for me?'

'The body of a male, early sixties, identified as Lord Orlando Stark,' said Robbie.

Pen tossed him a plastic-wrapped suit. 'Just when you thought you were free of all this … Suit up, Robbie, and lead the way.'

While Robbie assisted Pen and the team, I returned to the drawing room to wait. Serena had taken Mallory upstairs; with Wentworth displaying no adverse symptoms from his earlier whack on the head, Lucinda and Wentworth had, so Ginny told me, followed soon after.

Ginny and Richard waited just long enough for me to return before announcing they, too, were turning in.

'It is safe, isn't it, Philly?' Ginny asked with a too-quick smile that did little to mask her fear.

I lifted a shoulder in answer. 'While there is a murderer in the house, I don't believe you or Richard are their targets. Besides, the forensic team will be here all night, and DI Whitely will be here in the morning. It would be a very brazen person to try anything now.' I forced a smile. 'But lock your door just in case.'

Once they'd left, Tara asked, 'Do you really believe that? That none of us are in danger?' She was lounging on the couch, nursing a balloon glass of cognac, her slim legs tucked under her.

Pouring myself a coffee – it promised to be a long night – from the silver pot on the tea trolley, I shook my head. 'I don't believe Richard and Ginny to be in any danger.'

'But you think we might be,' said Piers, sitting at the opposite end of the couch from his wife.

Sitting in an armchair, I set my coffee cup on a coaster on the Liberty side table. 'I don't know.'

Rupert poked at the fire in the grate and added another log from the basket. 'No, you think *I* might be.' When I hesitated, he added, 'And you think it has to do with what happened to Jenny Black.'

'Why are you so interested in some woman who left here forty years ago?' Piers drained his whisky and stood to pour another.

Before I could answer, Rupert jumped in with his reply. 'Landy, Wenty and I all received a card with a symbol on it that Jenny and I used to use when arranging to meet.' His attention was still on the fire, his back facing us, his tone expressionless.

'You had a thing with her?' Tara unfurled her legs and straightened in her chair. 'Why didn't I know that? Did Serena know?'

He lifted a shoulder dismissively. 'Why would you need to? You and I were together years after that. Besides, Jenny and I were just a bit of fun. It was all ancient history.'

Tara glanced at her husband, whose eyes were on his friend's back. There was an undercurrent here I was missing – and too tired to decipher.

'What *did* happen to the girl?' Piers asked.

Rupert once again prodded the fire and nonchalantly shrugged. 'How would I know? I wasn't here. The accepted wisdom is she ran off with my brother. Who knows what happened to her after that.'

'Did you know she was involved with your brother?' I asked and took a sip of warming coffee.

Rupert turned to face me, still holding the fire poker and shook his head, the movement so slight I almost missed it. 'No.' Placing the poker back on its wrought iron holder, he said, 'You think that because Landy was killed and Wenty attacked, I must be next on the list as I'm the only other one who received a card?'

'Something like that.' That had been exactly what I'd been thinking.

He strode across to the drinks trolley and poured a large measure of whisky, downed it in one gulp and poured another. 'So what am I supposed to do with that? Sit around and wait for the killer to strike again?'

'Of course not.'

He smiled, but it was unpleasant, maybe with a hint of malice lurking behind it. 'What if I'm the murderer, and I planted one of those cards on myself just to distract the investigation and lead you all down memory lane?' The look in his eyes unnerved me. 'After all, I don't have an alibi for either the murder or the assault, and other than Wenty – who I think we can all agree didn't attack himself – I'm the only one who knows about that tunnel.'

'You also knew about the secret compartment where we found the knife.' I bit into the side of my mouth. Without Robbie here, the idea that I could be in a room with the murderer had caused my heart to race.

'Quite.' His eyes narrowed and held mine, a flicker in them telling me he was enjoying playing with me – or was he playing? 'Perhaps that was another red herring? Another piece of misdirection?' I remained silent. 'Then, of course, there's my anorak – yes, I know that's why you asked about that – presumably they'll take that away for testing. Out of interest, what are they expecting to find?'

As he continued to focus his gaze on me, I remained resolute, refusing to waver. 'Dirt from the tunnel and, if we're lucky, blood.'

The gasp in the background came from Tara. 'You can't possibly think it was Rupe?'

Finally, Rupert's eyes dropped from mine, and he swung around towards Tara. 'If not me, who do you think it could be?'

'I … I don't know. But you couldn't kill anyone, Rupe!' She flew to his side and grasped his arm, looking desperately into his face.

'Couldn't I?' He raised his eyebrows, and she shrank back. 'With the right motivation, I think anyone has the potential to be a killer, but you're right, Tara, of course it wasn't me. The evidence might point that way, but unless you actually find my fingerprints on the knife or the gin bottle, it's all circumstantial. Besides, what possible motive would I have to kill Landy? The money he owes me I can afford to lose, and it's not like he's slept with my wife. If that were the case, Piers and Wenty would have more reason to see him out of the picture, but Piers, at least, has an alibi for when Wenty was hit.'

Piers broke the ensuing silence. 'What will they be doing in there?'

'In the ballroom?' Piers nodded. 'Well,' I said, 'Their priority will be towards the body. Pen, the forensic pathologist, will examine the body where it lies. She'll note things like the body temperature and the ambient temperature and take photos of both the body and the pattern of blood pooling. Once that's all done, they'll prepare him for transport—'

'You mean put him in a body bag?' drawled Piers from the lounge. Tara flinched at the callousness of his remark.

I nodded. 'Yes. Pen will probably accompany him back to York in the chopper as soon as she can and leave the rest of the team to gather evidence from the ballroom, tunnel and barn. They'll take the items Robbie and I found for testing.'

'How long will they be here for?' The question came from Rupert, who had taken his customary position by the fire.

'As long as it takes. They should be done tomorrow – another team member will drive up in the morning – when we expect DI Whitely and his sergeant.'

'And in the meantime, I assume those areas are off limits?' Rupert set his whisky glass on the mantlepiece and turned to poke at the fire again.

'They will be – as will be your library.'

'I see.' He turned back to face us. 'Do you think I did it?'

I searched his face for something that could indicate guilt. A twist of the mouth, a flicker of his eyes. Did I believe he was capable of murder? 'I don't know,' I finally admitted. 'As you say, there's circumstantial evidence, but …'

He nodded once and raised his eyebrows. 'Thank you for your honesty – and your open mind.'

It was just past midnight when Robbie returned, his face pale, the bags under his eyes more pronounced. 'They're almost ready to leave with Lord Stark,' he said tiredly. 'I thought you might like to see him off.'

Tara's eyes filled with tears, and Piers stood and shook Robbie's hand. 'Thank you.'

Robbie and I followed the other three out onto the drive and watched as Pen supervised the loading of Lord Stark into the helicopter before climbing in after him. As the helicopter lifted off in a chug-chug of rotor blades, Piers touched his forehead with his finger in a mock salute, and Rupert muttered, 'Safe travels, old cock.'

As the lights faded from view, Rupert, Tara and Piers returned to the house, their arms around each other.

Robbie and I remained standing there in the dark, staring up at the now-clear sky. I'd come outside without my parka, so I hugged myself tightly against the biting cold. Robbie noticed and took his anorak off. 'Here you go.' He held it out for me to shrug into. While it dwarfed me, I snuggled into its warmth, the fabric smelling slightly woody, slightly earthy, slightly spicy – the scent, I realised, of Robbie.

Disconcerted by my sudden awareness of not just Robbie's masculinity but the comfort his practical presence brought me, it took me a second to realise he was pointing to the sky. A wisp of pale, milky, greenish smoke had appeared and was drifting slowly across the sky – like clouds but at the same time completely unlike them. 'Is that …?' I whispered as if any noise might startle them and send them back from whence they came.

'The northern lights? Yes, I think so.' He was whispering too and a stream of goosebumps ran up my arm.

I took my phone from my back pocket and focused the lens on the evanescent tendrils. The colour brightened through the lens, and the lights appeared to dance, swaying in and out and around themselves, twisting here and reaching out there.

Once we got our eye in, we saw them everywhere across the sky. When Robbie draped his arm over my shoulders, I allowed him to pull me closer to his side and nestled my head against his shoulder. The cold forgotten, we stood there in the dark and marvelled at the show, both of us forgetting for that short while the reality that waited for us inside while this miracle of nature performed just for us.

Chapter Twenty-Five

By the time Robbie and I went back inside, the others had, we assumed, gone to their respective bedrooms. Even though I should try to sleep, the effort would be pointless. Too much had happened; I was too wired and too unsettled.

'I'd like to read some of that book we found this morning,' I said as Robbie hung his anorak over the knob on the bannister. 'Rupert said Jenny found out about the tunnel from a book, and I can't help wondering if it was that book.'

'Given the book and the pot were found together, I'd say it's likely they were last accessed together. But' —he frowned and eyed me with concern— 'that can wait until tomorrow. It's been a big day and you should try and get some sleep. I don't mind staying awake and keeping an eye and an ear out … I need to get our notes into order for Chris Whitley.'

I shook my head. 'I can't. I just …' I rubbed at

my eyes. 'Even though I don't think anyone's in danger tonight, I …'

'Just can't?' he finished my sentence with a wry smile. 'I know. I could do with freshening up, though, so how about we do that and then come back to the library and see if we can't find some patterns in this mess?' When I hesitated, he said, 'I know you think the answer to Jenny's puzzle is in the book, but we need to concentrate on the case in front of us first.'

Reluctantly I agreed.

At some point during the night, I must've curled up in the armchair in Rupert's library and fallen asleep for an hour or so. When I woke, my reading glasses still on, it took a few seconds of stretching out the kinks to realise where I was. Robbie was in the other armchair, his reading glasses low on his nose, the crags in his face softened in sleep.

As if sensing my gaze his eyes flicked open. 'Good morning,' he said. Although his trademark half smile was in place, his voice sounded rough and tired.

Blinking a few times, I took in the weak sunlight beyond the curtains, the faint sounds of activity in the hall I assumed belonged to the forensic team. 'Good morning.' Another few blinks and I noticed an open notebook on his lap, a pen on the desk beside him. 'Find anything?'

He shook his head. 'I must have fallen asleep.' The side of his mouth twitched. 'If there's a pattern in all of this I didn't find it.' Glancing at his watch he grimaced. 'Whitely should be here soon.' Straightening in his chair he stretched his shoulders back, his eyes closing briefly once more before gingerly getting to his feet. 'And I want to tidy myself up a bit before he does.'

I uncurled myself from the chair and, groaned as the usual early morning aches were amplified by a few hours spent in an armchair – even if that armchair was a Chippendale.

Robbie extended his hand. 'Susan should be up and about by now, and I don't know about you, but I'm going to need a decent breakfast before dealing with Chris Whitely.'

Placing my hand in his, I allowed him to pull me to my feet.

We'd no sooner finished breakfast when the pealing of the front door had Susan scurrying off in that direction, muttering, 'Hold yer horses … I'm coming.'

Robbie and I exchanged resigned glances and followed, arriving at the door as the two detectives had their warrant cards out to introduce themselves.

'Good morning. I'm Detective Inspector Whitely from York CID, and this is Detective Sergeant Stanley. Aaaah, there you are, Robbie. And Mrs Barker too.' Without acknowledging Susan, he walked in and shook Robbie's hand, ignoring mine. Lewis Stanley sent me an apologetic glance, to which I grinned and lifted a shoulder.

'Now,' Chris was saying, 'what have you been using as your incident room? You'd better fill me in so I can work out what's been happening here.'

'I'm so sorry, Chris,' I interrupted. 'I've neglected to introduce you to Susan Phillips, the housekeeper here at Deverell Grange.' As he glared at me for calling out his rudeness – or was it because I used his Christian name? – I said sweetly, 'Mrs Phillips, would you be able to bring something restorative to Lord Deverell's library?'

Susan caught on quickly and, with a twinkle in her eye, said, 'Of course, Mrs Barker. Would the inspector be wanting coffee or tea?'

'Coffee, please,' Chris said grudgingly.

'I'd love a brew, thanks, Mrs Phillips,' said Lewis. 'If it's not too much trouble.'

'Not at all.' She patted his arm. 'You must've been on the road early, so I don't suppose I could tempt you with a bacon butty before you get to work?' As Lewis grinned, Chris opened his mouth to protest, but Susan got in first. 'After all, I'm sure Robbie and Philly have plenty to update you with.'

'Thank you, Mrs Phillips.' Resignation filled Chris' voice. 'If you could bring it through to Lord Deverell's library.'

As the two detectives ate their breakfast, Robbie updated them on the investigation.

Chris settled himself behind Lord Deverell's desk.

'This is nice.' He ran his hands across the leather top. 'The murder – who do you think did it?'

'While several of them have motives, we have no firm evidence pointing to anyone at this stage,' Robbie said evenly. 'Perhaps fingerprints might come back on the murder weapon, the bottle that was used to assault Mr Fitzroy and Lord Stark's phone, but I doubt it. The dirt on Lord Deverell's anorak will probably come back as a match for the tunnel, and the stain inside the jacket will be his blood, but everyone in the house had access to that, and I can't understand how it's only on the inside of the jacket. It's almost like it was deliberately placed there.'

Ignoring Robbie's last comment, Chris said, 'So what you're telling me is that Lord Deverell did it?' Chris groaned and ran his hand over his face. 'The super won't be happy about that – they're friends, apparently – although you might know about that Mrs Barker … or' —he smiled unpleasantly— 'I'm probably asking the wrong Mrs Barker.' His laughter was met with silence.

'Stewart does know him socially,' I said through gritted teeth. 'But if the evidence points that way, he won't interfere. I think, though—'

'We'd better get everyone in and take their statements,' he said to Lewis.

'We've already taken statements, Chris,' Robbie said, the tightness of his smile the only indication of his exasperation. 'Although when we spoke to Lady Stark she was intoxicated so you might want to question her again – while she's still sober.'

Chris raised his eyebrows. 'Like that is it?'

Robbie nodded grimly. 'Perhaps you'd like to be introduced to Lord Deverell first – given it's his house we're in.'

'Also,' I said, 'I don't think you can overlook the connection to Jenny Black's disappearance. Those cards with the daisy wheel clearly connect the murder and the assault with what happened to Jenny.'

Straightening in his chair, Chris rested his elbows on the desk, steepling his fingers under his chin. 'I already told Robbie this has nothing to do with a forty-year-old cold case, which, as I understand it, turned out not to be a case at all. No, Mrs Barker, I can already see there's only one person who had means, motive and opportunity – and that's Lord Deverell. Besides Mr Fitzroy and the housekeeper – he's the only one who knows about the knife in the hall, and he and Mr Fitzroy are the only ones who are aware of the secret passage to the barn. There's blood and dirt from that tunnel on his anorak. It has to be him.'

'What's his motive?' I asked.

Again Chris raised his eyebrows – this time, I suspected, in surprise at my temerity in questioning his judgement. 'It's always about money or sex, and I think you'll find this was about both. Lord Stark had borrowed heavily from Lord Deverell, and he'd had a sexual relationship with his wife.' He used his fingers to tick off the reasons.

'While we know Lord Stark slept with Lucinda and Tara, there's no evidence to suggest he also slept with Serena – and Lord Deverell said he didn't,' Robbie pointed out. 'I think you're taking a leap with that one.'

'Have you asked her?'

'Well, no,' I conceded. 'But … Rupert said …'

Chris held up his hand and flashed a patronising smile. 'You've had your fun, Mrs Barker, and thank you for helping us out, but I suggest you now leave the policing to the professionals.'

'But …' My hands balled at my side as he dismissed me.

'That will be all, Mrs Barker. We'll need Robbie, but you can find something else to do while we wrap this up. And arrange for some more coffee to be brought in, will you?' He added the last comment with a half smirk designed to put me in my place.

'What's the magic word?' As I held my ground, Robbie's lips twitched with growing amusement.

Eyes narrowed, he waited for me to drop mine. 'Sorry?'

'Is that sorry you don't understand the question, or sorry you seem to have forgotten your manners?'

Behind me, Lewis coughed, breaking the silence.

'You, Mrs Barker, are forgetting your place,' Chris

finally said.

'And what place is that?' I was being overly rude, but something about this man and his blatant disrespect for me made my blood boil. My tiredness was in danger of taking control of my temper.

Chris' eyes strayed to Robbie, who responded with a nonchalant shrug.

'Your place, Mrs Barker' —he stood and leant over the desk menacingly, a sneer in his voice— 'is as a witness – and a meddlesome one at that. Now do as you're asked and leave us to it. Oh, and mine is black with two sugars.'

'Only two? I would've thought you'd need far more than that …' I smiled tightly at his pomposity. 'In any case, if you want coffee, get your own.'

Refusing to let him see my anger, I forced a nod and swiftly turned to leave the room. Lewis' ears had tinged pink, and he couldn't meet my eyes. Robbie, however, saw me to the door. 'Don't let him get to you,' he whispered. Swallowing hard, I held my chin up and shut the library door behind me.

After taking their statements and acknowledging that their alibis were as watertight as Robbie had told him they were, DI Whitely (reluctantly) agreed to allow Ginny, Richard and Hattie to leave.

'The rest of you can stay put – I'll speak to you all again.' He tapped at his notebook as he said it.

'I don't understand why I can't go home,' wailed Mallory. 'It was my husband who died, and I have a funeral to prepare.' Her resentful glare was directed at Robbie, me, the DI, and his sergeant. 'You can't honestly believe any of us killed him. It's not fair for those other people to get to go home.'

'Don't worry, Lady Stark,' Chris said condescendingly. 'It will be some time before your husband's body is released for burial. You'll have plenty of time to arrange the funeral.' Chris' attention turned to Rupert. 'Lord Deverell, I'd like to speak to you now, if I may?'

After watching her husband leave the room, a concerned frown on her face, Serena placed an arm around the still-protesting Mallory and led her back to the sofa. 'There, there,' she soothed. 'I'll ring for Mrs Phillips to make you a nice cup of tea.'

'I don't want tea!'

Serena's eyes strayed to the clock on the mantelpiece and sighed. 'Perhaps something stronger? Now, you stay here with Lucinda while Philly and I say goodbye to Richard and Ginny.'

In the hall, Ginny and Richard were pulling on coats, bags at their feet.

'Are you leaving too?' Ginny asked me, slinging her handbag over her shoulder.

'No, not yet.' I grimaced. 'I'm sorry, Serena, but it seems you'll be saddled with Robbie and me for a little while longer.'

'Stay as long as you need. Do some more rummaging.' Serena smiled kindly. 'How's it going in there – with Inspector Whitely?'

'He's keeping his cards close.'

'I see.' Serena's narrowed eyes told me she'd read between the lines. 'I imagine he's quite … difficult?'

'That's certainly one description you could use. In any case, it seems I'm now surplus to requirements.'

Serena took my arm and patted it. 'I'm sure that's not the case.' Releasing me, she kissed Richard and Ginny goodbye. 'It's been lovely meeting you, Ginny; I'm just sorry about how the weekend turned out. I'm also sorry about Rupert's ghastly friends – but that's just between us.' Her smile was wry. 'Mallory's glass is probably empty by now, so I'd better go back inside.' She added as an aside to me, 'We'll be in the drawing room once you've let off some steam.'

Once we were alone, Ginny asked, 'Is the inspector being horrible?'

'That's one way of putting it.' Suddenly tired, I pressed the heel of my hand to my forehead, removing it when I saw the concern in her eyes.

'Did you get any sleep last night, Philly? You look exhausted.'

'Not much,' I admitted. 'Now that DI Whitely is here, I might try and sneak a nap this afternoon. He's certainly made it clear that I'm not welcome in the library.'

'See that you do,' she chided gently. 'Do you think you'll be home tomorrow?'

'Oh, I hope so,' I said with feeling. 'I'll need to ring Bell and let her know what's going on and check she's okay to have Bally a little longer …'

Ginny stepped forward to hug me. 'Don't you worry about that. I'll let Bell know what's going on. You know Bally will be safe with her.'

Swallowing a lump in my throat at her concern, and missing the waggy comfort of my pooch, I smiled my appreciation. 'I know Bally will be fine. Don't you go worrying about me. Now, you two drive carefully, and hopefully, I'll see you sometime tomorrow.'

I watched until I could no longer see them on the drive and stood there a little longer, breathing in the crisp air, the bleating of sheep floating across the moors. While the wind was still icy, the sky was clear and blue. Aside from some patchy snow where the sun hadn't reached, there were few signs of the storm that had wreaked such havoc.

Besides braving the elements to check on generators and search for blunt objects, I'd been locked inside all weekend; it was no wonder I wasn't thinking clearly and had allowed Chris Whitely to get under my skin. A walk would do me a world of good – and delay my return to the drawing room to make small talk with people who resented my presence. I zipped my parka, pulled up the hood and set off up the drive, hoping some alone time and exercise would help make sense of the jumble in my brain.

Chris Whitely was wrong in concentrating his efforts on Rupert as the chief suspect in the murder of Orlando Stark and the assault on Wentworth Fitzroy, I was sure of it. But if not him, who else?

Motive, means, opportunity. Aside from Rupert, who had all three?

With the exception of Serena, each of the others had their reasons for wanting to see Orlando Stark dead.

Mallory had the most obvious motive for her husband's murder. Everyone agreed her title, and the position in society that gave her, meant everything to her. If she'd known her husband had been cheating on her with two women who had been laughing at her behind her back, she might have been capable of murder. She professed not to know about Orlando's intention to divorce her or his precarious financial position, but while the others agreed she was probably in the dark, we only had her word for it. As for the means and opportunity? Her unfamiliarity with the house dismissed the means, and her over-familiarity with the gin bottle dispensed with the opportunity. Although the use of the gin bottle in Wentworth's assault pointed us in her direction, she and Piers Beaumont-Brown were each other's alibis for that attack. No, Mallory couldn't have done it.

Without checking the Beaumont-Brown finances, we had no way of verifying whether the amounts Piers had given Lord Stark really were as meaningless as he had made out. There was that hint that Orlando had something on Piers, but Piers hadn't let on what that something could be and if I were to take a guess, I'd say it had something to do with Tara and Piers not being keen on having news of her affair leaking out. That was, however, hardly motive for murder.

As for Tara, sure, she might have been jealous of Lucinda and had never explained where she was when Wentworth was attacked, but neither Robbie nor I seriously considered her a suspect. Further, we were satisfied neither she nor her husband knew about the priest's hole or the knife in the ballroom. Plus, Piers hadn't received the same card the other men had – and regardless of DI Whitely's opinion to the contrary, I remained certain that card – and its meaning in relation to Jenny Black – was important.

Wentworth and Lucinda were a different story. Wentworth knew his way around the Grange and was aware of both the knife in the ballroom and the tunnel through to the barn. He'd also lent money to Orlando, and while he appeared to be financially flush, Piers Beaumont-Brown was worth substantially more. Again, though, we only had Piers' word for that. More importantly, he wasn't as sanguine as Piers had been when we asked him about Orlando's relationship with

Lucinda. While he didn't say as much, his body language told a different story. He might have laughed it off, but Wentworth Fitzroy was not at all happy about his wife's fling with Orlando – and would've been less happy if he'd known of the element of coercion involved. Would that be sufficient inducement to murder? Possibly. Then there was whatever Orlando had on Wentworth – I'd love to know what secret of Wentworth's Orlando had been protecting. A secret that would've presumably died with its keeper. Yes, Wentworth Fitzroy had both the motive and the means. Even if he killed Orlando, who had attempted to kill him?

Lucinda's dislike of Orlando had been palpable – and for good reason – and her fear of her husband discovering an infidelity she thought had been hidden had seemed real to us. She, however, was unfamiliar with the house and its secrets, so while she had motive, she had neither means nor opportunity. Or did she? The Fitzroys had unwittingly provided alibis for each other at the time of Orlando's murder. If they'd both been involved, they could've rehearsed that alibi until it appeared natural.

How, though, to explain the assault on Wentworth? Lucinda's distress in that regard had been convincing. There was, however, something niggling at the back of my brain about that – something that didn't quite seem right.

While Rupert, Piers and Wentworth had all

attempted to convince us they'd lent Orlando money out of the goodness of their hearts to help him through a tight spot, and all three had said they weren't concerned about its repayment, it had felt to Robbie and me more like blackmail. Orlando knew something about each of them they needed to keep hidden. But what secret would be worth killing for?

We were also satisfied that, despite Chris Whitely's suspicions, Orlando hadn't slept with Serena. Knowing what we did about the dead man, if Orlando had slept with Serena, he would've ensured her husband and his friends knew about it.

As for Rupert? There was no denying Rupert had the means, and the dirt on his jacket indicated it had been worn in that tunnel recently and we were certain the stain would turn out to be Orlando's blood. As for opportunity? With no alibi for the murder or the assault, Rupert also had that. As much as I hated to admit DI Whitely could be right, Rupert was the most obvious suspect. Even so, something about it didn't feel right.

I couldn't shake the feeling that the answer was in those cards and the disappearance of Jenny Black. All my spidey senses knew it. I reached the end of the drive and turned back towards the house. While I wasn't needed in the library, and probably wouldn't be welcomed in the drawing room, Susan would be up for a natter – and she probably knew Jenny Black better than anyone.

Chapter Twenty-Six

After retracing my steps along the drive, I skirted the house, approaching from the rear through the courtyard. The blue and white police tape barring the barn door flickered and snapped in the breeze.

The estate manager's cottage still lay quiet and empty, but as I passed the narrow stone-built structure of the housekeeper's cottage, a knocking came from the window, and Susan beckoned me towards the entrance.

'Come in out of the cold, Philly,' she called.

As I stamped my boots on the mat, I made my way through the back door and found myself in a cosy room containing a large oak dresser, a round oak dining table, and a small fitted kitchen with an electric hob and under-bench oven. Through an open door, I spied a small sitting room and assumed the cottage's bedrooms were off that.

'You'd be wanting a brew? The kettle's just boiled.' Susan poured water into a teapot and removed two cups and saucers from the dresser without waiting for my answer. 'It's right parky out there. Where are you off to?'

'I've been for a walk. Needed some fresh air and exercise.' I removed my parka, unwound the scarf from my neck and hung both over the back of one of the oak chairs. 'But I was on my way to find you.'

'Oh, aye? Cake?'

'No thanks, Susan.' I took a seat in the chair she gestured to and waited for her to do the same. Eyeing the ball of wool and knitting needles peeking out of a bag beside the table, I said, 'I'm not interrupting you, am I?'

'Heavens no. I can knit and natter at the same time.' She chuckled. 'It's a talent. Now, what was it you were looking for me for?'

'I wondered if you'd tell me about Jenny – Jenny Black. What was she like?' I nodded my thanks as Susan poured tea into my cup.

A glint came into Susan's eyes; her mouth curved into a smile that held mischief and memories. 'She was a grand girl,' she said, sipping her tea. 'Our mothers were pregnant together, so Jenny and I were always going to be friends. And when Jenny's mam died' — she shook her head sadly— 'Jenny spent most of her time with us. Her poor father didn't cope – well, you wouldn't, would you? Jenny was just a girl – not much older than her bairn was when she went missing. I've got a photo of her here somewhere.'

She pushed her chair back, the legs scraping on the worn timber floor, and crossed to the old oak dresser, bending to open the cupboard door below the shelves.

'What happened to Jenny's mother?'

Susan paused and straightened. 'Childbirth. They were unable to save her or the bairn. You don't think that can happen in this day and age, do you?' She turned back to the cupboard, reaching inside with a little grunt of effort. 'Jenny's mother was a healer, you know – as was her mother and her mother and …' With her back still to me, Susan waved her hand to indicate how long the line went back. 'Ah, here it is.' She stood and returned to the table with a sizeable, worn, cardboard-covered book. 'They say it was her great-great-great-grandmother who killed the old viscount. Mary Flounders, her name was.'

A ripple of excitement ran across my chest. 'The witch Lord Deverell was talking about? The one he said cursed the house and its firstborn sons.' I replayed the conversation from that first night. 'Lord Deverell didn't mention she'd had children.'

Susan chuckled and placed the album on the table in front of me. 'He wouldn't, but Mary had a bairn alright – a girl.'

'How do you know that?'

'Jenny found an old book in the attic' — goosebumps ran up my arm— 'along with some pot

she thought had been Mary's. Right ugly it was, too —
the pot, that is.'

Attempting not to appear too excited, I reached
behind me for my jacket, pulled my glasses from the
pocket, put them on and opened the album – careful
not to allow the photos with their worn adhesive to
drop out. 'Did she tell you anything about the book she
found?'

'Aye. She was proper excited about it. Said it was
a ledger of everyone Mary had treated and a diary of
sorts, too.' She leant forward conspiratorially. 'Jenny
said she'd read enough to be convinced that the old
viscount had got Mary in the family way – if you know
what I mean.' I nodded. 'They all used to get up to
things like that in those days – thought the servants
were their property.'

'Mary was a servant, wasn't she?'

'Aye, a maid.' She smiled wryly. 'Jenny also said
she thought that even though Mary had dispensed the
poison that killed the viscount, she didn't give it to him
herself.'

I lifted my gaze from the album and met Susan's.
'Really?'

'Aye. It was the viscountess who had requested the
potion.' She raised her eyebrows. 'Jenny thought it was
probably her who had done for the viscount and then
blamed Jenny's great-great-grandmother – or whatever
number of greats she was' —she lifted a shoulder to

indicate the number of greats didn't matter— 'for the murder. Jenny said she thought it was for revenge. The viscount had his way with the maid, and the maid had a child from it, and rather than blame her husband, the viscountess blamed the maid.'

If Jenny found the pot with the book, Mary must have been arrested before she had a chance to hide it. 'If it's true, it's a sad story.'

'Aye, it is. After Jenny found the book, she became obsessed with the story and her family history. She kept saying the book was her birthright and spent her free time tracking her family history through church records and the like. It's understandable, really. The poor lass didn't know her own mam.' Susan pointed at a photo of two teenage girls sitting outside on a blanket, Deverell Grange rising behind them. 'That's Jenny there.' She indicated a slight girl wearing a striped T-shirt and shorts, her pale hair secured in two bunches with a plastic 'bobble'. 'And that's me. We must've been seventeen or so.' Susan traced the image with her finger, a pensive smile on her face. 'She was always scribbling in that diary of hers. I asked her once what she wrote in it, and she told me she was writing her family's story and that one day, everyone would know the truth about what the Deverells had done to her family and what sort of people they were.'

My head jerked up. 'A diary? Did the police find that?'

Susan wrinkled her nose. 'I couldn't say, but even if they had, it wouldn't have told them what happened to her.'

'I suppose you're right.' Unless what happened to Jenny had roots in what had happened to her ancestor. I turned the page. 'How old was Rupert in this photo?'

Susan pushed her reading glasses back onto the bridge of her nose and leant forward. 'That's not Rupert.' She chuckled. 'It's his brother, Teddy. They were very alike, though – they could've passed for twins.' She flipped the page. 'Here's one of Rupert. They may have looked alike, but in every other way, they were very different.'

'What do you mean?' On impulse, I snapped a picture of the two photos.

'Teddy was a good, kind, earnest boy who worked hard at school and university.' Her chuckle held warm memories. 'I have no doubt he got up to the same sort of shenanigans as any boy his age did, but he was never cruel and would've made a caring landowner. Rupert, though' —she shook her head— 'he was the apple of his mother's eye and spoilt with it. Thought the whole world and everything in it was his for the taking.' She grimaced as if tasting the bitterness in her tone. 'He could be so much fun, though – and that's what Jenny saw.'

'What do you think happened to Edward? Do you think Jenny ran off with him?'

Susan relaxed into her chair, removed her glasses and let them dangle from the chain around her neck. Tilting her head back, she closed her eyes briefly and rubbed her forehead. 'I don't know. I wouldn't have thought he had anything to do with Jenny's disappearance, but I know she didn't intend to go away with him when she met him that day.'

There it was – the hairs on the back of my neck stood to attention. 'She met Edward that day?' Again, I had to force myself to keep the excitement out of my voice.

'I can't say for sure it was Teddy she was meeting,' she said after a brief pause. 'But I know she was meeting somebody. She'd become quite excited by a card on the mail tray that morning and had asked me if I could watch the bairn for her. "If you can just watch Lucy for an hour or so, Suse," she'd said, "I'd be ever so grateful."' My pulse quickened. 'I never saw her again.' Susan stood and walked over to the sink, staring through the window into the gravelled courtyard across to the barn.

'The baby's name was Lucy?'

She shook her head. 'Nay, she was born Jennifer Lucy, but Jenny insisted John got it the wrong way round when he registered the birth. She said she always wanted to call her bairn after her mother, so that's what she did.'

'What do you think happened to Edward?' I asked gently. 'Do you think he's still alive?'

She shook her head, her shoulders hanging. 'No.' Her voice was so low I had to strain to hear it. 'I think he regretted what happened, and that's why he left. I think he …' She turned back to me. 'I think he probably couldn't live with himself afterwards.'

'You think Edward killed her?'

She shrugged and dabbed at the corner of her eyes. 'It would've been an accident, but why else would he leave the way he did?' She frowned. 'The way she acted that morning, though, I would've thought it was Rupert she was meeting – but he was in Oxford.'

Those little neck hairs were waving for attention. 'Did Jenny continue seeing Rupert after she was married?'

'I shouldn't speak ill …' Susan shut the album and replaced it in the cupboard.

'Nothing you say can hurt her now,' I said. 'But it might just help find who killed her.'

As she straightened, she almost overbalanced, using a chair to steady herself. 'You don't think it was Teddy?' The relief in her voice told me that while Jenny had been in love with Rupert, Susan had almost certainly had a crush on his older brother.

I shook my head. 'No, I don't. But I don't have any evidence for my suspicions yet, so what you have to say could really help.'

After giving it some thought, she finally nodded. 'If I can help. Would you like another brew?'

Although the last thing I needed was yet another cup of tea, I understood she needed to do something. 'Thank you, yes.'

Chapter Twenty-Seven

Robbie walked past the window as Susan was at the sink filling up the kettle. Susan waved at him and pointed towards the door. 'Come on in.' He held up a hand in acknowledgement. 'He seems to have a talent for knowing when there's a brew on offer,' she said dryly.

'He does. And he's always hungry too.' I chuckled.

'I'll cut some of this lemon cake, then. At least it won't be going to waste.' As Robbie walked in, she said, 'I was just getting us a brew.'

Robbie closed the door and sat beside me, stretching his legs under the table. 'I've timed my visit perfectly, then.'

'Susan was just about to walk me through what happened the day Jenny disappeared.' My eyes held his in a silent plea for him to allow me to go with this, telling him I'd explain later. He nodded his understanding. 'She'd mentioned that Jenny had arranged to meet someone that afternoon and had asked her to mind baby Lucy while she did.' Robbie raised his eyebrows at my slight emphasis on the baby's name but didn't comment. 'She also mentioned Jenny had a diary.'

'Did she?' He tilted his head to the side and frowned. 'We didn't find one when we searched the house.'

'Aye, that's right. Although' —Susan laughed— 'if she wrote *everything* in it, I daresay she would have had to hide it from John.' While the tea brewed, Susan cut an iced lemon cake and sat the slices on a vintage Meakin sandwich tray. 'Now help yourselves.'

Once Susan was satisfied that we all had tea and cake, she closed her eyes for a beat—as if taking herself back to that day forty years ago—took a deep breath, and began to speak.

'Memory's a funny thing,' she began. 'Sometimes I can't recall what I've come to the fridge for, but here it is, forty years ago, and I can picture that day clear as a bell. It was a Saturday in October, one of those days you get before the winter comes on proper-like – clear, blue, not much of a wind. John Black and the old viscount had gone to Skipton on estate business, and the viscountess was down in London. The viscount had said Edward wouldn't be in for dinner that night – he often went away on weekends – and as it would be just him, he was happy to settle for some cold cuts, so there wasn't much for Mam and me to be getting on with. My father had passed by then, you see, so it was just me and my mother in this place.' She waved her hand to indicate where we sat.

'Did you see Edward at all that day?' I murmured,

hoping my question didn't interrupt her chain of thoughts.

'No. I thought I heard him once, but' —she shrugged— 'maybe I didn't. Anyway, I was sitting right here doing some knitting – I was making a jumper for my Fred even though Mam had always said you never make a jumper for a man before you marry him or you'll never be married – when Jenny came in. Swept in, she did.' Susan warmed to her story. 'She was like that – like if you'd left the door open and the leaves swept in or the sun swept in.

'It must have been about ten in the morning, I'd say. She had Lucy in her arms and an excited look about her – it was how she always used to be if she was meeting Rupert. She'd carried on with that, you see – even after she'd married John. I'd warned her, but she'd always laughed it off and said, "Don't you be worrying about that, Suse. It's just a bit of fun!" But I knew it wasn't – not for her. She was in love with him – always had been – but the only thing he was in love with was himself.' She paused, took a sip of her tea and met my eyes.

'You're probably wondering why she married John. Well, I don't know this for sure, but I think she had to, if you know what I mean. John had been mad for Jenny for ages, but she'd never noticed him. Then, all of a sudden, they're getting married. He was as proud as punch on their wedding day – prouder even than when he won Supreme Tup at the Nidderdale

Show. His smile didn't even slip when Lucy was born so soon after they wed, even though he must have had his suspicions.' She shook her head sadly. 'He doted on that bairn.'

'Did the police suspect him of being involved in Jenny's disappearance?' I asked, glancing at Robbie.

'Aye, but I don't think they ever believed it. He didn't get home until around three that afternoon. It was he who raised the alarm, too. I'd been so consumed with what I was doing I hadn't realised Jenny hadn't come back for Lucy, so when he came over to see if I'd seen her, I was taken aback. Lucy, God love her, had slept the afternoon away, so I didn't notice the time until she woke up wanting something to eat. I suppose that must've been around four, and John came over soon after that.'

'Did you tell him where she'd gone?' Robbie asked, reaching for a second slice of cake.

'How could I when I didn't know myself? I told him she'd had to duck out for a few hours, and I hadn't seen her since. Then he asked me if I'd seen Rupert, and I told him I hadn't and thought he was away in Oxford. It wasn't really a lie – I hadn't seen him and he was in Oxford. Anyhow, it seemed to relax him, and he took Lucy home. When Jenny still hadn't turned up that evening, we went out to look for her – me, John and the viscount. We called the police the next morning, but they never found hide nor hair of her.

No one had seen her or heard anything. It was like she'd disappeared into thin air.'

'Did you think she'd met Rupert?' Robbie asked.

Susan nodded. 'I did – on account of her excitement, and there was also the card.'

'You mentioned the card before Robbie came in,' I said. 'How did you know it was from Rupert?'

'Because that's how they used to arrange to meet. Rupert would leave a card with a drawing of a daisy wheel on the back. It's the symbol that's in the wood in the barn, you see.'

'And that's where they used to meet,' I guessed.

'Aye. But it couldn't have been Rupert she met.'

'How do you know?' Robbie asked.

'Because when I called his rooms that night to see if she was there, Lord Stark picked up. He said Rupert was out at a party and hadn't left Oxford that day, so it couldn't have been him she was meeting.'

'When did people suspect she might have left with Edward?' I asked.

'Not until Thursday. The viscount was expecting him back, but he didn't show up. None of his friends had seen him, and the viscountess was called home.'

'What about Rupert? Had Rupert seen him?' While I didn't risk a sideways glance at Robbie, from the frustration I felt seeping from him, none of this had come out in the investigation.

'No, but he said Edward had phoned him from

the airport on Monday and told him he had to leave for a while.'

'It was after that the investigation found he'd purchased two tickets to Spain,' added Robbie. 'And Edward's car was in the long-stay parking at Heathrow.'

'That was also when they searched Jenny's house properly and found a suitcase and some clothes missing,' said Susan.

'No one had done that before?' This time, I did glance at Robbie, who shrugged.

'We were looking for anything with blood on it – or a weapon. We'd asked John if anything was missing, and he'd said there wasn't. She'd been wearing her good coat when she went out.'

'I see.' I tapped at my cup with my fingernail. 'Susan, you said earlier you thought Edward must've accidentally killed her and then ran to Spain where, unable to live with what he'd done, he killed himself.' She nodded. 'How do you explain the missing suitcase and clothes?'

'I think he ran in there before he left. John was away; I was occupied with the bairn, and he could've been in and out in minutes. Her make-up was still on her dressing table. Jenny wouldn't have left without her make-up.'

'I assume the police didn't ask you about this?' I asked.

'No,' Susan said ruefully. 'Nobody spoke to me

after that first day. And before you asked why I didn't volunteer it, well, by then, I thought Edward had done it.'

'And you didn't want people to think that too,' guessed Robbie.

'Aye.' Susan's cheeks tinged pink, and she lowered her eyes. 'Would it have made a difference?'

Robbie sighed and shook his head. 'I don't think so. We hadn't been able to find any evidence of her being killed, so …' He held his palms up.

'Did you think she'd been killed?' Susan asked.

'Aye.' Robbie nodded sombrely. 'Aye, I did.'

Chapter Twenty-Eight

'What's this about a diary?' Robbie asked as we walked back towards the house. 'I remember asking her husband about the existence of a diary, and he said she didn't have one. We searched the house thoroughly, but …'

'You wouldn't have been looking for one.'

'No,' Robbie conceded.

'Maybe John didn't know she kept one,' I said.

'Or maybe he'd found it and knew it held evidence of her continued meetings with Rupert,' said Robbie. 'No man wants the evidence of his wife's infidelity bandied about, especially if he doesn't think it has any bearing on the case.'

'But it might have pointed towards her killer,' I argued.

Robbie shoved his hands deep into his pockets and paused. 'Sure, Philly, it might have, but remember, as far as John was concerned, the evidence all pointed to his wife having run off with Edward Deverell. That's hard enough to bear without the world knowing she was involved with Rupert Deverell long after they were married and had a threesome with Rupert and Wentworth Fitzroy. John must have wondered whether his daughter was actually his.' He shook his head. 'No, Philly, if John Black had found his wife's diary, my money would be on him hiding it away and hoping it never saw the light of day again.'

'Speaking of books intended to remain hidden, Susan told me that Jenny had found the pot and the ledger in the attic. To summarise, the old viscount – Rupert's great-great-great-grandfather – had his way with Mary against her will, and she had a baby. As she was unmarried et cetera, et cetera, et cetera, the housekeeper who had been unable to have children with her husband took the child, a girl, to bring up as theirs. The viscountess knew about her husband's misdeeds, but this time, he was a little too taken with young Mary, so she decided to get rid of him and the girl in one fell swoop.' I told him how the viscountess had acquired the poison that killed her husband and framed Mary for the murder. 'Afterwards, Jenny became obsessed with tracking down her family tree and wrote all about it in her diary. She told Susan that one day she would see that her ancestor was avenged and that the world knew what the Deverells had done to her.'

Robbie looked sceptical. 'Two or three hundred years down the track, is anyone going to be interested?'

'Possibly not, but what if ...' I paused to organise my thoughts. 'What if John and Jenny's daughter found her mother's diary and inside wasn't just a story about how her ancestor was treated so many years ago, but also told in some detail how the current Lord Deverell treated Jenny – and how he passed Jenny across to his friends to use as well? You'd want revenge for that, wouldn't you? Not just on Lord Deverell but his friends too.'

When Robbie frowned, I continued. 'Think about it … You've been told your mother disappeared when you were a baby and ran away with the son of the lord of the manor, and you've been brought up by your father – who you probably adore. You aspire to get to know these people, turn yourself into one of them, and even marry into the circle.'

'You think baby Lucy grew up to be Lucinda and married Wentworth Fitzroy?'

'Why not? She's the right age. She told us she hadn't been brought up as a toff. What if, when her father passed away, she found her mother's diary hidden in his things? She read it, and everything she thought she knew was overturned.'

'But murder?' He scratched at the back of his head. 'That's a bit extreme.'

'To you and I, perhaps, but there's a symmetry to it. She kills one of them, a man who she told us had blackmailed her into having sex with him, the same man who stood back and watched while her mother was humiliated in a similar way, and manages to frame

Rupert for it. After all, she believes Rupert used her mother, and his brother was the one who had taken her mother away from her. Rupert deserves to be punished. Plus, Rupert's ancestor had falsely accused her great-great-great grandmother of murder, leading to her execution. How apt would it be if Lucinda could avenge her mother and her great-great-great grandmother simultaneously by setting up Rupert on a murder charge?' Another thought occurred to me. 'Now imagine you're not even sure whether your father is *really* your father.'

His face paled; he'd arrived at the same distasteful thought I had. 'You don't think …'

I shrugged. 'If John Black isn't her father, Rupert is the more likely candidate, but Wentworth had slept with Jenny too …' I wrapped my arms around myself against the cold creeping through my veins. 'How would you feel if you were worried you'd accidentally married your father?'

'Christ. What a mess.' Robbie covered his face with his hands. When he emerged from behind them, he said, 'How would she know about the priest-hole and the tunnel?'

'Jenny's diaries, of course. And what better way to lure Orlando there than by promising him sex?'

'From what we know of Orlando, he'd get off on having a clandestine meeting in Rupert's house with Wentworth asleep upstairs.' He frowned suddenly. 'But

Wentworth and Lucinda were each other's alibis. How do you explain that?'

For a second or two, I worried we would be back at square one, but then the final piece slid into place. 'That was the clever part. What better way to make sure of your alibi than to wake your husband? Rather than nudging Wentworth to stop snoring, she deliberately woke him as she got *back into* bed. It's why he could be so natural about it when he told us.'

'It makes sense,' said Robbie slowly, scratching his head. 'I don't know how we prove it, but it makes sense. And you think she assaulted Wentworth, too? Do you think she meant to kill him?'

'I do. I also think she left that ladder there at some time during the morning before Orlando's body was discovered so it would be assumed that's how the assailant got away. I then think she tossed the gin bottle out the window. Do you remember how it was opened slightly as if it had been lowered and sprung back up?'

He let out a short chuckle. 'I can't say I noticed. And the cards?'

'Aaah,' I said with the satisfied grin of a woman who thinks she knows all the answers. 'That's what gave her away. She wanted to lark about with them a bit first.'

'She certainly has done that.' Then, a wide grin spread across his face. 'Whitely has arrested the wrong person.'

'For the murder of Orlando Stark, yes, but …'

'Philly? What else is there?'

'I think Rupert Deverell killed both Jenny Black and Edward Deverell.'

CHAPTER TWENTY-NINE

'Where is everyone?' I wondered aloud, opening the door to the empty drawing room.

The house held an unnatural empty feeling, almost as if anything that had existed in it had left.

The clatter of bags being thumped down the stairs shattered the silence. Piers and Tara Beaumont-Brown.

'There you are,' said Tara. 'We wondered what had happened to you.'

'If you're looking for anyone else,' said Piers, 'Rupert is still being questioned by that inspector, and his sidekick has called Serena in.'

'Wentworth and Lucinda?' I asked.

'Upstairs, I believe,' said Tara.

'Tara and I are allowed to leave, but he still has questions for Wenty.' Piers rolled his eyes. 'He seems determined to pin this on Rupe.'

'We're getting out of here before he changes his mind.' Tara swung her scarf around her neck.

With a slight lifting of her fingers to signify a goodbye, the pair were gone.

'I don't know about you, Philly, but I need a drink.' Robbie led me into the drawing room and poured whisky into two glasses.

I sank into the couch with relief, luxuriating in the way it supported my aching back. 'God, I'm tired.' Taking a sip, I closed my eyes as the amber fluid did its job and warmed my chest from the inside. The second sip, reaching to soothe the exhausted edges of my brain. Groaning, I straightened in my chair. 'I know I only just got comfortable, but I'd like to see the ledger and confirm what Susan has told us. Please tell me forensics haven't taken it away.'

Robbie tilted his head back and sighed. 'I handed over all the other evidence, but Pen said she wasn't interested in that.' He eyed the whisky bottle on the trolley. 'I know it's cheeky, but …'

'Somehow I don't think Lord Deverell will miss the bottle,' I said with a grin.

'Besides, I suspect he'll be otherwise occupied with Whitely for a while yet.' Robbie picked up the bottle, a small smile playing around his lips as he waited for me to coax my body out of the comfort of the lounge and back into a standing position.

Robbie's room had the same layout as mine, but while mine was chintz and plaid, his was decorated with more masculine occupants in mind. The plaid used on the upholstery on the armchair and duvet cover was stronger in tone than that in my room, with accents of navy, burgundy and forest green.

While I hadn't been in Robbie's house, I would have expected it to be neat – the way he'd left this room. His suitcase was sitting on the window seat, yesterday's clothes folded neatly beside it.

Waving his hand for me to sit in the armchair (Serena had continued her dog-themed cushions with a border collie), Robbie fiddled with the lock on his suitcase and lifted out the ledger, still wrapped in my jumper. He handed it to me and sat on the edge of his bed as I carefully unwrapped it, a thrill running through me at the possibility I was about to read something that had been written by a young woman who had no idea she hadn't long to live.

'For something that old, it's in good condition,' commented Robbie as I carefully turned the brittle pages. Even though the first measure had gone straight to my head, I nodded when he held up the decanter of whisky.

'It is, but the ink has faded and it's very difficult to read.' I reached into my pocket for my loupe and pushed my glasses to the top of my head. 'This is better,' I said, placing the glass lens to my eye.

Robbie poured us each a fresh whisky, placing mine on a coaster on the side table, and waited by the window as I skimmed through the pages.

'I think this is it,' I said, the excitement in my voice bringing Robbie quickly to my side, his hand lightly resting on my shoulder as he leant over to read. 'I'll need to study it closely for the whole story, but while I can't make out all the language, it seems to be as Susan told us.' As my fingertip ran lightly down the page I fancied I felt the hum of emotions from hundreds of years ago. 'What I can understand is she was afraid she was going to be arrested so created a charm to protect her.'

Robbie looked down at me. 'Do you think that's the pot?'

'I do. I think she intended to hide the pot in the tunnel – presumably the daisy wheel was put there years ago to mark the entrance – and she intended to give this ledger to the housekeeper for safekeeping until her daughter was old enough to learn the healing arts.' Replacing the loupe with my glasses I gingerly flipped through the pages. 'There are more entries after that so the book must have been passed down the female line as Mary had intended.'

'Aye,' said Robbie, reading over my shoulder. There's an entry from the eighteen hundreds.'

Nodding my agreement, I said, 'Jenny's grandmother or great-grandmother, I expect. It seems to have stopped there.'

'Until Jenny found it.'

'Her birthright. I can only imagine how she felt when she read about what had happened to Mary – the injustice of it.' Closing the book, I looked up at Robbie. 'What she found in here' —I tapped the cover— 'is what led to her death.

Robbie stepped away from me and towards the window. Taking a sip of whisky, he gazed out over the courtyard that only a day ago had been covered in snow. 'I think you're right.' He spoke slowly as if thinking out loud. 'But what makes you think Rupert killed her?'

I rewrapped the book, set it on the side table and picked up my whisky. 'Remember when we asked him about the card and wondered whether Jenny was back? He said it was impossible. At the time, I thought he was panicked that maybe she had come back, but now I realise the only person who would know for sure it was impossible would be the person who'd killed her. That panic was the fear that someone else knew she was dead.' Another sip and more parts of the puzzle slotted into place. 'I think it was him who met her that day – Susan said she only ever had that level of excitement for Rupert – and I think the alibi Orlando gave him is what he had over Rupert. That and the threesome, of course.'

'If you're right, he would've had plenty of time to duck back to the house, grab a suitcase and throw some clothes into it.'

'And the body?' I wondered.

'They probably disposed of it down one of the old mine shafts.' He drained his glass and placed it on the bedside table.

'They?'

Robbie nodded, now on the same track as me. 'Yes, they. I wouldn't be surprised if Wentworth Fitzroy wasn't an accessory after the fact.' He paced the floor as he spoke. 'What if Jenny reached out to Rupert because of … the baby, perhaps? Or something else she knew that would give her leverage against him? Maybe she threatened the family honour with the information in that book.'

In my brain, a puzzle-shaped piece jostled for position – what wasn't I seeing?

'She gets a message to him telling him they need to meet. Maybe she wants money for the baby or money to run away and start a new life. They meet and she's killed.' He paused, a thoughtful expression on his face. 'But none of that explains Edward and the reasons he left. Maybe Susan is right, and Edward killed Jenny and subsequently fled.'

I pondered that briefly before shaking my head. 'No, I think it's more likely that Edward never left here either. Yes … that would make sense … He came across Rupert and Jenny – maybe after Rupert had killed Jenny – and Rupert had no choice but to kill his brother, too. Wentworth had to be with him – one of them drove Edward's car to Heathrow, and the other drove back to Oxford. What if …' I thought aloud. 'What if it was Edward who Rupert had come up here to meet and he took the opportunity to see Jenny as well? What if Edward had found out about Rupert and Jenny's baby – assuming the baby is Rupert's, of course – or what if Rupert had done something more serious?'

Robbie paused. 'What could be more serious than a baby?'

I tapped at my lower lip. 'What is it these families are interested in?'

'That's easy.' He counted the reasons on his fingers. 'Family honour – or the integrity of the family name – is always at the top of the list. Then there's money – these old families are always looking for ways to bolster the coffers, make sure they can fix the roof or the electrics … that sort of thing. There's the title itself and ensuring the estate is passed intact to the next generation. In these old families, the responsibility for all that falls onto the oldest son; the spare is left to fend for themselves.' Robbie pulled a chair out from the writing desk and sat down. 'The parentage of Jenny's baby wouldn't, in this day and age, bring the family honour into disrepute, but any funny business regarding the estate – or Rupert, himself – Edward might want to nip in the bud before it reached the ear of the viscount or, worse, the tabloids.'

That puzzle piece in my head waved at me. What was it I wasn't seeing?

'Okay,' Robbie said slowly. 'If we accept that Edward was also killed here – accidentally or otherwise – who used that ticket to Spain?'

'Rupert, of course.'

Robbie shook his head. 'No, Philly. We visited the travel agent and showed them a photo of Edward. They were able to confirm it was he who bought the tickets, and his credit card records corroborate that. We also established that Edward used his passport to exit the country, and there was no record of anyone using that passport to return to Britain. I'm sorry, but that theory won't hold up.'

I took another sip of whisky and tilted my head back, gazing at the intricate plasterwork on the ceiling, working through the potential scenarios. Bringing my attention back to Robbie, I said, 'What if Rupert bought that ticket using Edward's credit card, left the country using Edward's passport, and then flew back to England using his own passport?'

'I don't know …' Robbie frowned.

'Was Edward's credit card used again? After buying the tickets, that is, I'm assuming you checked.'

Robbie's eyes narrowed as he consulted the case file in his mind. 'Aye, we checked. It was used twice: to rent a car in Barcelona – which was returned to Valencia the following day – and to pay for a hotel room and room service meal in Valencia.'

'Did you check Rupert's credit card?'

He shook his head. 'There was no reason to. And before you ask, there was no reason to check if Rupert's passport had been used either. But Philly, my point remains – the travel agent positively identified Edward from the photo we showed him.'

I pulled my phone from my back pocket, opened the photos I'd snapped from Susan's album and walked across to where Robbie sat. His eyes widened as he examined the image. 'Did you show the travel agent a photo of this man, or' —I selected the next photo— 'was it this man?'

Robbie took the phone and used his fingers to zoom in on the images. 'Are these both Edward?'

I shook my head, the beginnings of a smile curling around my lips. 'No, one is of Edward and the other Rupert. I can't recall which was which, but Susan said they were so alike that plenty of people thought they were twins. They're certainly alike enough that a travel agent would make a positive identification and alike enough to get through passport control as well. I bet that if we looked, we'd find that Rupert Deverell travelled back to England from Valencia on Wednesday using a ticket purchased on a credit card registered to Wentworth Fitzroy – I don't think he'd be stupid enough to use his own – caught the train back to Oxford and then told his family that Edward had flown out of the country. In the meantime, his friends covered his absence.'

Still flicking back between the two images, Robbie said, 'Are you now saying you think Orlando knew Rupert had killed Jenny and Edward?'

I shook my head. 'No, I don't think Orlando knew about that, and I don't think he knew Rupert had gone to Spain, but he did know Rupert had lied about his whereabouts on the weekend his ex-girlfriend went missing – and that's what Orlando had on him.'

Robbie handed the phone back with a resigned sigh. 'All of this is circumstantial and gives Rupert a primary motive for killing Lord Stark and attempting to kill Wentworth – it's one way of ensuring the secret never comes out.'

I collapsed back into the armchair and drained the last of my whisky. Robbie was right. Every way we looked at this, Rupert had the most compelling reason to commit murder.

'Maybe I'm wrong about Lucinda.' I rubbed at my eyes and sighed heavily, my limbs feeling heavy and tired. 'It's so far-fetched that Whitely would laugh at me if I tried to talk him through it.'

'I don't know, Philly. It makes a sort of convoluted sense – and sometimes the most unlikely scenario is the right one. Even so, we should take our suspicions about Rupert to Whitely. If he's unable to extricate a confession from him, he may want some other sort of leverage. In the meantime, we can at least prove that Lucinda is who you suspect she is – birth and marriage records will show that.' A twinkle came into his eyes. 'Perhaps we can use her great-great-great-great-grandmother's book to draw her out. Using the information in that would allow her to complete her revenge on the Deverell family – possibly one she can't pass up.' Robbie stood and stretched. 'Alright, there's no time like the present.' When I sighed and drooped in an exaggerated way, he said, 'Come on, Philly, the sooner we see Whitely, the sooner we know what we've got to follow up on ourselves.

Chapter Thirty

Serena and Lucinda met us as we came down the stairs.

'There you both are.' Serena grasped my hands in hers. 'The detective still has Rupert in for questioning; I'm certain he will charge him. I don't suppose you could talk to him …'

'It's only circumstantial evidence,' said Lucinda, rubbing Serena's back. 'He can't charge Rupert unless there's physical proof.'

'But what if they find that?' wailed the usually poised Serena. 'He can't have killed Landy! Do you think he's the murderer?'

Realising the question was directed at me, I said, 'No, I don't.'

Lucinda raised her neat brows, yet she remained silent.

'You must talk to that detective, then!'

I shook my head. 'I don't think he'll listen to me. We didn't exactly get off to the best start when we met.'

A single tear ran down Serena's face. 'But we'll try.' I squeezed her hands and extricated mine.

'Thank you.' Pressing at her eyes with the back of her hand, she forced a bright smile. 'Have you two eaten? There's soup and sandwiches in the dining room if you're hungry.'

I suppressed a grin at the way she'd moved back into hostess mode so quickly. 'Thank you. Now that I've stopped to think about it, I'm quite hungry.'

'And I'm always hungry,' added Robbie.

The two women accompanied us into the dining room, but while Robbie and I ladled soup into bowls (today's was a creamy potato and leek) and loaded side plates with sandwich triangles, they opted for coffee.

'I meant to ask Philly,' said Serena, stirring sugar into her cup. 'Did you find anything interesting in the attic yesterday?'

'We did. There are a few paintings and some quite saleable pieces of furniture.' Robbie was at the sideboard pouring tea into two cups. 'We found a couple of things that were quite exciting though …'

'Oh good! Tell me more!'

'When I say exciting, it's more interesting than valuable – although there is a market for items like these …' I nodded my thanks when Robbie handed me a cup of tea and sat beside me.

'Now I really am intrigued.' She leant forward, her forearms on the table.

'Well, this is the exciting part. We found what's known as a witch's pot, and we believe Mary Flounders used it – the woman accused of murdering Rupert's great-great-great-grandfather.'

Lucinda's head snapped up.

'A witch's pot – what exactly is that?' Serena wrinkled her nose in distaste.

'Essentially, it's a bottle – this one was pottery. Mostly, these were used either to break a curse you believed had been put on you or to protect you against harm. In this case, we believe it to be the latter.'

'You mean you think this Mary Flounders made it to protect herself against …?' Lucinda leant in, her eyes wide with interest.

'Yes, in this case, she most probably wanted to protect herself against being arrested,' said Robbie. 'It's an ugly thing, but there you go.'

'But if she poisoned her employer, surely she didn't think a bit of pot was going to save her,' said Serena.

'That's the thing. We also found an old book belonging to Mary. It's part ledger, part journal, and Mary used it to record what she'd dispensed and to whom. She also used it as a diary.'

'Did you read it?' asked Lucinda.

'Enough to know that while Mary dispensed the poison, it was the viscountess who gave it to her husband.'

'So this Mary was innocent?' Serena frowned

slightly, her elbow on the table, her cheek resting against the back of her hand.

'It certainly appears that way. By this time, they'd repealed the witch laws, so she couldn't be tried as a witch in any case. But if what she wrote was correct, she was innocent of the murder she was hanged for.'

Serena's hand flew to her chest. 'Oh, that's so sad.'

'Where's this book now? Lucinda stood and walked across to the sideboard to pour more coffee. 'I'd love to see it.' She held the coffee pot up to Serena who shook her head.

Taking a deep breath I risked a sideways glance at Robbie. As if knowing the direction of my thoughts he inclined his head. 'We left the pot where we found it in the attic, but the book is still in the library. When we talk to the inspector, I'll try and retrieve it. It's a few hundred years old so can't have a bearing on the case' —I forced a laugh— 'so I can't see he'll have a problem with that.'

Robbie's eyes went to the clock on the sideboard, and he wiped the corners of his mouth with a cloth serviette. 'Speaking of which, Philly, we probably should do just that.'

Draining the last of my tea, I stood. 'We had.' I gave Serena a reassuring smile. 'I know it's easier said than done, but try not to worry.'

'Thank you, Philly.'

As we left, Lucinda reached for Serena's hand and gripped it tightly.

•

Chris shook his head. 'You expect me to believe that this crime was perpetrated by somebody as revenge for something that happened forty years ago? No. It's a ridiculous idea. Where's your evidence, Mrs Barker?' Without allowing me to answer, he continued. 'Exactly. You have none. This is nothing but a fanciful story you've concocted. Next thing you'll be telling me that this missing woman didn't really run off with Edward Deverell and has been in a shallow grave ever since.' He held up a finger, a smirk on his face. 'No, I'll go one better. You'll be telling me that Edward Deverell didn't bugger off to Spain and has been lying in the same shallow grave for forty years.'

'That's close to what I think *has* happened,' I said indignantly, my hands on my hips.

'Robbie, what do you have to say about this?' Chris asked with a sneer in his voice.

'I think Philly's right,' he said. 'I think Jenny Black's daughter murdered Lord Stark and assaulted Wentworth Fitzroy, and I think we should consider the theory that Rupert Deverell murdered Jenny Black and his brother and – probably with the assistance of Wentworth Fitzroy – disposed of the bodies and made it appear they'd run away together.'

'You're as mad as she is!' Chris threw his hands in the air. 'Sergeant, what do you think?'

Lewis tilted his head to the side, his lips pursed. 'I think it's worth considering, sir.'

Chris contemplated us both for a few seconds. 'What will you do if I tell you not to investigate this far-fetched theory any further?' I lowered my eyes. 'Just as I thought – you'll go behind my back to your ex-husband or one of the other contacts Robbie still has on the force.' My cheeks burned. 'Here's what's going to happen. You two can make whatever calls you want to make to confirm – or discount – this theory of yours, and Sergeant Stanley and I will continue with the real police work.' His stern face took in the pair of us, and I had to stop myself from shuffling my feet as if I were waiting outside the headmaster's office. 'The only thing I ask is that you bring any evidence you find to me – and not your ex-husband.'

'Agreed,' I said quickly, not wanting to give him the time to change his mind.

'In return,' Chris said slowly, 'I don't suppose you can talk to that housekeeper and rustle us up some sandwiches or something?' Before I could answer, he added, 'Please.'

Chapter Thirty-One

After grabbing some Post-it notes from Rupert's desk, Robbie and I set up our personal incident room in my bedroom.

'We can use the window as a murder board,' Robbie decided. 'I don't think we can prove Lucinda is our murderer, but what we can do is prove she's Jenny Black's daughter. That, at least, gives us a starting point.'

'Okay. Do you know anyone who can access those records? Because while we're at it, we should probably also check the date John Black died.'

'True. We also need to check if there was any record of Rupert's travel back from Spain during the week following Jenny Black's disappearance and if there was any activity on his credit card. We won't have the authority to check Wentworth Fitzroy's, but we might get lucky.' He grinned. 'I'll make the calls.'

As Robbie pulled out his phone and called his colleagues, I began making notes of the other questions we needed to verify.

Why would Rupert want to kill Jenny Black?

A) It was an accident

B) She was blackmailing him over the baby's birth.

C) She'd discovered he was up to something dodgy.

D) She'd threatened to expose the misdeeds of his ancestor.

Why would Rupert want to kill his brother?

A) It was an accident.

B) Edward came across him as he was attempting to dispose of Jenny's body.

C) Edward discovered he was up to something dodgy.

But what could be dodgy enough for it to be worth killing for? Again, the niggling thought ducked out from behind my brain and waved at me. I sat on my bed and replayed what I'd been doing each time the same thought had come to mind. Frames. Canvases. Closing my eyes, I visualised the ballroom again and imagined walking its length, examining the pictures that lined the walls. All those dead relatives and dead animals. What was I missing?

Robbie was off the phone, his eyes full of concern when I opened mine. 'What are you thinking?'

'I need to see the Stubbs again,' I said. 'I think it's important.'

'As a painting or for the case?'

'The case. I can't get past the question I had when I first saw it – why would you lock a painting like that away?'

'Because you don't want it to be stolen?' Robbie suggested. 'It's definitely got more security locked away in the ballroom than if it were on display in one of the more public rooms.'

'True. But I think it's more that they don't want it to be seen.'

Chris had raised his eyebrows and sighed in resignation when we interrupted his questioning of Rupert to ask for the keys to the ballroom. 'You shouldn't need them – the forensic team is still there.'

As Chris had said, although the entrance to the ballroom was protected by police tape, the doors were unlocked. Inside, there were signs of police presence, the dusting of powder on the wooden rails and benches, the dark stain in the floor where the body of Orlando Stark had lain for almost twenty-four hours. The door to the priest-hole was open and portable lights set up to illuminate the tunnel.

Robbie greeted one of the officers who was scraping blood stains from the timber, but I ignored it all and made directly for the Stubbs. This time, I stood and absorbed it, allowing the painting to weave its magic on me, but again, the prickling sensation I felt was not the usual excitement I'd expect when looking at a painting as beautiful as this. I wasn't sure whether it was in the line of the horse or its musculature – and it would need to be confirmed by an expert – but my every instinct told me this painting was a fake.

Serena and Lucinda were still in the drawing room, but a subdued Wentworth had now joined them too.

'How are you feeling?' I asked him.

'Like I've been clouted with a gin bottle,' he said dryly. 'I'll live.'

'Is Rupert still in with DI Whitely?' Robbie joined me in the doorway.

'Yes,' said Lucinda. 'I know you said to try not to worry, but they've been questioning him for hours. And the sergeant said they want to see Wenty now.' She sighed, all the worry she'd been trying to hide in that one exhalation. 'What are you two up to?'

'I have one question,' I said. 'Possibly not related to anything else …'

'At the moment.' Serena laughed. 'That's the very best sort of question! What do you need to know?'

'The Stubbs …'

'The horse picture in the ballroom? Astonishing, isn't it?'

'It certainly is – and it seems such a shame it's hidden away where no one can see it.' Wentworth had straightened in his chair. Good, that meant I was on the right track. 'Has it always been in the ballroom?'

Serena frowned. 'Yes, well, it's been there for as long as I've been here. Is it important?'

'It could be,' I said.

'Wenty,' Serena began. 'I can't very well ask Rupe at the moment, but can you remember if the Stubbs has always been locked away in the ballroom?'

Wentworth squinted and wrinkled his nose as he tried to remember. 'I can't say as I've paid much attention to the painting, but I can't see why it would be moved and don't recall it being anywhere else.' He chuckled, a forced high-pitched laugh. 'Maybe one of Rupe's ancestors didn't think it was as astonishing as you do.' The way Lucinda frowned at him, I guessed he'd probably just lied to me.

'Perhaps.' I laughed with him. 'You're probably right. Well, don't let us keep you … oh, and good luck with DI Whitely. As long as you tell the truth, he'll go easy on you.'

Once we were out of earshot, Robbie let out a chuckle. 'He'll go easy on you as long as you tell the truth? Even for you, that's a step too far.'

'You two seem more chipper this afternoon.' Susan was wheeling through a tea trolley.

'Actually, I'm glad we caught you,' I said. 'I've been wanting to ask you about the Stubbs – the horse painting in the ballroom … Has it always hung there?'

'Heavens no!' said Susan. 'The old earl used to

say it was the favourite part of his collection and he wanted to show it off. The story is he stayed here, you know, back in the late seventeen hundreds. Stubbs, that is. Commissioned, he was, to paint that horse. Edward loved it too. It was only after his father died that Lord Deverell moved it out of the drawing room and into the ballroom. I always thought it must have reminded him too much of his father. Such a shame, but there you have it.'

As she continued on her way, Robbie turned to me. 'You think the Stubbs is a fake?'

I nodded. 'I do. It's the only explanation for why I don't get the feeling I get when I look at other great pictures. I couldn't explain it, but when I set eyes on the Stubbs, the back of my neck didn't prickle the way it usually does. It's an excellent copy, but a copy it is.'

Robbie laughed. 'Somehow, I don't think you should be telling Whitely that.'

'Possibly not. Anyway, I don't know what's wrong with the painting, but I suspect it was switched. Rupert pocketed the coin, which is why, as soon as he could, he moved it into the ballroom where there'd be fewer chances of anyone who knows about these things suspecting there was anything wrong with it. I also think either Edward or Jenny – or possibly both – found out about it.'

'However it was done, Wentworth Fitzroy knows about it too – I was watching him when you asked

Serena. Everyone has said Lord Stark could procure what you needed – perhaps an artist to copy that painting was what Lord Deverell needed from him.'

'If that's the case, it's no wonder Rupert continued to pay for his silence,' I said. 'If we get confirmation that Rupert travelled back from Spain, we've got him.'

Chapter Thirty-Two

Robbie's phone rang. 'Thanks for getting back to me … Right, I see. He died when? No, that's not what I expected … Really? That's great. Yes, thanks for that … I know, some retirement, right? … My regards to the wife and kids … I owe you a pint.'

'Good news?' I asked.

'Some of each. We've got confirmation that Rupert travelled back into the country that week, so that's certainly enough for Whitely to put pressure on him and prompt a full investigation. Lucinda isn't our murderer, though. Her maiden name was Grant, and her mother passed away from breast cancer when she was in her teens.'

I slumped against the stone wall in disappointment. 'I was so sure it was her.'

'I know you were.' He reached out a hand and gripped my shoulder. 'Nor is it Mallory.'

My heart beat faster. 'I'm sensing a but …'

He cast his eyes around the hall to ensure we were alone and lowered his voice. 'To make sure we'd covered all bases, I also requested a check on Serena.'

'And?'

'There's no record of Serena's birth. My colleague wants to know if she'd been known by another name.'

Robbie's voice was becoming a whirr of white noise. Serena? Surely not. 'Philly?'

'Um, I heard you, but …'

'I know it's not what you expected, but we need to think.' He gripped my shoulders. 'Right, what was it Ginny told us? That Serena had lost both her parents in a car accident and was brought up by her aunt?' I nodded. 'John Black committed suicide two years after Jenny disappeared, so if we find the aunt, we can trace the daughter.' He looked into my eyes, willing me to get my thoughts together. 'Philly?'

'She has no alibi, and we didn't even consider her.'

'I know, but we need to consider her now.'

'She hinted she sleeps away from Rupert because of hot flushes – perimenopause – but she's only forty-one.' It was such a plausible explanation, but it hadn't occurred to me that it could've been a lie. 'I thought she was older – even though she looks younger. But Richard said she looked up to him as a big brother …' I was rambling, but it was the only way I could get my thoughts together. Serena? 'I'll phone Richard.'

Robbie released my shoulders and grinned his

approval. 'That's my Philly.'

His approval filled me with a warmth I didn't want to think about. I dug my phone out of my pocket and dialled Ginny.

'Philly, this is a surprise. Is everything okay there?'

'It's coming along, Ginny. Hey, is Richard with you?'

'Yes.' She sounded confused. 'Did you need to talk to him?'

'Please.'

There was some muffled muttering, and then Richard was on the line. 'Philly, Ginny said you needed to speak with me?'

'Yes … Please don't ask why I need to know this, but can you remember the name of Serena's aunt?'

'Her aunt?' He sounded puzzled.

'Yes. Ginny mentioned how her parents had died when she was young and she was brought up by her aunt.'

'Yes, that's right … I'd have to check with my parents. I know she died recently – maybe three months ago. Mum was saying Serena came back to clean the house out. I suppose you need the information in a hurry?'

'Please. Thanks, Richard.'

I turned to Robbie. 'Serena's aunt died a few months ago, and Serena came back to clean the house out.'

'That could be when she found Jenny's diary,' Robbie guessed.

'You really think she's Lucy Black?'

'Aye. And I think what she read in that diary made her snap.' He frowned and added, 'I'd like to bet that's when she stopped sharing a bed with her husband – and the reason has nothing to do with hot flushes.'

As we stood in the hall outside the ballroom digesting this possibility, Lewis came haring around the corner. 'There you are! The DI needs to see you urgently. Forensics found traces of blood inside the cuff as well as the inside lining of Rupert's anorak. It's a match for Orlando Stark, but as you pointed out, anyone could've accessed that.'

'Where's Rupert now?' Robbie asked as we walked with Lewis to the library.

'We weren't getting anywhere, so the DI has allowed him to go back into the drawing room.'

'What have you got for me?' Chris pounced on us as soon as we entered the library.

'Enough for you to question Lord Deverell about the disappearance of Jenny Black,' said Robbie.

Chris rolled his eyes. 'Not that again. This had better be good!'

'Oh, it is.' Robbie's face lit up with a wide grin. 'We've had confirmation that Rupert flew out of Valencia to London on the Wednesday following Jenny Black's disappearance, but there's no record of him leaving the country, although a one-way ticket was purchased in Valencia using Rupert's credit card.'

'What's the significance of Valencia?'

'A car was hired in the name of Edward Deverell at Barcelona airport on Monday and left at Valencia on Wednesday.'

The beginnings of a smile played around Chris' mouth. 'And Mr Fitzroy?'

'We believe he was involved as an accessory – at the very least, he gave a false statement regarding Lord Deverell's whereabouts that weekend.' Robbie paused briefly. 'It's enough to question them both.'

'And motive? Do we have a motive?'

'Aye. There's a very important painting owned by the estate which has been switched out for a fake – I'd say Edward found out about it.'

'Do you have proof?' This time, Chris looked at me.

'I'm almost positive, but an expert will confirm it and I suspect so will Lord Deverell's financial records.'

'And Orlando Stark?'

'I was wrong about that,' I conceded. Before Chris could say 'I told you so', I added, 'It wasn't Lucinda … We're waiting on confirmation that Serena Deverell was originally Lucy Black, the daughter of Jenny Black, and that her aunt changed her name when she adopted her.' Biting my bottom lip, I contemplated the massive favour I was about to ask. 'I know this is unusual, and highly irregular, but before you talk to Rupert and Wentworth about Jenny, could I try something?'

'What?' Chris' eyes narrowed.

'I think Serena has read Jenny's diary and knows what Wentworth, Orlando and her husband did to Jenny – how they humiliated her. She would've also read about how the Deverells falsely accused her ancestor of murder. I don't think she intended to kill her husband but rather set him up for murder. She used his anorak in the tunnel, she made sure he didn't have an alibi, and if she's read the diary, she knows about the compartment and the tunnel and has had time to test them both. If she thinks she's failed, that we're looking elsewhere for Orlando's murderer, she might show her hand. She'll also want to get her hands on her ancestor's book. Other than her mother's diary, it's the only physical record of the tunnel, and without it there's no link to what happened to Mary Flounders.'

Chris pursed his lips as he contemplated my proposal. 'You're right, it is completely irregular,' he said. 'But as you say, we have no evidence. How sure are you she is this Jenny Black's daughter?'

'I'll have that confirmation very …' My phone rang. It was Richard. 'I'm sorry, I have to take this.'

'Philly…' He sounded worried. 'I've got the information you needed, but I don't understand it.'

'That's okay, Richard. We probably will.'

'Okay, well, her surname was Grace, but my mother said soon after they arrived, there was one time when little Serena told my mother that her name was really Lucy Black, but she wasn't supposed to tell anyone because now she was Serena which was so much nicer than Lucy. My mother said she always assumed her aunt changed Serena's name when she adopted her.'

'Thank you, Richard.'

'Philly … please tell me this isn't about what I think it is.'

I paused for half a beat. 'I'm sorry, Richard, I'll explain when I can.'

'It's her,' I said to the waiting room. 'Serena Deverell is Jenny Black's daughter. And Chris …'

'What now?' he barked.

'There's the possibility that Serena could be Lord Deverell's daughter – or possibly Wentworth's. I think that's what made her flip.'

Chris put his hands over his face and groaned. 'This just gets better.'

Chapter Thirty-Three

Monday 4 pm

It was a subdued quintet gathered in the drawing room when Robbie and I walked in. 'This had better work, Philly,' Chris had muttered before we left the library. We'd moved onto Christian names, so maybe things were looking up – or at the very least, he was beginning to accept me … even if it was much like one accepts an annoying insect.

'You two look exhausted!' Serena stood to greet us.

I nodded wearily and waved her back to the lounge she was sharing with Mallory. 'I feel as though I could sleep for a week.' Smiling faintly I said, 'How are you doing Rupert?'

Rupert sat in one of the armchairs nursing a glass holding a generous measure of amber fluid. He shrugged. 'Well, I haven't been arrested yet.' As if remembering his hosting duties, he said, 'Help yourselves to a drink.'

'Are they close to making an arrest?' asked Mallory.

By the colour of her cheeks, the drink she sipped was far from her first gin of the day.

'I'm not sure,' said Robbie, standing in Rupert's usual position by the fireplace.

'Has DI Whitely given you any indication about his next move?' Serena asked anxiously.

Robbie shook his head. 'No, I suspect he's waiting on the results from forensics, but he seems to be struggling with finding a clear motive.'

'Tell me about it. I asked if I could have the book we found and he got quite angry with me.' I poured tea for Robbie and me from the trolley. 'As if something that old could have any links to this case.'

'Philly, you know how it works; everything is important until it's found not to be.' Robbie spoke as if he was explaining a concept to a truculent teenager.

I rolled my eyes, selected a curd tart from the trolley, placed it on a plate and handed it, and a cup of tea, to him.

Lucinda chuckled. 'It sounds like you've had words with DI Whitely.'

'Let's just say he's not a fan.' I took my tea and curd tart and sat in a free armchair. 'Hopefully the fresh air will improve his temper.'

'Oh?' Serena stood and took Lucinda's empty glass from her.

'He and DS Stanley are conducting their own search of the barn,' said Robbie. 'Even though forensics have already been over it, sometimes it helps to get a feel yourself.'

'I see.' Serena poured gin and slimline tonic water into Lucinda's glass. After passing it to Lucinda she said, 'If you'll excuse me, I just need to check something with Mrs Phillips.'

With Serena gone the conversation dwindled. Lucinda fussed over Wentworth who was, I noticed, still avoiding alcohol; Rupert appeared lost in his own thoughts, a slight frown on his face as he sipped at his drink; Mallory half-slumped into the corner of the lounge.

I stood and walked across to Robbie. 'Too much?' I asked softly.

'The eye roll was a nice touch. Now we wait.'

We didn't, however, have to wait long before Chris walked in with Serena whose cheeks were flushed.

'I found Lady Deverell in the library,' he said. 'And when she explained she'd been looking for me to get an update on the case I thought I'd tell you all at the same time.'

Serena kept her eyes downcast as she took her seat next to Mallory.

Chris stood with his legs wide, his hands behind his back. 'This is rather unorthodox, but nothing about this crime has been ordinary.' He cast his eyes around the room. 'The forensic team have now finished in the ballroom and the barn, so you're free to move around those areas.'

'Do you know who killed my hushband, Inspector?' asked Mallory.

'Unfortunately not, Lady Stark. You are, however, free to go.'

'But … I thought …' Serena frowned her disbelief. 'You're not arresting Rupe for it? That's … that's great news.' Her bright smile didn't make it to her eyes. 'Isn't that great news, Lucinda?'

'I'm afraid there's insufficient physical evidence to charge Lord Deverell with the murder of Lord Stark.' While Chris appeared nonchalant, Robbie and I were watching Serena closely.

She let out a little laugh. 'Well, that's great news. I was so worried when they took away his anorak in case they found blood on it.'

'We did find blood on the jacket, Lady Deverell, but anyone could've used it. We also found some of your hair on the collar.'

'Really? But as you say, anyone could have worn it. I probably did … yes, I did … last week. I'd forgotten to bring mine downstairs, so I grabbed Rupe's when I went for a walk.'

'Yes, that would be it.' Chris smiled benignly.

'Besides, it couldn't be me.' There was Serena's high-pitched laugh again. 'After all, I knew nothing about the tunnel or the compartment.'

'Oh, but I think you did, Lady Deverell.' Sergeant

Stanley walked in, nodded and handed Chris a book. 'After all, you read about it in your mother's diary.'

'My what?' The colour drained from Serena's face. 'You've been in my room?'

'We have. When we first arrived, Lord Deverell offered us his full cooperation and gave us permission to search wherever we needed to. But yes, your mother – Jenny Black.'

While Mallory looked bored, Lucinda gasped. Wentworth and Rupert looked at each other with horror, the latter's face turning puce. He put his hand over his mouth and rushed for the nearest bin.

'Your husband has just contemplated the possibility he could also be your father,' Chris said calmly. 'How long have you known Jenny Black was your mother?'

'That's ridiculous,' Serena snapped. 'I don't know where you got such an idea.'

'Your father committed suicide on the second anniversary of your mother's disappearance,' I said gently. 'You wouldn't have even been three. Your aunt took you in and adopted you, changing your name to Serena Grace.'

Serena shook her head. 'That's ridiculous,' she said again. 'My parents died in a car crash when I was a baby. Ask anyone.' Scowling at Chris she said, 'It's no wonder you haven't arrested anyone for Landy's murder if you've been running around making false accusations like that.' She rushed to Rupert and grabbed his arm. 'Don't listen to him, darling. None of it's true.'

As Rupert began to look hopeful, Chris said, 'But it is true, isn't it? You were born Jennifer Lucy Black.'

Serena turned to me. 'Ask Richard – he knows.'

'I did ask him,' I said. 'Richard's mother remembered a time when you told her your name was really Lucy Black, but now you had to be Serena.'

Serena's eyes filled with tears, her shoulders slumping. 'I see.' She twirled her wedding ring around her finger. 'I don't remember telling her that.'

'She said you were very young. How long have you known?' I asked quietly. 'That Jenny was your mother?'

'I've always known I was adopted,' she finally said. 'To be honest, I don't remember anything about my mother. As you said, I was very young. I've always known my mother grew up here and she left here with another man, but my aunt wouldn't speak of her. She was always "that woman". She told me my father was so heartbroken he couldn't live without her, so I've always known the Deverells destroyed my family.'

Rupert's face twisted in horror and he collapsed into the nearest chair.

'What did your aunt say when she found out you were marrying into the family?' I prompted.

'She was so angry. She told me she wanted nothing more to do with me. The Deverells had taken her brother from her, and she'd never forgive them.'

'But you wanted to know who they were?' Serena seemed to have forgotten there were people other than her and me in the room.

'I couldn't believe it when I met Rupert at a party, and when he asked me to marry him, it felt so right. Being here, I felt close to my mother and could put aside everything else that had happened.'

'And then your aunt died.' She nodded. 'And when you were packing up her possessions, you found your mother's diary.'

'It was in a box that had belonged to my father. I don't think anyone had looked inside that box since he died.' She chuckled mirthlessly. 'If my aunt had read it, she would've certainly destroyed it – and stopped me marrying Rupe … Although now,' she added wistfully, 'I wish she had.'

'What was in the diary, Serena?' asked Chris.

She shook her head, her eyes clouding with the memory. 'Terrible things. At first, it was teenage stuff, like how she had a crush on Rupe and then, later, how he took advantage of her.'

'It was never like that,' Rupert protested. He leapt from his seat, his face red.

'Sit down Lord Deverell!' barked Chris.

'Of course it was,' she spat back. 'My mother was young, and you were the son of the viscount. I was nearly sick when I read about the night that you and him' —she pointed at Wentworth, her mouth twisted—

'shared her with Orlando looking on. You plied her with alcohol and drugs, and you took advantage of her.'

'Is this true, Wenty?' Lucinda gripped her husband's arm.

'It wasn't like she makes it sound,' Wentworth mumbled. 'Besides, it was Landy's idea.'

'Thash convenient,' mumbled Mallory. 'Poor Landy ishn't here to shtick up for hishelf.'

Serena ignored her. 'She wrote about how she was messing about in the attic and found the ledger belonging to Mary Flounders and the witch's pot and how the Deverells killed her.'

'That's rubbish!' exclaimed Rupert. 'Mary Flounders poisoned my great-great-great-grandfather and paid the price for that. Besides, I didn't think she had children.'

'She gave the herbs to the viscountess for another purpose, but she used them to kill her husband,' I said.

'Why would she do that?' Rupert asked, crossing his legs and sitting back in his chair, his posture that of a man ready to defend his family's honour.

'Because the viscount had got Mary pregnant. Mary tried to hide it, and when the baby was born, she gave it to the housekeeper to bring up, but the viscountess must have known, so she poisoned her husband and blamed Mary. Jenny tracked her family tree and learnt that Mary Flounders was her ancestor, so when Rupert threw her over, she realised history was repeating itself, and she had an opportunity to right a generational wrong. She was going to expose the Deverells for what they were.' I paused, my gaze meeting Rupert's. 'Did she tell you that?'

He dropped his eyes and shook his head. 'Of course not. It's completely fanciful.'

'How did that make you feel?' Chris asked Serena, attempting to regain control of the situation.

'How would you feel if you'd read about the humiliation of your mother and then realised you might've married your father?' Serena spat the words out, her face red, her eyes blazing. 'I felt sick to the stomach! The Deverells had ruined my life when I was a baby – they'd taken away my parents – and now they'd ruined it again. So I wanted to ruin them!'

'Is that the reason you contacted Philly? You wanted her to find Mary's book?' Robbie spoke for the first time, his tone gentle, encouraging.

She nodded. 'I knew it was in there somewhere, but I hadn't been able to find it and didn't know what I was looking for. Also, my mother had mentioned something in her diary about seeing a painting get switched' —Rupert and Wentworth exchanged glances— 'and I knew Philly's reputation, so I figured if she found something wrong with one of the paintings, that would discredit Rupe further.'

'And what better way to wreak revenge than to have your husband accused and convicted of a murder he didn't commit?' Chris shook his head. 'That must've felt like it would bring history full circle.'

'It would – and in saving Mary's soul, I could save my own in case I had married my father.'

'Oh Christ.' Rupert bowed his head, his hands resting on the back of it.

'And Jenny's diary told you where to find the secret compartment in the ballroom and the priest's hole,' Robbie guessed.

'All you needed to do was find a way of luring Orlando to the barn, and what better temptation than yourself, the one prize that had always been off limits,' I said.

She shrugged. 'Orlando always wanted what someone else had.'

'Is that why you broke into my room yesterday? In case we'd found Mary's book and learnt about the tunnel?'

She nodded. 'I needed for Rupe and Wenty to be the only people who knew about it.'

'And that's what you were snooping around in the library for when we caught you in there,' guessed Chris.

'And the power cut?' asked Robbie.

'All I had to do was switch the generator off and let the storm do the rest,' she said with a shrug. 'It was just to buy me some time.'

At Chris' nod, Lewis stepped forward, and Serena stood. 'Lady Serena Deverell, I'm arresting you on suspicion of the murder of Lord Orlando Stark. You do not have to say anything. But, it may harm your defence if you do not mention when questioned something which you later rely on in court. Anything you do say may be given in evidence.'

Mallory's face twisted, and she dropped her glass and flew at Serena, her fists balled. 'How could you?' Serena stood expressionless through the onslaught until Sergeant Stanley pulled Mallory away. 'He wash my hushband,' she wailed. 'Now I have nothing!'

Rupert also stood and shook his head sadly. 'You killed Landy?'

Serena shrugged. 'And Wentworth's lucky he has a hard head.'

Rupert stared at her in disbelief. 'You would've let me go to prison for murder?'

'It would've been the least you deserve,' she snarled.

Chris stepped forward. 'Lord Deverell, I'm arresting you on suspicion of the deaths of Jennifer Black and Edward Deverell.' Chris read Rupert his rights. 'Wentworth Fitzroy, I'm arresting you on suspicion of being an accessory after the fact in the deaths of Jennifer Black and Edward Deverell.'

'What?' blustered Rupert, standing in shock.

'You've got to be joking, man!' Wentworth cast a desperate look towards his wife. 'It isn't true, darling.' She, however, sat there, too shocked to move or speak.

'On what jumped up evidence?' A scowling Rupert demanded.

'You shouldn't have used your own credit card to buy your ticket home from Valencia,' I said, straightening with a new release of energy. 'And the Stubbs is a fake.'

As Robbie and I left the room, Serena's manic laughter followed us to the foyer.

CHAPTER THIRTY-FOUR

Once the evidence of his attempted cover-up had been presented, Rupert had confessed all – as had Wentworth.

It had been as we'd surmised – Jenny had sent a message to Rupert threatening to expose the Deverells over what had happened to her ancestor and tell the world that the baby she had was Rupert's. At the same time, Edward had noticed some discrepancies with the Stubbs and called Rupert home to explain.

Rupert and Jenny had fought, and Jenny had knocked her head on a beam in the barn. Edward had come across them, and Rupert had lashed out at his brother, leaving him with two bodies to dispose of.

Wentworth and Rupert had driven up together, so he helped Rupert load the bodies into the boot of his car and tip them down one of the old mine shafts. The rest was as we'd deduced. As to whose idea it was to pose as Edward, both Rupert and Wentworth credited each other.

'Well, Susan.' I embraced the housekeeper warmly. 'I'd like to say it was a pleasure, but …'

'It's certainly been an eventful weekend for sure,' she said, walking Robbie and me to the door. 'One I'd prefer not to repeat in a hurry!'

'Your teacakes were the bright point,' said Robbie. 'I've never had any so good.'

'Oh, away with you.' Her cheeks tinged a delicate shade of pink. 'Happens I've parcelled some up for you.'

'You're a grand woman, Susan.' He leant forward and kissed her cheek.

'What will happen to you now?' I asked gently. While Hattie had a job and a home away from Deverell Grange, Susan had grown up here – it was all she knew.

She shrugged. 'It depends on what they decide to do, I suppose. I imagine Lord Deverell's eldest son will take over the running of the estate, although he won't inherit the title yet. In any case, I'm due retirement, so I might do that.' She patted my cheek, and it was such a sweet gesture. 'Don't go worrying about me, Philly, I'll always have a home with Hattie. And tell your Ginny I'll email her those recipes she was after.'

'Thank you.' I hugged her once more before walking out of Deverell Grange.

Robbie stopped the car at the same point on the drive as when we arrived just two days ago. We both got out of the car and stared down at the Grange.

'Hopefully it's the last time I see that place,' he said.

'Me too.' I turned to him. 'You've got to be happy that you finally got a result for Jenny Black, though?'

'Aye, thanks to you.' He opened his mouth to say something else, then closed it.

'We make a good team.' I couldn't help but smile, our eyes holding for a moment.

'Aye, that we do.' He turned to head back to the car and stopped. 'What do you say to a detour via Hawes? There's not much daylight left, and seeing I'm so close …'

'Are you suggesting we call in on your brother?'

'I reckon he'd like to know we got a result for Jenny, too.'

A comfortable-looking woman came out of the stone farmhouse when we pulled up. She wiped her hands on the apron around her waist and peered through the car window.

Robbie had barely uttered a word on the drive down – one of the most steeply picturesque roads I'd ever travelled. At one point, I said, 'I feel like I'm in an episode of *All Creatures Great And Small.*' To which he swerved to avoid a sheep wandering in the middle of the road and replied, 'Aye, it's not bad.'

Now, he sat in the car, silence weighing heavily. I placed my hand over his, giving it a reassuring squeeze to let him know I understood what a big deal this was for him. 'Aye, you're right. We'd better be getting this done then.'

Robbie stepped out of the car, shutting the door behind him. The woman threw her hands in the air. 'Robbie? It's yourself, then?' Then she called into the house. 'Ken! It's our Robbie! He's here!' Robbie stepped forward and wrapped his arms around her.

An older, more weather-beaten version of Robbie appeared at the door, a tan and white collie beside him. 'What are you blathering about, Fern?'

Robbie extricated himself from his sister-in-law's embrace and held out a hand to his brother. 'It's about time you called by.' Ken took Robbie's hand before wrapping an arm around him in an awkward man-hug that was over as soon as it started. 'And who's this in the car?'

Robbie opened the door for me and waited till I'd slid out. Ken, Fern, this is my friend Philly Barker. Philly, my brother Ken and his wife Fern.

While Ken eyed me narrowly through suspiciously moist eyes, Fern held out her hand. 'Well, it's nice to meet you, Philly Barker. Now, get yourselves inside, out of the cold. The wind does fair rip through the fells.'

As with most other Yorkshire farmhouses I'd been in, we entered through a boot room and into a cosy kitchen warmed by an Aga.

'You'd be wanting a brew?' asked Fern, fussing around the kitchen, collecting cups and saucers from the oak dresser.

'Be damned with a brew,' said Ken, indicating the kitchen chairs to sit on. 'This calls for an ale.' Without waiting for an answer, he went to the fridge and took out two tall bottles of a dark ale and some beer glasses.

'You are staying tonight, aren't you?' Fern asked. 'I've a stew on, and it's no problem to make up the guest bed – or beds.'

Robbie looked at me and raised his eyebrows. I nodded. 'If that's okay,' he said. 'We've had a bit of a day – and that would be two beds, thanks Fern.'

She smiled conspiratorially at me, and my cheeks grew warm. 'Right you are. So what brings you this way?'

'We've been up at Deverell Grange,' Robbie said.

Ken paused, the beer bottle held aloft. 'Oh aye?' He passed full glasses across to Robbie and me. 'The storm hit there badly.'

'Aye. Philly was doing some work there, so I tagged along.'

'What sort of work do you do, Philly?' Fern lifted the lid on the cast iron casserole pan on the stove and stirred the stew, filling the kitchen with a rich, herby aroma.

'I'm an antique dealer in Chipwell, but Lady Deverell had asked me to rummage through her attic to see if there was anything worth selling.'

'Oh aye,' Ken's face and tone were expressionless. Now I knew where Robbie got it from.

'We've got justice for her, Ken,' Robbie said

quietly. 'For Jenny.'

Fern stood behind her husband and laid a hand on his shoulder. 'You found her?'

'We haven't found her yet, but they will. We found her killer, though – Rupert Deverell. He killed her, and when his brother came upon him attempting to dispose of her body, he killed him too.'

'Poor Jenny,' said Ken. 'She didn't deserve any of that. What happened to her bairn?'

'That's another sad story.' Between sips of brew, Robbie relayed the events of the last two days. 'If it hadn't been for Philly finding the compartment and the priest-hole, Serena would've gotten away with it.' When I protested that Robbie had found the priest-hole he waved my words away.

'Well,' said Fern, 'All's well that ends well. 'What will happen with the witch's pot and the ledger you found?'

'I'm not sure, but they belong in a museum.' I said. 'I doubt any of the Deverells will want to keep them in the house as a reminder.'

'I daresay you're right. Ken, have you locked the hens up for the night?'

'No, I'd forgotten. I'll do it now. Robbie?' Robbie nodded, and the two men left the kitchen.

'We've got some foxes that would love to get into that henhouse,' Fern said. 'Now tell me, Philly, how did you and Robbie meet?'

Understanding that I was about to get the third degree, I smiled to myself. 'We met when Robbie called my shop to ask me to be on the lookout for some fake china, and then when my shop was broken into, Robbie helped out. He's become a good friend.'

'Oh, aye. And that's all it is?'

I nodded.

'Well, friendship or nowt, you've brought him back, and we're right chuffed about that.' She busied herself mixing the suet dumplings. 'After Audrey passed, he retreated from everyone and threw himself into his work. We tried to reach out to him, but he wasn't having any of it.' She rolled the dumplings into small green-flecked balls. 'I think it's been harder for him to deal with as they never did catch who shot her.' As she shook her head, my heart began to beat faster. 'She'd been looking forward to her visit to London for so long – she was catching up with her friend, you see – and to get caught up in a drive-by shooting on the way back from the theatre ...' Again, she shook her head. 'It's no wonder he's never recovered.' She cast me another meaningful glance. 'I happen to think you're good for him, though, Philly. Friend or nowt.'

Chapter Thirty-Five

The men returned soon after this, so the conversation turned to farm matters, what Ken and Fern's kids were up to (both married with children), and how Robbie's Jim had been offered a new job in Wellington, New Zealand.

'Do you think he'll take it?' asked Ken.

Robbie shrugged. 'Probably. He's got nothing keeping him in Sydney.'

'What about you, Philly? Do you have children?' Fern asked.

'I have a daughter in Australia too – but she's on the Sunshine Coast with her husband. They don't have any children yet, but my son in York has twins – Ada and Alfie – they're five next week.'

Fern's stew was served, pronounced to be 'exactly what I felt like' by Robbie, and her apple crumble and custard were demolished.

Despite my best efforts to stay awake, my eyes grew heavy and started to drift shut after dinner.

'I think Philly's jiggered,' Robbie said, a laugh in

his voice.

'I'm sorry,' I said. 'As my dad used to say, I'm Jatz-crackered … knackered. I didn't sleep much last night.'

Fern chuckled. 'Don't apologise, Philly, you two have been through a lot from the sounds of things, and I imagine you wouldn't sleep well knowing there was a murderer in the house. I'll show you to your bed.'

'Thank you,' I said gratefully.

Despite being both physically and mentally exhausted, I didn't drop straight off to sleep, instead lying awake listening to the wind roaming around the house. While at Deverell Grange, it had been fighting for a way in; here, the wind was almost comforting, encircling the house, bedding it in for the night. As the weight of the duvet calmed my body, my mind was full of what Fern had told me about Audrey, Robbie's wife – and whether I should mention it to Robbie. I couldn't help but feel that how I broached the subject with him – and his reaction to it – could have a massive bearing on our relationship.

Fern sent us off the next morning with a full Yorkshire breakfast and, through moist eyes, made Robbie promise not to be a stranger and to visit more often. There was a gruffness in his tone as he made the promise, emotions spilling over. Ken gripped his hand as he'd done yesterday. 'Ta ra,' he said lightly and patted Robbie on the back. For me, he had a slightly awkward half hug and a wish that I'd come back soon.

We'd been on the road for half an hour or so before Robbie broke the silence. 'They both seemed in fine fettle,' he said.

'It was nice of them to welcome me so warmly,' I offered, my eyes on the landscape skimming by.

'Aye, well, I'm glad we stopped, and Fern does a good stew – although' —I turned, and he flashed me a quick smile— 'yours might just be better.'

'I wouldn't let her hear that,' I retorted, still grinning.

Another short silence followed. 'Did she give you the third degree while I was out with Ken last night?'

'A little.' I inhaled deeply and then decided to go for it. 'She also mentioned how Audrey died.'

A pulse beat in the side of his jaw, his hands tightening on the steering wheel. I held my breath, waiting for a response.

'Oh aye, I thought she might have. He kept his eyes focused solely on the road. 'I probably should've told you myself before now; it's just ...'

'You find it hard to talk about her?' I guessed.

'Aye.' He swallowed. 'I don't want sympathy, and' —he briefly turned his eyes to mine— 'sometimes I feel like I'm losing sight of her.'

'How do you think she'd feel about that?' I asked gently.

'She'd tell me not to be a great berk and to let her go.' He grinned wryly. 'And she's right.'

'You know you can talk to me about her and what happened?'

'Aye, Philly. I know.' He shot me another quick smile.

Anything else he might have said was interrupted when my phone rang. It was Stewart.

'I just thought I'd check in, Philly. You okay?'

'Thanks, Stewart, I'm fine. I slept well last night, and we're almost back at Chipwell.'

'Good. I also wanted to say well done – to both of you. Chris told me you and Robbie virtually solved this one.' The praise from Chris Whitely rendered me speechless for a few seconds. 'Philly?'

'I'm here. It's just … well, a compliment from DI Whitely?'

'He's alright when you get to know him,' Stewart chided. 'Anyway, must go. Will we see you at Ryan's for the twin's birthday on Saturday?'

'You sure will. Thanks, Stewart.'

When I rang off, I said to Robbie, 'Fancy coming to the twin's birthday with me on the weekend? I can't promise it will be as action-packed as this last weekend has been.'

'Count me in, and Philly …?'

'Yes?'

A slight hesitation and then, 'Would you like to come out for coffee sometime?'

Coffee? We often had coffee at the Barn. Then it

twigged … He was asking me *out* for coffee. A warmth filled my body, and I couldn't stop the smile that spread across my face. 'Yes, Robbie, I'd like that. A lot.'

If you enjoyed *Murder at Deverell Grange*, I'd love it if you left a review in the usual places. If you'd like to stay up to date with what Philly, Robbie and the crew at Chipwell Barn Antiques get up to next, you can sign up for my newsletter at my website: https://joannetracey. com

You can also drop by and see me – virtually speaking, of course – here:

My Substack: https://brookfordkitchendiaries. substack.com/
My blog: https://andanyways.com
Facebook: https://facebook.com/joannetraceywriter
Instagram: https://instagram/jotracey
Recipes from the books: https:// brookfordkitchendiaries.wordpress.com/

Acknowledgements

This story was inspired by just one thing – lunch at the Tan Hill Inn on a blustery Saturday in October 2022. This pub, the highest in Britain, is about as in the middle of nowhere as you can be if you're a pub in Britain. Set high in Swaledale, the scenery might seem bleak, but it is astonishingly stunning and worthy of the overdone adjectives I toss at it. The local black-faced sheep wander willy-nilly, unphased by roads, cars, cyclists or ramblers. They're tough sheep. The patrons here are also resilient – this place gets snowed in relatively often. One famous occasion was November 2021, when dozens of patrons were trapped for days after visiting to hear an Oasis tribute band.

Walking into the pub with its exposed beams and flag-stoned floor, I said to my husband, 'I've just found my new Philly story.'

'You can't set a story in a real pub,' he pointed out.

No, I couldn't, but Philly and Robbie could visit it, and I could invent a grand house – Deverell Grange – and plonk it down in the middle of nowhere somewhere near Tan Hill. I could also rustle up an unseasonal storm and a cast of characters. And that's what we have here. Don't go looking for Deverell Grange when visiting Tan Hill Inn – you won't find it. But do go to the pub – the scenery really is spectacular.

During the writing of this novel, our beautiful cocker spaniel, Adventure Spaniel, Best Dog In The World, our darling Kali, passed away at the grand old age of almost sixteen. She lived a wonderful life – mostly at my feet – and was loved by everyone she met. While I still listen for her snores in the corner and have a massive Kali-shaped hole in my heart, she lives on in the spirit of Balthazar, Philly's cocker spaniel, and Nigel, the spaniel in my Brookford series. It is, however, why I couldn't bear to have Bally appear too much in this novel – he was too close a reminder of our loss.

As for thanks, the usual goes to my fabulous editors, Nicola O'Shea and Jo Speirs. Not only do you make my words read so much better than they did when I first wrote them, but you also inspire me to continue to improve my craft and push myself. One day, I might even learn the difference between en and em dashes – and the focus to apply that knowledge … but I wouldn't hold your breath.

Thanks to Louisa West for nailing the cover and Keith Stevenson for making it look and feel like a real live book. Thanks also to Bel Williams for helping me with the blurb.

The feedback and support from my early reading team are invaluable, so thank you from the bottom of my heart to my sister-in-law Pieta (who has read every one of my books before anyone else) and the members of my simply stunning book club – Donna, Sue and Deb.

Massive thanks to my writer's group – the Friday Writing crew. You guys are the best!

I couldn't do what I do without Grant and Sarah, but sorry, Sares, this time the dedication in the front goes to Kali.

Mostly, though, my thanks are to you, dear reader, for supporting me and picking up this book to read when there are so many you could have chosen. It means the world to me.

9 781763 776821